CW00376326

THE
MISPER

Kate London graduated from Cambridge University and worked in theatre until 2006 when she joined the Metropolitan police service. She finished her career working as part of a Major Investigation Team on the Metropolitan Police Service's Homicide Command. She has since written four novels in The Tower series, which is now a major ITV drama, starring Gemma Whelan.

Find out more by following her on Facebook
and Twitter @K8London

The Tower series

The Tower (previously published as *Post Mortem*)
Death Message
Gallowstree Lane

THE
MISPER

KATE
LONDON

CORVUS

First published in hardback in Great Britain in 2023 by Corvus,
an imprint of Atlantic Books Ltd

This paperback edition published in 2024 by Corvus

10 9 8 7 6 5 4 3 2 1

A CIP catalogue record for this book is available from the British Library.

Paperback ISBN: 978 1 83895 451 2
E-book ISBN: 978 1 83895 450 5

Printed and bound by CPI (UK) Ltd, Croydon CR0 4YY

Corvus
An imprint of Atlantic Books Ltd
Ormond House
26–27 Boswell Street
London
WC1N 3JZ

www.atlantic-books.co.uk

MIX
Paper | Supporting
responsible forestry
FSC® C171272

To my mother.

PROLOGUE

1

It was a boy he knew a bit from school who made the connection. It was when Leif was suspended. Jaydn was two years older and he was wavy. He had all the stuff, the trainers, the jacket, but it wasn't just the garms that made Jaydn cool. Whatever that other thing was that made you cool, that deep thing; he had that. At first, they were just smoking weed. Then Leif met Mo, who was kind of dirty, but he let you hang at his place. Jaydn said, 'You could do this. You do as much or as little as you want. Your mum can't tell you anything.' That was during the time his mum had taken his PlayStation away. Jaydn said, 'You can make money and any money you make is yours.' He gave Leif a phone and a weed crusher. 'Just a little something,' he said. 'Hey, man, believe.' Then he said, 'You know I gave you this, you do something for me?'

That's how Leif started running with the Bluds.

PART ONE

THE INCIDENT

2

The gun springs back in his hand and Ryan thinks, Wow, I didn't shoot myself. But, in almost the same instant that he has this thought his eyes communicate to his oh-so-slow brain that the guy in front of him has jerked backwards, as if pulled suddenly by a hawser attached to his back. The bang almost deafens the exhalation the man makes. But the exhalation is definitely there. You've shot him, he thinks. That's crazy. Things are moving both super-fast and very slowly at the same time. How is that possible? And the look on the man's face. No one could be more surprised than he is! One minute so cool and in control, using big words, and calming him down, the next, well, not so cool. It's nothing like the telly. No holding your hand to your chest. No big speeches. The man falls onto the floor and sort of gurgles.

Ryan stands for a second with the machine in his hand. In the next instant there's a blast downstairs. Steve says, 'Throw the gun away or they'll shoot you.' Feet hammer up the stairs. Ryan throws the gun into the corner of the room just as a man appears in the doorway. Helmet. Balaclava. Ballistics vest. *Armed police, don't resist!* No chance of that; the room is full of them. The whole thing has been a dream, or this is a dream; his brain is struggling to catch up, to seize an understanding of what is happening, while the other Ryan, the physical Ryan, is swept away. A tornado has got hold of him and lifted him into the air and then thrown him on his front, face down on the floor, guns pointed at his head, hands in cuffs behind his back. It doesn't even hurt. The main thing is astonishment because even though it's all clearly been some sort of massive illusion, he still can't work out what the illusion actually is.

Can't see much but black boots. Although he's shot someone, he's surprisingly irrelevant; no more than the subject of a kind of packaging service. It's Feds Amazon! Black boots everywhere. There must be loads and loads and loads of them. He's pulled to his feet and put to stand with his back to the mantelpiece. The snitch, whose fault this all is, Steve, stands beside him. Out of the corner of Ryan's eye he sees that Steve has blood on his hands, his face, his chest. Hopefully that's from the guy on the floor. He can't have shot him as well, can he? They don't look each other in the face. They stand and watch what is unfolding in the room. Ryan thinks, Even though I've actually shot someone, it's not about me. There seems to be some information there about his whole existence. Any case, the most important thing is, without a doubt, the guy on the floor. Turns out the black boots weren't just police. There are lots of medics in green with their dead bags, and side pockets and heavy stuff that must do something important. Screens and tubes and canisters. They are crowding around the guy and every single one of them looks busy. The guy's a fed, for fuck's sake. Kieran, he said his name was. And just about a minute ago he was promising Ryan could get off lightly. That having the gun, and holding Steve prisoner, wasn't so bad, all things considered, but murder was, so better steer clear of that one. And now the guy who told him to steer clear of murder is lying on the floor surrounded by medics because Ryan's shot him. What a joke. For another stupid second Ryan thinks, *Mum will kill me*. The window is shattered – when did that happen? What remains of the panes of glass are splashed with blood too. The whole room is like someone's been throwing cans of red paint. There's a woman. He recognises her. Lizzie, that's it. She arrested him about one hundred thousand years ago. She's crying and trying to get close to the man on the floor and the man says, 'Let her come.' And she says, 'You're going to be all right.' So, it's calm after all. It was an accident, and like the woman said – Lizzie – the guy's going to be all right. But for all that the medics are very busy. There's dressings and shit all over the floor and the thump thump thump of helicopter blades.

That was what he thought then, but it turned out that wasn't even the half of it. Because his lawyer told him when they talked in the police station – Ryan in a white paper suit – that Steve wasn't a snitch. He was a fed too. An under-cover officer. Like in a film. And the man he shot? Detective Inspector Kieran Shaw? He died.

At the magistrates' court, he's remanded. The lawyer warned him that would happen. It's standard, he said, as though that made it better. For a murder charge, he said. Standard. Don't worry, he said, it's just the beginning.

Oh, thanks, man. Yeah, great.

It's SERCO now, not police. Out of the court in handcuffs, up three steps to the door at the side of the truck. Then into one of the compartments. Three feet wide, three feet deep, just big enough to hold a man. A hard moulded seat facing forwards. He sits. The guard locks the door. He expects them to drive away but nothing happens. How come they call these things sweatboxes? It's freezing. More packaging. He's an Amazon delivery again, not a human, and he's stuck in here with his thoughts.

Other people. The doors of another compartment opening. He stands and looks through the darkened pane of the small window. He can see the yard of the court. People moving around. What it's like to be free. Then a voice from inside the truck.

'Oy, you the cop killer?'

Even in this little box with its darkened window he already has a sense of how important it is to be respected by the people he is confined with. It is vital to say the right thing. He has to learn quickly. But his lawyer said, Don't talk to anyone. Anyone can witness against you.

Another voice. 'It is. I saw him. Ryan Kennedy.'

Suddenly the truck is full of voices.

'Killing a fed, Ryan. Well done, bruv.'

'Murder, that's life. Minimum twenty years.'

'Killing a cop? He'll get whole life for that. Never get outside again.'

Then there's the joker.

'You innocent, Ryan? Just like Andy Dufresne in *Shawshank*.' The voice does a passable Morgan Freeman imitation. 'You gonna fit right in.'

Ryan pulls his feet up onto the seat and wraps his arms tightly round himself.

And they're off. The van surges. He steadies himself on the bulkhead. Pulling out of the gates there are flashes at the window. 'That's for you, Ryan. You're famous!' He stands up and immediately there's a bright flash through the dark glass.

10

They've got him. It's gonna be everywhere. His poor mum. His sister.

I'm a celebrity, he thinks. Get me out of here.

Out into London's streets. Simple things, seen through the frame of the small square of glass. It's like a boring film on Channel 4 that normally you'd bin in five but which has suddenly become completely engrossing. A boy on a bike. An old man with a dog. A park with a playground empty except for three youngers hanging out on the swings smoking weed. The van pauses like a labouring beast then swings heavily left onto the main road that runs along the edges of the Deakin. The concrete line of home spools out. The ramparts and walls. The walkway where he and Spence stood as kids looking down on the chuntering tube trains. The meadow that the newcomers planted with flowers. They used to go there and lie on their backs and smoke weed. The Deakin will carry on without him and Spence. Spence is under the earth. Ryan may never get back there.

'You been in prison before, cop killer?'

'You wait,' another voice shouts. 'Prison smells like a junkie's arse.'

The smell hits him as soon as he enters the prison and wraps itself round him as he walks along the landing to his cell carrying the bag of stuff his mother brought to the court for him.

He understands at once what the smell is: it is the sweaty fearful molecules of boys confined. Boys eating, shitting, wanking and staring at the ceiling in a cramped space with a window that doesn't open.

The door is unlocked but he stands on the threshold for an instant.

'In you go, son.'

He steps inside and the pain of the door locking behind him is a little explosion under his chest. He puts the bag on the floor and presses his hands against his face.

He tells himself he's on remand. Not guilty yet. Not yet. He can still wear his own clothes and they are endlessly precious to him these sweatshirts and trousers and socks and T-shirts. He sits on the bed and sticks his face in the bag and smells his mother's washing powder.

He takes one of the T-shirts out, leans forward and opens the locker. Inside, on the top shelf, is a brand-new pair of black Balenciaga trainers. Five hundred quid's worth. He shuts the door. He opens it. They are still there. What the fuck? He holds them in his two hands and is afraid.

He's only been in three days. They are on something called the red regime. Not enough staff so just one hour for exercise. Standing in the yard thinking how he can't even see the sky properly. How long before he will see it unconfined again. How long before he can take a shower whenever he wants one. How long before he can get on a bike.

One of the lads told him there was a sweepstake on his sentence running. 'Killing a fed. You could get whole life for that. Never get outside again.'

He hasn't even been found guilty yet. Aren't there any odds running on that?

None of his usual stuff works. He can't imagine his life as a professional footballer because the walls press on him and, instead of the daydream, into his mind comes reality. He can't get up and go out. He can't take his ball and kick it about with his friend.

He is shut in with a preoccupation. They asked him about that when they booked him in.

'Any thoughts of self-harming?'

All the time.

'No, boss.'

Not so easy, in any case. They have him on a watch to stop that. At night the screws open the hatch on the window and shine a light in on him. Every hour. 'You still with us, Ryan?'

They have an hour for socialisation but down the corridor it is kicking off. The alarm sounds. Ryan gets up and moves to the doorway of his cell. A youth, big like a door, stands outside.

He nods for Ryan to move back into his cell. Ryan wonders whether he should try to get past him, but that's impossible. He steps back. The youth says, 'Got something for you.'

He pulls something out of his pocket. It is a tiny phone and a piece of paper with a phone number.

'Dial that number and eat the paper. Screws will get this shut down pretty quick. I'm outside.'

Ryan sits on the bed, the little window above him, the picture of his mum and his sister in its frame on the table.

The phone only rings once before it is picked up. The voice is deep, distorted, monstrous. What the hell is going on?

'The Federation has taught you that conflict should not exist. But without struggle you would not know who you truly are . . . Struggle made us strong.'

'Who is this?'

Laughter.

'It's Krall. Former Starfleet captain.'

Then he knows who it is. Shakiel. What a doughnut.

'You got what I sent you, fam?'

'The trainers was from you?'

'Who else? Bluds still got you.'

Ryan doesn't answer. They are in his cupboard. He hasn't dared wear them.

'Listen, Ry, what you did. It was good. Don't worry about it. It's like the man says. There are things that have to be done and you do them. You just do them. Then you forget it.'

'What man, Shaks?'

Laughter. 'The man, Ry, the man. The Godfather.'

That's the voice, the voice he's done so much to please. The voice he's wanted so much to turn its attention on him. Now he is afraid of its focus. He feels the pressure, reaching him as if there are tentacles winding their way through drains and cable lines and stretching into his cell. He's locked away here but Shakiel can get to him if he wants to. The fighting down the corridor – all that so he can have this little chat?

'Don't worry about the time, Ry. I've got guys in there gonna look out for you. Like I said, you're family.'

But nothing comes free. Ryan knows that.

'I'm getting off most of it,' Shakiel says. 'Gonna be out in about ten, I reckon.'

Ten. Ten years. How can anyone do ten? And Ryan's looking at a lot longer. He can only catch glimpses of the sky. He wants to be able to get on his bike and ride. Just that one thing. He would give five years of his life for that. On the first night one of the boys sharpened the plastic casing of a biro.

Stuck it in a milk carton. All night he was cutting himself with it. Lot of blood, the boys said, but no real harm.

'Grenades was dummies,' Shakiel says. 'Who'd a thought I'd be pleased about that?'

'What about Lexi?'

'Lexi? They've dropped that. Course they have. Nothing to link me.'

'And Jarral?'

'Jarral can't duck it but he can hope for something else. Death by dangerous driving, his lawyer is saying. Or manslaughter.'

'Jarral's not snitching, then? My lawyer said he was. Going Queen's.'

'Shh, Ry. What would he talk about anyway? Like I said, nothing to link me to Lexi.'

Ryan sits on the bed and draws his teeth down his top lip.

Shakiel says, 'Any case, Jarral's not a snitch.'

There it is. That's what this is all about. Shakiel doesn't even need to tell him not to say who gave him the gun.

'You happy with your lawyer? You know I can help with that.'

A lawyer reporting straight to Shaks? No thanks.

'No, but listen, thanks for the offer. You're all right. My lawyer's sound.'

'So, what's your plan? What you gonna do? What you gonna say?'

'I dunno. Still trying to work it out.'

'OK, but roughly.'

'The lawyer says plead to the gun, plead to the lesser stuff, but fight the murder charge.'

'That sounds good.'

15

Course it does. Plead to the gun. Then you won't have to say who give it you.

He should say something but he can't speak. Any case, Shakiel's doing all the talking. He's never talked so much. He says, 'Your mum. Is everything blessed at home?'

'I guess.'

'And your sister. What's her name?'

'Don't say her name, Shaks. I know you know her name.'

'OK. OK, Ryan. Don't be thinking bad thoughts. I'm just gonna make sure they're looked after.'

Looked after.

'My man, who handed you the phone, he's gonna look out for you. They move him, there'll be someone else.'

The cell feels so small. He wants to pour his heart out, say, Life, Shakiel, they're talking life. Tell him about the sweep-stake running on how much time he's got to do. Twenty years would be short, everyone's saying. You killed a fed, what do you expect? Twenty? He'd be thirty-five. Thirty-five! All his youth wanked out in a tiny room. But he's got to bury all this deep. There's no place or time left to cry about it.

Shakiel says, 'What did I say?'

'I dunno.'

'There are things that have to be done and you do them. Then you forget it. Who said that?'

'The man.'

'That's right. The man, Ryan. Which man?'

'The Godfather.'

'You got that?'

'I got that. Thanks, Shakiel. Appreciate it.'

'Gotta go. Hold your head up. You did well. All you got to do, Ry, is what you always gotta do: learn to firm it.'

The line goes dead. The big guy steps back in and holds his hand out. Ryan gives him the phone.

'Yeah. Safe,' the guy says. 'I'm Costello. Gonna be looking out for you.'

Then he's gone. *Looking out for you.* There's been a lot of talk of looking out. Could mean one thing, could mean another. That's the beauty of it.

Ryan lies back and stares at the ceiling. What the lawyer really says is that he should apply for the National Referral Mechanism; go to the judge, say he's been groomed. He was fifteen when it happened: a victim, not a perpetrator. But he can't do that. Whatever the sentence he won't dodge prison, not after he's killed a police officer. So, he can't go live somewhere Shakiel can't reach him. He's got to do that thing Shakiel told him: firm it. And then there's that other thing Shakiel's told him to do, which was to forget it.

PART TWO

R V KENNEDY

3

On the pavement outside the Bailey the camera crews are massing. DC Steve Bradshaw steps onto the road to avoid them as he makes his way towards the court's lesser-known entrances. In the trial of R versus Ryan Kennedy he has been given anonymity; he will be known to the court as Officer V23, and his evidence will be given from behind a screen. Nevertheless, as he shows his warrant card and slips into the building, he feels a kind of nausea at what is about to unfold and into his mind comes a wildlife documentary he once half-watched, eating his dinner in front of the telly.

The light had glinted greenish gold off the scales of the bigger, slower fish as they began to pick off the littler ones. The pulse of the music quickened. One of them, dead-eyed, had a smaller fish in its mouth, the tail still flapping. A low, curiously thrilled, BBC voice narrated and it was this curious thrill, he thinks, that had so nauseated him.

'Waiting in the wings, to pick off any injured fish, are the piranhas.'

He imagines his words followed by such a feeding frenzy, his experience gobbled up. What do they have nowadays, these people who live on their phones? Hashtags and trends and memes.

Transcript: Examination in chief of undercover officer V23 in the trial of R v K

(The defendant cannot be named for legal reasons.)

Q: Officer V23, you had been working undercover on Operation Perseus for a couple of years at the time of Detective Inspector Kieran Shaw's death.

A: Yes.

Q: You had infiltrated yourself into the community where the Eardsley Bluds, an urban street gang, are based?

A: They are a lot more than an urban street gang—

Q: Please, confine yourself to answering the questions.

A: I had developed a cover over two years.

Q: And Ryan, the fifteen-year-old who fired the shot that killed Detective Inspector Kieran Shaw, what part did he play in this process of developing your cover?

A: The targets of Operation Perseus were the leaders of the Bluds, most importantly Shakiel Oliver, and the European gang that were supplying them with firearms. It was an organised crime network—

Q: As I said, please limit yourself to answering my questions.

A: Ryan was not a target for us. He was someone who happened to come into the orbit of the operation because he was close to Shakiel Oliver.

Q: Very well.

A: Ryan was what drug dealers call a roadman.

Q: A roadman. Explain your understanding of that word.

A: A roadman is a young person – usually a boy, but sometimes a girl – who spends a lot of time on the streets. He's kind of a runner, delivering drugs, getting into all sorts of trouble, in Ryan's case committing robberies too, that kind of thing.

Q: So how would you describe Ryan's relationship to the Bluds?

A: He was on the edges. I can't be more precise than that. It's not as if the Bluds have got membership cards and ranks. They can't be identified and called to account. They're not like us. They're not the police.

Q: Thank you for that, Officer.

A: I'm explaining the real-life difficulty we faced. It's hard to assess precisely the status of someone like Ryan. He was a hanger-on. Someone who was maybe looking for more involvement, or someone who might in the course of things drop out and have no further criminal involvement. But he was not one of our targets.

Q: The jury have been given transcripts of recordings made by you over the period of the operation. Based on those transcripts, can you tell me how much time you spent with Ryan?

A: A hundred and seventy-six hours, but that's over a period of two years. Two hours a week.

Q: I'm sure the jury can do their own maths.

A: If you say so.

Q: In any case, the time doesn't average out over two years. In the first year, how often did you meet Ryan?

A: Five times.

Q: And who else was present at these meetings during the first year?

A: Shakiel Oliver, Ujal Jarral, other people whose names I did not always know.

Q: And where did you meet?

A: Clubs. Pubs. Once in a betting shop.

Q: Whereas in the last nine months you met how often?

A: I don't have that figure to hand.

Q: Look at the schedule. Take your time.

A: OK, so . . . thirty-seven times.

Q: In the three weeks before Shaw died, how often did you meet?

A: Eight times.

Q: And where were most of your meetings in those last three weeks?

A: In the flat.

Q: The flat?

A: The flat the operation had rented for me to live in.

Q: And who else was present at those meetings in the flat?

A: It was the two of us. Ryan and me.

Q: The last three meetings? How long did they last?

A: The first lasted two hours, the second two and a half, the third an hour and a half.

Q: And why did you, a highly trained undercover police officer, choose to spend so much time one-to-one with someone who wasn't even a fully-fledged member of the Eardsley Bluds? With someone who, as you just said, was no more than a roadman? Just fifteen years old and a hanger-on?

A: I didn't choose. We can't choose who comes to us. We are in the business of infiltrating a community. Ryan was close to Shakiel Oliver and he made himself available.

Q: And do you know why he 'made himself available', as you say?

A: I can't say. I'd infiltrated the Bluds. Shakiel knew me. Jarral knew me. From time to time, Ryan came to me with things he had stolen. He thought I was a fence.

Q: Ryan came to you when his friend, Spencer Cardoso, was murdered.

A: He came to me because he had stolen a phone. He wanted money for it.

Q: How had you assessed whether that stolen phone wasn't a pretext for a boy who was in great distress?

A: I refer you to real life. I was undercover. Ryan came to my door and told me he had stolen a phone and he asked me to fence it.

The phone was subsequently traced to a robbery. My job was to maintain my cover and to gather intelligence. I offered him money for the phone.

Q: I refer you to the transcript of your conversation when Ryan brings the stolen phone to you. This transcript was exhibited by you and is in the jury bundle {SB7478/5}. The defendant enters the flat. You offer him a drink of Coke. Please tell me what you say to him at line three.

A: I say, 'You all right?' A normal thing to say to a person.

Q: Thank you.

A: And he replies, 'Yeah.' Also normal.

Q: What do you say at line five?

A: I say, 'Only you sounded like you were going to break the door down.'

Q: 'You sounded like you were going to break the door down.' Then at line twelve you say?

A: 'Cheese and Branston, mate?'

Q: Why do you say this?

A: Because I was making him a cheese and Branston sandwich.

Q: Can you tell the court anything else that you offered him.

A: I give him crisps and cigarettes.

A: You say? Line twenty-three?

A: 'Help yourself, mate.'

Q: Then, at line thirty-seven, he starts to tell you what?

A: That he was there when Spencer Cardoso was murdered.

Q: What was Spencer Cardoso to the defendant?

A: They dealt drugs together.

Q: Officer, please read line fifty-seven of the transcript that you signed as a fair record.

A: It says that Ryan Kennedy is sobbing and that I am rubbing his back.

Q: And at line sixty, you say?

A: I say, 'You're all right, mate. You're all right.'

Q: Mr Kennedy replies?

A: Spence, he was so frightened and he didn't know what was happening and then he sort of lay down.'

Q: To which you say?

A: 'Mate.'

Q: Then Mr Kennedy tells you what?

A: That he has gone to Shakiel and told him that they have to do something about it.

Q: Specifically, he says, line sixty-four, please, Officer.

A: 'We have to do something about this, pay them back.'

Q: Pay them back.

A: I immediately told my superior officer about this disclosure.

Q: That was not the question.

A: What was the question?

Q: We're getting to it. It's clear from your own transcript that Ryan confided in you and that you did everything you could to encourage him to trust you. You must have known that he was on the edge. How did you mitigate this risk?

A: It was my job to infiltrate the Bluds and Ryan made himself available. He was involved in criminal activity and he sought me out because he believed I was too. His contact with Operation Perseus had been overseen by higher ranking officers than me. He had information. What was I to do? Blow my cover? Tell him to go away?

Q: You made him very welcome. You made him a cheese and Branston sandwich. You rubbed his back and called him 'mate'.

A: I did my job. Nobody asked him to come to me and offer me stolen goods.

Q: What did you know of Ryan's home circumstances?

A: He lived with his mother and sister.

Q: Where was his father?

A: Dead.

Q: Was that all you knew about his father?

A: He had been murdered, when Ryan was three.

Q: How long had Ryan known Shakiel Oliver?

A: Since he was a child.

Q: Why was that?

A: I believe because his father and Shakiel had been friends, criminal associates probably.

Q: Do you know they were criminal associates, or are you assuming that?

A: I have no evidence that I can put in front of the court that they were criminal associates.

Q: How did it affect your relationship with Ryan that his father had been murdered when he was an infant?

A: I don't understand what you're asking me.

Q: By your evidence Ryan was vulnerable. His father had been murdered and he was close to a dangerous man, Shakiel Oliver. Ryan had told you that he was looking for vengeance for the murder of his friend. How did you execute your duty of care to Ryan?

A: Ryan's contact with the operation was assessed and agreed by people with more rank than me.

Q: You were just following orders?

A: I'm not answering that.

Q: I'll rephrase. Beyond the referrals you made to your superiors, did you ever feel that you, personally, had a duty of care to Ryan Kennedy?

A: Of course I did.

Q: What adjustments did you make?

A: I did my best. I didn't encourage him to commit offences. But Ryan was not a key member of the Bluds and he wasn't central to the operation.

Q: But still, he was considered close enough to Mr Oliver to be useful?

A: No one could have anticipated that he would be supplied with a firearm.

Q: Mr Oliver was dealing in firearms. That was indeed the focus of the police operation.

A: We knew Shakiel was intending to take delivery of firearms. We had no intelligence whatsoever that he was already in possession of a firearm.

Q: But you knew that he was a very dangerous man. It was a dangerous environment.

A: That was why he was the target of an operation. Because London, and indeed the United Kingdom, needs protection—

Q: If I can finish my question. Mr Oliver was a man who fully intended to use firearms—

A: No, we did not have intelligence that he intended to use firearms, just to acquire them. To deal in them in order to increase his power and his wealth. We had no intelligence that he had a firearm at the time. Nor could we have anticipated that he would give a firearm to a fifteen-year-old boy. On London's streets firearms are expensive commodities, and difficult to obtain. Top-level criminals don't just give them away to teenage boys.

Q: Prior to Detective Inspector Shaw's death, Shakiel's right-hand man, Jarral, had been arrested. You didn't anticipate either that that would have a destabilising effect on the handover of the illegal imported weapons.

A: That kind of assessment is above my pay grade. I'm just the

28

officer on the ground, getting information. I'm the cannon fodder, you know, the one you throw under the bus—

Q: An hour or so before the shooting of Kieran Shaw what had happened?

A: Shakiel Oliver had been arrested accepting delivery of automatic weapons.

Q: And you?

A: I was with Shakiel at the time of his arrest.

Q: What do you know of Ryan's involvement in that?

A: CCTV showed that Ryan was acting as lookout. He cycled past the vehicle that I was in with other police officers after the arrest. I knew nothing of this at the time.

Q: Ryan said he saw you shake one of the officers' hands.

A: I can't give evidence as to what Ryan saw.

Q: But you can tell the court whether you shook one of the officers' hands?

A: I shook one of the officers' hands. It had been a long operation. We had seized an armoury. I was relieved it was over.

Q: You were someone Ryan confided in. He saw you at the scene of the weapons handover, and he may have seen you shaking the hand of a police officer. Shakiel Oliver had been arrested in front of him. You didn't anticipate any fallout?

A: What can I tell you? It's dangerous and risky dealing with dangerous and risky criminals.

Q: And after the arrest of Mr Shakiel Oliver you did what?

A: I went back to the flat.

Q: With the intention?

A: To arrest Ryan.

Q: How had you risk-assessed that decision?

A: Do you think that if I'd had any idea he might have a firearm, I would have put my own life in danger? In any case, I was not

29

intending to let him into the flat at that time. If he'd appeared at the door, as I'd expected, I'd have called for assistance to have him arrested. I encountered him on the street.

Q: How had you managed the possibility of meeting him on the street?

A: It was bad luck. Two minutes either way and—

Q: Bad luck?

A: In the real world you can't plan for everything.

Q: So, you were unlucky. You did meet him on the street, where he knew you resided and where you had often met him. He had come looking for you after he had seen that you were not what you had seemed to be. He forced you into the flat. This fifteen-year-old boy had seen you as someone he could turn to. A father figure, even.

A: Father figure? Come on.

Q: A friend, then?

A: His fence. A man he sold stolen goods to.

Q: You were a highly trained undercover officer. It was a part of your job to assess the states of mind of your targets. What do you think Mr Kennedy's state of mind was when he entered your flat? What is your professional judgement as to his ability at that time to form clear intentions?

A: As to his intentions, Mr Kennedy said – and it will be on the recordings – he said, If I shoot you, it won't be by accident. Then he shot my friend.

Steve Bradshaw slips out of the court and back onto London's busy streets. He blends in: he's good at that. He needs to walk quickly, but it's almost impossible: there are too many people. Time and again he has to step off the pavement onto the road.

He tries to shake off the feeling that it has gone badly. Whatever he said in court they would find a way to misunderstand him.

Spy cop is one of the ridiculous catchphrases the journos are using about him. Silly, silly, silly, telly talk. Not one bit like the reality: living in a shit flat for most of two years, putting his own life both on hold and in danger, constantly having to make important decisions quickly. The lawyers only ask the questions they want answered. One of the things they don't ask is how it feels to see a friend shot.

He realises that he has stopped walking. London continues around him. What will he do now? One option is to slip into the underground, crash in front of the TV with a beer. He decides instead to walk briskly home. It will take two hours. It will physically tire him. He needs that. Tomorrow he's seeing Lizzie. He's taking Kieran's son to the zoo.

4

Lizzie wears an apron over her blue suit and silk shirt. She wipes the work surfaces in the kitchen.

'How did you feel about your evidence?' she says.

Steve shrugs. 'No worse than expected. It was always going to be our fault that a criminal killed one of us.'

Lizzie shakes her head, although what the meaning of that is is unclear. Steve wonders about Lizzie, but he cannot bring himself to ask. Does she blame him? He can't get out from underneath that question. And then he's angry because why did Kieran have to come to the flat? Acting the hero. What a fool. Steve would have handled it much better on his own. And in his darkest moments he thinks he would have coped better too with being dead than with being the one in the room when Kieran was shot.

Lizzie holds out a Spiderman duffel bag. 'Well, V23, everything Connor needs is in there. I've made you both sandwiches.'

'You didn't have to. I was going to treat us.'

'Just taking him to the zoo will be treat enough.'

Connor has his feet on the seats of the tube train and Steve taps his shoes. 'Come on, little man.'

Connor shuffles forward and stretches out his little legs. His feet dangle into space.

Steve says, 'What's your favourite animal, then?'

'Elephants.'

'Course it is. Stupid of me.'

Steve remembers those little wooden elephants in the hospital. Lizzie told him Kieran bought them in a stall in Hackney. They'd come all the way from Africa.

'We can see them first if you like.'

'No elephants at the zoo,' Connor says.

'Are you sure? They always used to have elephants.'

'One of them had a sore foot.'

'What?'

Connor speaks emphatically, as if Uncle Steve is being a bit slow. 'One of them had a sore foot.'

Steve narrows his eyes. Oh yes, now he remembers. One of the elephants killed a keeper. That must be what Connor is talking about. In spite of himself, he smiles. Sore foot: it's the perfect defence. Temporary loss of control: manslaughter. Couple of years. He sighs. Unless the jury particularly likes elephants. In which case it will be not guilty.

'There's elephants at Whipsnade,' Connor says.

'We could have gone to Whipsnade.'

'There's giraffes and zebras at the zoo.'

Steve says, 'OK, so we'll see them then. I like giraffes and zebras. Spots and stripes, they've got it covered. What's not to like?'

'And the turtles.'

'Yes, and the turtles. Nice shells.'

'And the otters.'

'Yes, the otters too. Sweet little ears.'

'And the lemurs.'

Steve laughs. 'We'll see all the animals, Connor. Any animals you want to see, we'll see.'

The tube pulls into the station. An old lady with a stick

and a red felt hat gets on. In a second Connor's jumped onto the floor. He looks a bit wobbly on his little legs and Steve wonders whether he's old enough to stand on the moving train. But Connor's grabbed the rail and Steve decides to let him be. The lady sits and turns to Steve.

'What a well-behaved little boy.'

'I blame his mum.'

Connor is swinging on the standing rail and Steve smiles because Connor's just like his dad: cocky.

'Your daddy must be very proud of you,' the lady says and turns back to Steve with an indulgent smile and a nod of appreciation.

'Uncle Steve's not my dad,' Connor says.

The woman looks between them. Her face has clouded. It isn't the pretty scene she had imagined after all. Steve can read her mind. She's jumped to divorce and he's the boyfriend.

Connor swings out like he's a compass drawing a circle and Steve stops himself saying, *Careful*. Kieran wouldn't have mollycoddled his son.

Connor says, 'My daddy's dead.'

'Oh.' The lady's eyes widen. 'I'm very sorry to hear that.'

Connor carries on swinging. 'My daddy was a hero.'

The lady smiles kindly. 'He was a hero, was he? Good for him.'

'A bad man shot him.'

The woman recoils at this. Her hand goes to her mouth. There's a moment before she speaks. 'Your daddy, he wasn't Kieran Shaw, was he? The policeman?'

Connor is completely unperturbed. 'Yes. Kee-Ran-Shaw. He was my dad.'

'Then he *was* a hero.' The lady fumbles desperately in her purse.

Steve puts his hand up. 'No, no, no. Thank you. But, no.'

She has tears in her eyes. 'But won't you let me buy him a treat?'

Steve says, 'We don't need money.' Realising that sounds brusque he adds, 'But thank you for your kindness.' He stands up. 'Come on, Con, it's our stop.'

'No it isn't. One more stop.'

'We're getting off here; the walk will do us good.'

But it is too far for Connor, and Steve carries him most of the way piggyback.

5

They don't call Lizzie to give evidence. She saw Kieran dying, but that is irrelevant. She was out of the room when the shot was fired. Neither prosecution nor defence consider that her evidence contributes to their case.

The jury retire just before lunch. Lizzie waits with Elaine, her family liaison officer, in the room for family members. One of the DCs from the MIT team brings them takeaway coffees and sandwiches. They scroll through their phones. Steve texts to say there will be pizza when she gets home. Connor wants to watch *Horton Hears a Who!*.

Lizzie's mum has Connor from Wednesday. By lunchtime it has become clear that it isn't going to be a quick verdict. Elaine produces some playing cards. She teaches Lizzie cribbage. On Thursday, at lunchtime, they are called into court. But the jury hasn't come to a finding.

Instead, a young woman in heavy make-up whose glittery nails Lizzie spotted a few days into the three-week trial passes a note to the clerk to give to the judge.

He unfolds it, reads it. He passes it to the defence and prosecution.

'I don't think this need bother us too much.'

The jury are dismissed but told not to go all the way back to the jury room. After a short discussion they file back in.

'DNA and fingerprints don't go to the issues in this case,' the judge explains. 'The defendant doesn't deny that he was in the room or that he was holding the gun. The issues at this trial are not forensic . . .'

But the jury member who passed the note is having none of that. She purses her lips and shakes her head. Presiding might be the learned His Honour Judge Mark Knapman QC, but she knows better and she isn't going to be hoodwinked; the forensic evidence is very material to the decision the jury has been struggling with for so long.

Lizzie is scalded by fury. The whole criminal justice system having to be so patient around such stupidity! This three-week trial, its learned QCs with their keen juniors, the laborious laying out of evidence, the meticulous reconstruction of events; all of this in the hands of someone who has watched too much *CSI* and is completely missing the point.

The judge smooths his hands out across the bench.

'To help you focus your discussions, and with the agreement of my learned friends, I am going to deliver a reminder of the facts that you have to decide upon.

'You do not have to decide whether Mr Kennedy fired the gun or that the bullet caused the death of Detective Inspector Kieran Shaw.

'What you are called on to decide upon is the state of mind of Mr Kennedy when he released the bullet. You must decide what, if anything, Mr Kennedy intended, and what he knew.

'You should consider the murder and manslaughter charges in order, and the first charge that you should consider is that of murder.

'To be guilty of murder a person must intend serious harm or to kill. That is, that at the time he performs the act that leads to death, the defendant must mean for serious harm or death to occur. Without this intent a person may kill, but still not commit murder.

'So, in respect of the murder charge, the questions before you are: are you sure that Mr Kennedy released the trigger on the gun intentionally, and if he did so, was this with the intent of causing serious harm or death?

'Whether this intent was towards Detective Inspector Shaw or to the man he had seen in the street, Mr Jermaine King, who he believed had murdered his friend, Spencer Cardoso, is irrelevant. If you are sure that Mr Kennedy intended to cause death or serious harm to either man at the time of the shooting, then you must find him guilty of murder.

'If you cannot be sure that Mr Kennedy had formed this intent, then you must find him not guilty of murder and move on to considering whether he is guilty of manslaughter by unlawful act.

'Manslaughter is sometimes called a "lesser charge" than murder. That is because the person committing manslaughter does not need to intend to cause serious harm or death to be guilty. The prosecution say that Mr Kennedy knowingly and unlawfully possessed a firearm. If that is the case, there is no defence to the charge of manslaughter.

'However, the defence say that Mr Kennedy did not know that the weapon in his possession was a real firearm and not an imitation . . .'

Lizzie closes her eyes. The judge's words swim over her into meaningless sound. She no longer wants to try to make sense of them. This fine slicing of time and intention, as if by a mandoline, seems to have no bearing on what had happened in that flat. Hearing the gunshot in the street and running up that narrow flight of stairs. Kieran on his back in the small room, surrounded by medics and police. His chest soaked in blood. Blood splashed on the broken window.

That boy, Ryan, who sits now so still and so carefully suited in the high dock, standing then in handcuffs by the flat's boarded-over fireplace, blood on his chest and face.

Suddenly privileged in the police family that created itself in an instant around the wounded officer, she moved towards Kieran. His face was white and sticky, his lips pale. This man, in such pain and extremis, was already not the man she had known.

She said, 'Love you,' and he moved his head and looked at her and mustered something that may or may not have been a smile.

'Don't be ridiculous.'

That was the last thing he said to her. Don't be ridiculous. Even with her eyes closed here in this courtroom, she presses her hand to her forehead. Don't be ridiculous. For goodness' sake!

No point in trying to make sense of it, the counsellor told her. Kieran's brain was already dying when he said those words, all possible meanings slipping away from it. Still how many times has she gone over those three words and tried to find the salt of them sweetened by humour, by love too, if only by love.

She said, 'You're going to be all right,' and he nodded and turned his face away, too busy with dying to stay with her. She stood back to let the medics work. How she regretted that now. Each second, so precious, and she had given away whole minutes. They lifted him onto the trolley bed and he was carried away from her down those narrow stairs.

The judge finishes talking. Lizzie opens her eyes and takes

in the burnished solemnity of the court. The wooden panelling, the precise words, the meticulous arguments and counter-arguments: all this ceremonial makes not a dint on what happened in that flat. She glances at Ryan, who sits almost motionless, mostly staring straight ahead of him.

Connor had been too young to retain any memories of his father.

The jury are getting up, beginning to file out, and her eyes travel over the people who are struggling to make up their minds about something that seems so obvious. A tall guy in a blue drill workwear jacket who has been making notes throughout. Taking his responsibilities seriously. Taking himself seriously, too. A dumpy woman, who wears every day a different patterned dress, all in polyester. How many can she have? A grey-haired man in suit and dark tie. They are a lucky-dip assortment of London to have to rule on these arcane shades of meaning.

She thinks of them going home at the end of each court day. Catching the tube and sitting there, anonymous, with their store of new knowledge. Are they wise enough to know that this violence is something they do not comprehend? To be humble before the fact of it? Kieran lying there with his life leaving him. The *CSI* know-it-all with the manicured nails glances towards her. Lizzie should look vulnerable, try to arouse her sympathy; there is a lot more going on in this courtroom than the arguments of the lawyers. She turns back to Ryan. He is looking at her too but when she meets his eyes, he looks away.

He was there. He pulled the trigger. He must know he is guilty.

The jury has left and the prosecution barrister, Margaret

Williams QC, is putting in a request to the judge – bearing in mind, My Lord, the circumstances of the deceased's families. The childcare issues. The defence does not object. The judge is sympathetic: the interested parties can go home. Provided they can return within an hour, the court will wait for them to hear the verdict when the jury is ready.

The judge rises. The remaining entourage, pressed up against each other, are forced to dawdle their way out through the narrow doors. The defence barrister is deferential and sympathetic: doing his job but still enough room in his heart for sympathy. As they move down the stone steps the prosecutor – very grand in her gold-heeled court shoes and bright lipstick – smiles at Lizzie. 'Won't be long now, either way.'

She has the look of someone who doesn't want to be detained but Lizzie puts a hand on her arm and pauses her on the stone steps.

'It's been a few days. Do you think they're going to be hung?'

The prosecutor draws Lizzie aside and speaks quietly.

'They won't be hung. Not on every count, anyway. Maybe on the big one, but on the manslaughter charge the judge seems to have given fairly unambiguous directions that he's guilty. He clearly knowingly possessed the firearm.' She smiles and rows back on her certainty, just in case. 'But you never can tell.'

'And if they are hung on the murder charge, then what? A retrial?'

The QC winks conspiratorially. 'We're not there yet. Let's wait for the jury.'

Margaret Williams QC is already walking briskly away,

her wig in her right hand. She doesn't want too much contact with the families. Just that exuberant introduction on the first day, like a galleon under full sail, and then every day afterwards a bright don't-bother-me-I'm-busy smile. Probably nervous herself. A big job, and a difficult one. High profile. She'll be wanting the guilty finding.

Outside the court are the usual protestors with their various agendas. Elaine puts her arm round Lizzie's shoulders and begins to walk her through the blizzard of strongly held opinions. Lizzie takes in the metal crash barriers. The grey slabs of stone. Someone has a noose. A blue flare spills into the air. Hard to tell what point they are making. A group with a big sign: *Abolish the Police*. A black cab drives past with its taxi sign lit up orange. Margaret Williams flags it down, steps into it discreetly and slips away. A camera flashes in Lizzie's face. In some way, she senses, this is fun for everyone involved.

A bunfight feels very different when you're the next of kin. Though, of course, Lizzie isn't the next of kin. That is Kieran's wife.

She won't put herself through this again. If there is to be another trial, she'll leave them to it.

Friday and through the weekend she is on compassionate leave at home. Her mother stays so the flat is very clean, all the washing done and neatly folded.

Elaine calls her every day. 'Just checking in.'

After Kieran's death the Met looked after Lizzie. Found her what the Fed Rep described as a nice little desk job working in the criminal justice unit. Case papers. A disclosure course for when she is ready to resume her career. 'Get you back into proper policing when the time's right,' Detective

Chief Superintendent Trask said. Part time and no one ever asking questions if she leaves early. The whip-round that officers organised on social media went towards a large down payment on a flat that includes a spare room for her mum to help out with childcare. And, every month, a trip in the new little blue Volkswagen down to the coast to see Kieran's widow so that Connor can get to know his sister. Rachel and Lizzie are doing their best. Hard enough for the children, they agree. At least they will have each other.

On Sunday Lizzie and her mum drive Connor out to Whipsnade to see the elephants.

While Connor watches the seals perform, Lizzie's mother says quietly, 'I never wanted you to go into that world. It's not that I don't think we need the police. But getting caught up with criminals. Look what's happened to your life.'

And then, in the evening, as they stack the dishwasher while Connor watches *Horton Hears a Who!* for the thousandth time, she says, 'You know, it's not too late for you, Lizzie. You're still young. And pretty.'

On the Monday afternoon Elaine calls. Still no news.

'The jury's hung, aren't they?' Lizzie says.

'No way of knowing, but yeah, they are taking fucking ages.'

Then on Tuesday, at 11 a.m., there is a call to get to court.

The guy in the blue drill jacket is the jury foreman. He stands and speaks the two verdicts clearly.

Not guilty of murder.

Not guilty of manslaughter.

Elaine squeezes Lizzie's hand tightly. There is a little noise from the gallery, quickly suppressed. Not a cheer but a cry. Lizzie glances to her right and sees Ryan's mother, Loretta, who is sitting with her head in her hands.

The judge thanks the jury for their service. A date for sentencing on the other matters is set. Reports are requested. Lizzie thinks she might faint.

Margaret Williams is waiting for Rachel Shaw and Lizzie in the family room upstairs. Her wig is in her hand and she is standing crookedly. This is a terrible result for her and Lizzie guesses that she'd love to take her shoes off and slump on one of the sofas. Yates, who has led the investigation for the police, is in the room too, leaning against the wall, his arms folded. He's normally a quiet self-effacing man, but right now his expression is thunderous.

Rachel says, 'What just happened? I mean, the judge practically told them to find him guilty on the manslaughter.'

The barrister says, 'It must be jury nullification.'

'What?'

Yates says, 'When a jury finds not guilty even though it's clear as day the defendant has broken the law.'

'Why on earth would they do that?'

Yates says, 'I think we can guess—'

Williams interrupts, 'No, that's not right. We can't guess and we'll never know. The jury's deliberations are secret. You can never second-guess a jury.'

Lizzie catches Yates's eye. It's clear what he thinks about Williams and how she has conducted the prosecution.

Rachel says, 'Can we appeal?'

Williams shakes her head impatiently. 'The law doesn't allow an appeal against a jury finding.'

Lizzie looks around the room. There's nothing to say

really. It's plain as day what's happened: the jury felt sorry for Ryan.

She says, 'I need to get back to Connor.'

Elaine says quietly, 'Let's both pop to the loo, then I'll drive you home.'

When the toilet door shuts behind Elaine, Lizzie takes the opportunity to slip away down the stairs and out into the street. Elaine is brilliant. Kind. Cynical. A fabulous swearer. Perfect. But Lizzie just can't be with anyone who will try to form this into words.

Guilty wouldn't have brought him back. She hadn't realised how much she wanted it.

Kieran's widow, Rachel, stands outside the court giving a statement to the press. Amazing that she's managed to put her response to this into words so quickly. Lizzie feels that she will never be able to vocalise what she feels. Kieran's girl, Samantha, dressed in a dark woollen coat, stands next to her mother. Lizzie tries to commit to the thought she needs to adopt: we all deal with loss in different ways. She walks briskly away, avoiding the cameras. Her phone rings and she glances at the screen. It is Elaine. She rejects the call. A text follows swiftly.

I'm still in the court. Let me know where you are. I'll come get you.

Lizzie hails a cab. The childminder will be home, waiting with Connor. Lizzie longs to be there, to hold her son. He won't want that. He'll want to go to the park, or to make gingerbread or to get his trains out. But that will still be good.

Her phone is ringing: Elaine again.

'I'm sorry, Elaine. I'm on my way home . . . No, I'm in a

cab. I'm nearly there. Thank you for everything. Yeah, yeah, not to worry. Listen, thank you. Really. You've been great. Yeah, I expected it. I did. A lot of doubt thrown . . . Yeah, OK, maybe not the manslaughter. No. We'll speak later. I gotta go.'

The driver's eyes are on her in the rear-view mirror. He is a white guy with a big round close-clipped head. As they turn into her street, he says, 'You're DC Griffiths.'

'Sorry, I don't want to talk about it.'

'It's not what you think. I'm ex-job myself.'

'I'd guessed.'

'That obvious, is it?'

'It is, yeah. Sorry.'

'Well, all I want to say is they're a bunch of bastards who know nothing and I hope it bites the lot of them in the arse. They'll get the police service they deserve.'

'Yeah, thanks.'

He pulls over in front of the flat. She fumbles in her bag for her purse.

'I won't be taking your money today. You stay safe out there.'

And then there she is, looking for her house key, alone in the street with the bare fact of it.

PART THREE

DOING TIME

6

Lucky.

That was how Ryan's mum, Loretta, tried to think of her son's prison sentence. He had been found guilty of robbery, possession of a firearm and false imprisonment. But still, she told herself, it could have been so much worse. And after all, it was only half an hour on the train from Waterloo to Feltham. She got there at least once a month. She could still glimpse the boy in him.

But now he was to be transferred to the adult prison and she had to battle despair again. It felt as if the son she knew was dying. Who would he be when he came back? She sat with him in the visitors' room.

'I'll try to get there,' she said. 'I think there's a bus.'

She'd always been thin, but in the years since it happened, she had become all bone. There were deep pools at the base of her neck and her eyes were large in her hollowed-out face.

'Don't worry, Mum,' Ryan said. 'I should be out in a couple of years, with a bit of luck.'

She smiled bravely. 'I can't wait.'

It was more than two years since he had been outside the walls of Feltham and in spite of the purpose of the journey Ryan's spirits lifted. But as the hours drew on, he began to feel as if his identity was being stretched out, thin as a strand of candyfloss. Through the window of the sweatbox, he saw an unpeopled landscape. Humpback bridges over zigzagging streams. Remote white stone pubs with cars pulled up in front. A stand of wind-blasted trees. White stone walls bright with green moss. He was unimaginably far from London. As they climbed it became foggy. Through the small window, across misty fields, he caught a glimpse of HMP Dartmoor. But he wondered whether he had imagined it, because the prison looked unreal, like a film set. Big as a town. Huge grey stone buildings with long rows of tiny square windows, slate rooves and tall chimneys. The sight of it made him suddenly desperate to get out of the little tin cell that trapped him. The van climbed, panting and sawing from side to side. It threaded its way through a small, bleak town. A fish and chip shop. A café. A bus stop at which no one waited. A man walking briskly along the road in the black uniform and lace-up boots of a screw. The van followed a line of the stone walls and ancient grey buildings, swung right, paused, moved forward. The gates closed around it.

For three days on the induction wing he waited for the fog to lift. Then he realised it never would.

The smell was different, but it was still the smell of prison. His heart was fluttering inside his chest, longing for freedom.

KJ said, It's the Kingdom of the North here. Ryan nodded and KJ said, I hope when the White Walkers wake up that the wall is high enough to keep the fuckers out. KJ was from his ends and it was funny; as if they were already back in London laughing at this big old freak show somewhere in the middle of nowhere. But then they moved out into their permanent cells and KJ and him were separated. Then Ryan wished he hadn't said that thing about the White Walkers.

In Feltham he'd had the first hint that he was being

watched. He'd tried to put it to one side: a sense of someone lingering at the end of a corridor perhaps, or behind a door. But that first night on G Wing he glimpsed two faces at the window, five storeys high with the wind blowing a gale outside.

The exercise yards were small, surrounded by high walls, the sky still confined, now by ancient rocks. The old-timers said the black birds hopping around and circling above were the ghosts of prisoners from the Napoleonic Wars. The prison wings looked to him like a huge grey stone ribcage, as if he had been buried inside the skeleton of a whale. Five storeys with almost vertical iron stairs that the wind rattled down.

Always cold.

There was a window in his cell with bars. If he stood at it, he could see out to the moors. The guys on the landing said they were lucky. Lower down and all they would see would be an exercise yard. But one night he saw a great big white bird flying past and he didn't like that because he wasn't sure whether it was real or not and he didn't have anyone he could ask.

He'd be out soon. He got a care package with a jacket and some trainers. Even here Shakiel reached out to him. Most of the time he was all about getting out, back to London, but not always.

A girl worked the landing. Too pretty for her warden's uniform, she was probably not much older than him. Very short very blonde hair. Eyes blue as Cinderella's. A pierced left nostril. First day he said to her, 'You've got beautiful eyes, miss.'

'That's not appropriate,' she said.

'Those eyes, miss, they just cut me down.'

51

'I'm happy to talk to you,' she said. 'But that's not appropriate.'

Still, she had smiled.

The landing was life. This was what you had to hammer yourself to. There was the usual stuff. One of the screws got potted and so for three days they were all banged up. There was a guy, Cuts, they called him, who sometimes shouted in the middle of the night to be let out of his cell. He got beaten in the showers for disturbing everyone's sleep but it didn't stop him.

Ryan caught a break. He was allocated a job in the gardens. Through the fog the sun was on his face and the wind blew. The trees were covered in moss with little red berries and the pretty screw's name was Lily.

7

Detective Inspector Sarah Collins was in the middle of a murder trial at the Bailey.

The case was R v Edward Holliday, a man who had killed his father. His barrister was running the 'last straw' defence: that after years of humiliation Holliday had momentarily lost self-control. Holliday's father, the defence said, had bullied him since childhood, had beaten his mother in front of him, and forced him to work unpaid. A week after his mother's death from cancer he told his father that he had had enough. He was leaving and he wanted the money that was owed to him. His father threw fifty pounds on the floor.

'Pick it up then,' he said.

But Sarah's team had found messages from Holliday to his sister about how much he hated his father and how one day he would take his revenge. There was one message in particular: One day I will kill him. And there were internet searches too, made before the killing, on how to destroy forensic evidence. Far from losing control, the prosecution said, Holliday had planned his father's death and had therefore no defence to murder.

The trial proceeded, the essential question not being whether Holliday had killed but rather the state of his mind at the time. Once Sarah would have been absorbed by the cut and thrust of the argument. The trial was when you had done the legwork and you gave it to the court. You could sit back, talk it over with your team in the police room. But this time she was restless and ill at ease. The jury listened, watched, made notes, and Sarah felt as though she were elsewhere. She imagined Edward Holliday, not the cipher the court somehow made him, but as a real son with a knife in his hand, stabbing his own father. She remembered, too, the jury in Kennedy's trial: the woman in her polyester dresses and the man in his expensive workwear.

At twelve o'clock, she gathered her things and stood, bowing quickly to the judge before she slipped out to make her way across London.

King's Cross station was a changed world from the dark low-ceilinged maze of her youth. There were shiny metal escalators and wide ticket halls with silver signage. She stepped out from the station's curtilage into a newly made district. A magic wand had been waved and the spell cast: smarter, cleaner, richer.

The banks of the Grand Union Canal were renovated, the brickwork cleaned and repointed; the once derelict and soot-stained warehousing spruced up and carrying heritage names: Coal Drops Yard, The Granary. The gasometers had been transformed into award-winning apartments.

Sarah could just about picture the old quarter as it once was: industrial, run-down and poor. The workers walking quickly in woollen coats and leather shoes. The women with prams and the children playing out. And later the fall into dereliction. Heroin-addicted prostitutes working the service roads, stepping forward to the men who pulled up in cars and wound down their windows. The director of public prosecutions had been arrested here a lifetime ago. Ghosts, Sarah, thought. All erased by the washed cobbles and bright little lights sunk into the pavement.

Her task today was to give evidence at Kieran Shaw's inquest: the last stage, she hoped, in the legal arguments about his death. The state would hear the evidence and draw its conclusions. Mistakes had been made and recommendations would follow. But beyond the court, the press would swarm again. The same facts would lead to very different conclusions. Sides would be taken.

And what about the pictures in her mind? The walkways and the bicycles. The excluded boys, the drug deals, the violence. And the officers, too, at three in the morning, taking a break between the tough jobs, standing together by their cars by the river, drawing strength from the company of the only people who understood their experiences.

She was early, so she turned right just beyond the court and took the steps into St Pancras Gardens. There had been a fall of rain and the many broad-leafed trees were still dropping sudden unexpected splashes. The garden was almost entirely in shade, dotted with green-stained tombs and memorials. She paused in front of a Victorian sundial and the weathered statue of a dog. Habit drew her towards the church with its sign: *Everyone Welcome*. She stepped inside. The walls were white plaster, the windows plain and arched. A man was sitting in one of the dark slatted chairs, a coffee in his hand and a folded Brompton bike beside him. She thought to leave, but, hearing her footsteps on the stone floor, he turned: Detective Chief Superintendent Baillie. He nodded and gestured with his hand for her to come and sit beside him. She stepped towards him.

'Have you given evidence?' Sarah asked.

'Not yet.'

'I shouldn't speak with you until we've both been called.'

'Up to you.'

After a moment's hesitation she sat.

'Going to do my legs, are you?' he said.

'I'm going to tell the truth.'

'As you see it.' Baillie smiled, as if expecting Sarah to agree with this inflection, and she braced herself for what was to come next. He said, 'You made a note of the meeting in your day book.'

'Didn't you?'

'Not in so much detail.'

'I'm not going to discuss my evidence.'

'Everyone warned me to be careful around you. I should have listened.'

'It's taken a long time to get to this point. Not easy for any of us.'

He shrugged. 'Doesn't matter what you say anyhow. Not bad enough that someone died on my watch and I've got to live with that. No, the big black cloud has settled over me. They need to find someone guilty, and obviously it can't be the boy who pulled the trigger. I wonder what bit of Siberia they'll move me to.'

There was a pause.

Sarah said, 'But do you honestly care about that? After everything that's happened?'

'I do care, yes. And I'm not going to be shamed into saying that I don't. I worked hard. I earned my rank. I liked leading important work and I was good at it. It mattered to me.'

Sarah stood up. 'I better go.'

Baillie ignored her intended exit.

'That's the risk you run, taking on difficult investigations.

Bit of good luck, bit of bad luck: that's what makes the difference. At my rank, it's nine-pin bowling. Last man standing, all that.' He looked at her keenly. 'Or woman.'

'You think I care about rank? After all this?'

He smiled nastily. 'I thought you'd say that. You've always been too grand for personal ambition.'

A chill passed over Sarah. She wanted to leave before he said his piece, but something else made her stay and listen.

'Think you're better than just doing the job well, better than just bringing a job home. Too pure to let a little lie pass. They'll never find you in any way responsible for Shaw's death. But you are responsible.'

8

Ryan sat in a steel chair with a blue plastic seat. The room was in one of the outbuildings. The walls were white plasterboard, the windows plastic-framed and double-glazed, as if he had escaped the Kingdom of the North into a fragment of the modern world. But it was an illusion. The White Walkers were just outside the door. One of them peered through the window. What a joker. Ryan moved in his seat to block it with his shoulder. He needed to convince this woman if he wanted his probation.

She said, 'I see you haven't written down who your victim was.'

'That's coz I don't know their names.'

'What do you mean, *their* names?'

'I pleaded guilty to the robberies, so I never got to know their names.'

The woman's expression did not change. She had a solidness about her: like a no-light-reflects kind of thing. No one would think you could push this woman around. But her name was Colette and that name meant the softer side must be there, behind that stern face. The first day he met her he said, 'You make me think of my auntie.'

And she laughed; it was like the sun coming out. But she was only briefly shaken out of her seriousness. She said, 'I'm here to help you, Ryan, but I'm not your auntie.'

Now she interlocks her fingers.

'I don't mean the robberies, Ryan. I mean the shooting.

You haven't written down the name of the man you killed.'

'But I was found not guilty of that, miss.'

That first meeting she gave him this little pamphlet. On the cover it said, Victim Empathy Booklet. It went towards his probation so it was in his interest to fill it out. He sat at the little table in his cell, pen in hand, and stared at the entries.

What did you gain from your crime?

That was baffling. He reached back to those days when him and Spence ran. The time they stole the posh boy's ball on the Astroturf and the boy chased them and nearly caught them. They'd laughed so hard. And then they'd given the ball to some of the youngers on the estate because it was never about the ball, was it? Course not. It was just for bants. Robin Hood, wasn't it? Thanks, Ryan, the YGs said. And he said, It's calm. And they walked away, him and Spence, feeling good.

Happiness. Maybe that was what he'd gained.

But he guessed that wasn't a good thing to write, not if you wanted probation. You couldn't say that robbing stuff made you feel happy. He wrote: Money.

What did you lose from your crime?

That night when they went to supply Lexi and, instead of finding her, there were two boys waiting for them in the darkness of Gallowstree Lane. Please don't. That's what Spence had said. The glimpse of the blade under the street light as the boys moved towards him. Spence collapsing and lying down. Ryan standing in the street as the helicopter hangs in the sky above them and a man slows his car and leans out of his wound-down window.

'Wannabe gangster. Hope he dies.'

Then, the rest of it. A long fall into destruction.

What had he lost from his crime?

Everything.

But that wasn't right. It wasn't the robberies that caused him to lose everything, it wasn't even the possession of the gun. What was it that had caused him to lose everything? It was everything, every single thing that had ever happened: that was what had caused him to lose everything.

He'd sold some wraps, stolen a few phones. Shakiel had given him a gun. Those were his crimes. And what had those crimes cost him?

He wrote: Freedom.

Write down who your victim was.

And he wrote, I don't know.

Now Colette said, 'But you did kill a man. Don't you know his name?'

Where was she coming from? It was like he'd filled the whole form out wrong! He didn't need to write about the dead police officer. He wasn't guilty of that.

'It was an accident.'

'Let's talk about Kieran Shaw for a minute. How do you feel about that? About him being dead?'

Ryan put his weight on the arms of the chair and lifted himself up. He'd thought he was going to enjoy these meetings. Bit of a change. Away from the landing and all that. And Colette, she looked like she'd turn out to be fun for all her stern face. But, fuck it.

'Can I go back to my cell?'

'You don't want to talk about it?'

He kissed his teeth.

'What do you think you're here for?'

'It's a game, innit?'

There was a pause before she replied. 'That's what they call drug dealing too, isn't it? A game?'

He shrugged. 'I dunno, do I? Could be anything now. Man's always switching it up. Been away a long time.'

'Calling it all a game. It kind of protects you from reality, doesn't it? But you killed a man.'

'I was found not guilty. He moved towards me and the gun went off. I never meant to kill him.'

'But you had the gun in your hand. What was it doing there?'

'Someone gave it to me.'

'You accepted it. You had it in your hand. Whether the jury found you guilty of murder or not, you did kill him.'

Ryan rubbed his eye. 'I told you already. I don't wanna talk about this. I don't see what it's got to do with anything.'

He was being disrespectful, and it made him uncomfortable. If this woman was his auntie, he would never talk to her like this. But this was different because he couldn't get away, which is what he'd do if she was his auntie. Get away. Get on his bike. Cycle round the estate. What he'd give to be out on his bike.

She said, 'Talk me through what happened.'

He rubbed his eye again, like it was the most boring thing ever.

'So, I was in the flat. Steve's flat. I thought he was a snitch. And, I can't really remember what happened, it's like a big noise in my head; but the gun, it went off. By accident. And no one was hurt. Then Mr Shaw came in. He was talking to me. He said everything was going to be all right. He said it wouldn't be so bad. He said he knew about my dad.'

'Then what happened?'

'The boy that killed Spence, he come walking down the street, and I had the gun and I was opening the window. And there was a woman in the street too, a police officer, Lizzie Griffiths. And I *knew* she was police because she arrested me once. But Kieran Shaw, he said sumat like, She's just a young woman. How do you know she's a fed? And I thought, Oh yes, all that fine talk, but turns out you're a liar just like everyone else. And then he came at me and—' He stopped speaking. Then he shrugged, and exhaled. 'I dunno, miss.'

'One minute this man is being kind to you. You maybe even like him. It sounds like he's going to look after you. He says he knows about your father. Maybe he feels for you? Is that possible? But the next minute he's lying to you. And then he moves towards you, and you shoot him.'

Ryan leaned back in his chair. 'No. I been through this, like a hundred times. It was an accident. The gun just went off.'

'The gun went off because you had it in your hand. You were waving it out the window. Your hand was on the trigger. You were excited. You were upset. You felt powerless. You were looking to shoot someone. And then he moved towards you.'

'I was found not guilty.'

'OK, but if you tie yourself too hard to that, it's going to be like dragging a stone behind you your whole life. You want to move forward, you've got to face what you did.'

'I wasn't guilty, though, was I? I don't have to face anything.' He stretched out his hands. 'You even qualified for this shit, miss?'

Colette was silent.

Then she said, 'Kieran Shaw had a little boy. I believe he

was a toddler when you killed his dad. You must think about that. I can't believe you don't. How old were you when your own dad died?'

Ryan stood up. 'I wanna go back to my cell.'

'That's OK. The meeting's nearly over for today. Step outside and call the guard.'

But he didn't move. He said, 'What do you know about my family? You're lucky I don't hit you.'

She raised her eyebrows. 'And if you hit me, that would be my fault, would it?'

He stepped towards her. 'Why are you going on like this? You trying to make me feel bad or something?'

But she didn't blink. 'Oh Ryan, I'm not trying to make you feel bad. I don't have to do that. You feel bad already.'

He jerked his head back. 'What then?'

'I'm trying to help you.'

He shouted, 'And how the fuck does this help?'

9

The coroner's court was too small and too old. The participants sat on hard wooden benches. There had to be a relay for the press. This was the broken-down criminal justice system where the causes of death were laid out in a building that was not fit for purpose.

Detective Inspector Sarah Collins raised her hand and took the affirmation. David Holfield QC, who faced her, was fair and not very tall. He was dressed in a well-fitted dark suit and a plain white shirt, with a patterned orange silk tie that added a bit of fizz. Sarah glanced at his hands: so neat they must have been manicured.

He began. 'On the evening of Tuesday 11 October, you were called to a meeting with Detective Chief Superintendent Tim Baillie?'

'That's right.'

'Also present were?'

'Detective Chief Inspector Jim Fedden, who was my boss at the time, and Detective Inspector Kieran Shaw.'

'What was the purpose of the meeting?'

'There were operational issues.'

Unasked, Sarah's mind retrieved memories so different from the words that had popped into the air with such simplicity. The dead woman hidden from view under the scene tent and outside the honking of London's thwarted cars. Then later that night, Baillie's office high in Scotland Yard: the exhaustion of the three detectives who gathered there, and the pressure to make decisions. None of this could be felt in the courtroom. Her account was a partial story, constrained by the shape of Holfield's questions, and glimpsed as if through a narrow viewfinder.

'You wanted the juvenile known to the court as D to be arrested?'

'For his own safety. Not because I for one moment identified that he posed a threat to others.'

'You wanted him to be arrested because he was vulnerable. His friend had been murdered. He was in the orbit of serious criminals.'

She understood the question. The lawyer was attempting to steer the evidence in such a way that it would convince the coroner that while Ryan might have killed Kieran Shaw with the bullet that flew out of the gun he held in his hand, it was the Met that bore the responsibility. Ryan had been found not guilty at trial. Now the Met's guilt would be inferred in the coroner's court. Perhaps the service would even be ordered to pay Ryan compensation.

'I wanted him arrested because I thought that Jermaine King or his associates would try to kill him if they thought he was giving information to the police.'

She had sworn to tell the truth, the whole truth, and nothing but the truth. But how was this possible? The truth was glimpsed – as her father would say – only *through a glass darkly*.

The examination moved on.

Here was the failed arrest of Jermaine King. Him crawling out of a Velux window and along a pitched roof three storeys high because DS Robyn Oakley had allowed him to use the toilet.

Fedden had told Sarah after the event that it hadn't taken the job long to anoint Robyn with her new nickname, which would be with her until her retirement and probably beyond. Robyn would always be the officer who didn't make King use the toilet with the door open. And if she'd made him leave the door open, she would have been the officer who didn't respect his right to privacy and respect.

Kami-Khazi either way.

She remembered her own bitter pang of irritation at the young show-off officer who for all her confidence had turned out to be as fallible as everyone else.

And with that something happened and Sarah was flooded with a memory of her father praying desperately after her sister's sudden death in a car crash. Even as a child she had understood; his faith was shaken.

She said, 'Kieran Shaw told DS Oakley to lie. King's escape might not have mattered if she had, but I countermanded Shaw's order. I told her to tell the truth. That was one of the things that went wrong: me telling her to tell the truth.'

The barrister, caught off guard, shuffled his papers. 'Give me a moment.'

But the coroner leaned forward. 'Go on, Detective Inspector. What do you mean by that?'

Sarah took a sip of water, put her two hands flat on the lectern.

'Do you need to sit, Officer?'

'No, I'm all right.'

'Go on then.'

'You have to understand, most of this, it was the least bad option.'

'Detective Inspector Shaw told another officer to lie. Go on.'

'He was trying to protect Ryan, not anyone else, certainly not himself. He told Robyn to lie to King when she gave the reason for King's arrest: to say he'd been seen on CCTV that linked him to a serious assault. But we hadn't viewed all the CCTV at that time. We are not allowed to misrepresent evidence. I wanted to ensure the arrest was lawful, that the evidence obtained would be admissible, so I countermanded Kieran Shaw. I instructed DS Oakley to tell the truth, to say that the arrest was based on intelligence. And King assumed – wrongly – that "intelligence" meant Ryan was a police informant. That was what had him walking down the street coming after Ryan, and Ryan waving the gun at the window. The fact that I told the arresting officer to tell the truth.'

The barrister was on his feet objecting, grasping that this was somehow not fair, a radical attempt to upset the apple-cart. What on earth were they going to do now? Recommend that the Met lie more? The legal argument began. Not caring to follow it, Sarah sat down. After the shooting they had viewed the relevant CCTV and King was indeed there, just as Kieran had counted on him being. And if he hadn't been, then what? He would have fudged it somehow. No one would have died.

10

That night the faces were at the windows. Ryan was asleep but he woke and caught them at it. They were watching him, noticing the things he got wrong.

An old man lived on the landing. Walking back to the wing from the garden Ryan asked Lily why he hadn't been moved to F Wing and she said, 'Coz of the fish. He doesn't want to leave them.' The man's name was Joseph but everyone called him Quint, who it turned out was the gnarly old captain in *Jaws*. There was a big tank on the landing and Quint's job was looking after the fish. The tank was crazy: bubbles rising through blue light and colourful fish swimming through an underwater garden.

Lily said she'd heard Quint used to be one of the top guys. Used to swagger down the hallways – people would do everything for him. Now look at him.

And Ryan did look at him, tied up to his oxygen, moving down the landing, taking care of the fish.

Colette said, 'I was looking through your record. One of the prison officers says you've been sleeping badly.'

Ryan shrugged.

Colette said, 'Do you want to tell me about that?'

'No biggie. I think the fog's getting to me. It's always fucking foggy.'

'Last meeting, you said, I don't remember your words

exactly, but you said something like that I was lucky you didn't hit me.'

'Sorry about that.'

'Thank you.' Colette thought for a moment. 'But you didn't spend the whole of the session threatening me. Most of the time you were polite. So perhaps we could have a think about what prompted you to feel like that.'

'If you want.'

'If I want?'

'Yes. Up to you.'

'It's a game?'

'Like I said, I don't know what the point of this is.'

'OK, so we'll do what I want.'

'Whatever.'

'You said you felt like hitting me immediately after I brought up Kieran Shaw's little boy and you losing your own dad to violence at about the same age.'

Ryan kissed his teeth. 'You must be qualified after all.'

Colette smiled. They were rare her smiles, but when they did come, they were bangers. 'Every time I bring up the coincidence you say something hostile. What's that about?'

'Bit obvious, innit? You didn't have to go to uni or nothing to notice that. My dad died. His dad died.'

Colette smiled again. 'It being obvious, does that stop it causing you pain? It must be hard having to ignore something so obvious. That not sleeping thing, you reckon it's just the fog?'

Ryan thought of those faces at the window. No way was he telling her about them. Don't want to end up in the madhouse just as you're about to get out.

'OK, Doc. Let's do it your way. Tell me how to feel better.'

There was a short silence.

Colette said, 'I think that's going to be difficult.'

Ryan looked over his shoulder, as if he expected someone to be there.

'Great.'

'In a way, it is.'

'How's that?'

'Because it means you're not a psychopath.'

Ryan glared at her. 'That meant to be funny?'

'Not at all. Some of the people I meet in here, they're wired differently. They don't feel any guilt about what they've done, or, if they do, they can't use that to change. There's nothing I can do to help them. But that's not you, and that's good because it means you can change. But the downside is that thinking about what happened and your part in it makes you feel very bad. It's not going to be easy.' She waited but Ryan didn't speak. She leaned forward. 'It also means you can have a better life. Real relationships with people. The things I think you want.'

'I want to get out of here. I want to go cycling again.'

'Of course you do.'

'So?'

'The problem is that these feelings are going to follow you, maybe even when you're cycling. You feel *really bad*. You can't sleep. You can't bear it. You don't know how to deal with those feelings, so you do everything you can to avoid them. When I bring up Kieran's death you get angry. You say you want to hit me. Or you insult me, try to humiliate me – you ask if I'm qualified. That's you diverting the conversation away from what happened and the feelings you have. And it kind of works in the short term. Most

70

people will be convinced. Some are even impressed by your aggression. They call you cop killer on the landing, don't they?'

Ryan puffed out his cheeks. 'I don't ask them to.'

'Still, it's tempting? Cop killer – sounds kind of cool? Very different story to feeling bad about killing someone who was loved, who was a father. You're probably a bit weak if you feel ashamed about taking away a little boy's dad because a big man would be proud, wouldn't he? He'd be a cop killer.'

'I'm not proud of it. It was an accident.'

'You had the gun in your hand. The first step is admitting that to yourself. That's the first step to feeling better.'

'Are you deaf or something? It was an accident. I didn't mean to kill him.'

'They found you not guilty?'

'That's right.'

Colette sighed. 'But still. You can't sleep.'

11

Sarah tapped out at Colindale station and turned with the other police flooding in the early morning along the too narrow pavement towards Hendon. Uniform and detectives alike knew each other as belonging to the same breed but, in the way of police, did not make eye contact. Judgement was reserved until such time as more information had been received. So many of her tribe, from all the different possible walks of police life. Youngsters, self-conscious, on their way to training. The old sweat never-anything-but uniform types. Walking briskly. Short hair. Every problem could be solved if only the brass would enforce better discipline around ironing and shoe polishing. Her subtribe, the detectives: men and women in a variety of mostly blue suits. Ahead, two grey-haired male tecs suddenly recognised each other and she witnessed an outbreak of police warmth and friendship. The pat on the back, the laugh, the handshake. Evidently – although she did not know them – two people who had worked the long hours and seen stuff and had each other's backs and then unexpectedly bumped into each other on a grey nothing-special London morning. The two men fell in step, heads down, talking.

Sarah passed through the turnstiles, tapping her warrant card. Her feet slowed only momentarily by the memorial flame. She waited for the secure lift to the third floor. Her team were huddled round a computer and when they saw her stirred with the uneasy embarrassed friendliness of children caught red-handed. They nodded to her. 'Morning, Sarah.' She nodded back. 'Morning.'

She found a computer at a deserted table and opened her email account. So that was what they were looking at. The report was embargoed but someone on the team must have access to it. Sarah hadn't smoked in years but the sight of it gave rise to the old craving. She tapped in the password, which had arrived by separate email.

Inquest into the death of Detective Inspector Kieran Shaw
Report to prevent future deaths

This is a report under schedule 5 of the Coroners and Justice
  Act . . .

It was a long read, beginning with the events leading up to Kieran Shaw's death. She would go back, read the report again in detail. But now she skipped straight to the conclusions. There were a number of Matters of Concern, all marked in bold and numbered.

16. MC1 *The handling of vulnerable parties in covert operations.*

She scanned it quickly: more guidance, more suggestions of rules to protect young people caught up in criminal networks.

She went back to her team. 'Anyone got a cigarette?'

Looks were exchanged. A couple of them shook their heads. 'Sorry, guv.'

She tried for a joke. 'No problem. I don't smoke anyway.'

Devan, the detective sergeant, did his best and laughed and said, 'Good one, Sarah.'

17. MC2 *The need for senior officers to take seriously concerns raised by subordinates.*

This was every public report ever written about any institution's failures. But it was also her and Fedden and Baillie.

Here were the words they would hate her for.

20. *Detective Inspector Sarah Collins suggested in her evidence that if she had allowed the arresting officer to lie in giving her reasons for the arrest of King it might have prevented the later death of Kieran Shaw. However, I find that it was an earlier action advocated by DI Collins that might have prevented the death; that is the prompt arrest of the juvenile known as D, who subsequently shot Detective Inspector Shaw.*

21. *A decision was made by DI Collins's superiors to safeguard the efficacy of Operation Perseus over prioritising the safeguarding of a juvenile. DI Collins was put in a position whereby the failure to respond to her advice led her subsequently to question her own decision-making. However, she behaved with integrity and carries no responsibility for the officer's death.*

She couldn't stop herself. She rested her head in her hands. How could these words that were so supportive of her make her feel so disgraced? She hadn't meant to provoke this when she said she should have told Robyn Oakley to lie. She took a breath, placed a hand on her chest. Her face heated with the shame of it.

Turned out Baillie had been right then when he'd talked to her in that church. She hadn't intended to damage her colleagues with her evidence, but she had. There was indeed no Matter of Concern in bold from the coroner recommending that officers consider lying if it might save a life.

But she could not be so clear as to what should have been done, because she remembered the car that was still outstanding when Baillie made the decision to delay arresting Ryan. She'd seen the crime scene photographs of the vehicle after it was seized. Black nylon holdalls crammed together in the boot. Milled-steel Kalashnikovs. Four Skorpion machine pistols. A grey-muzzled suppressor. Grenades. A little war had been packed into the back of that BMW, just waiting to burst out onto the streets of London. Baillie had wanted to make sure that nothing jeopardised the seizure of those weapons. Had he not been right, and she wrong?

It was good, she reminded herself. Careful appraisals of what could be done differently were the mark of a civilised society.

She felt so tired.

She looked across the large open-plan office of the Met's brand-new operational and training centre – IKEA, some of them called it – and saw her boss, Jim Fedden, looking at her.

On the last page was the determination.

Kieran Michael Shaw was unlawfully killed.
One of the officers under his command was being unlawfully detained and threatened with a firearm by a juvenile male who cannot be named for legal reasons. With no concern for his own safety, Kieran Shaw gained entry to the flat and tried to negotiate a peaceful resolution. Unfortunately his efforts were interrupted by the

appearance of Jermaine King in the street below. King had murdered the young man's best friend. He became agitated and Kieran, believing that the lives of others were in immediate danger, selflessly tried to disarm him. In the course of that attempt Kieran was shot in the chest. Despite the best efforts of police officers and paramedics at the scene and subsequent treatment at hospital the wound was not survivable and Kieran Shaw died an hour later.

Sarah resisted the impulse to put her hands over her face. She closed the report. Went back to her emails. Here was the one she had already opened from Midshire Constabulary, the one she was delaying her reply to. She clicked on the reverse arrow on the top and typed.

Dear Sir . . .

Fedden was walking over to her across the long floor. Fedden: the bulldozer. The DCI famous for his party turn dancing to 'It's Not Unusual'. The guy who was a bastard but never bore grudges. The boss who liked a grafter and who, in spite of everything, had liked her. She finished her email and pressed send. She stood up, waiting for him. She couldn't have this conversation sitting down.

'Sarah.'

'Jim.'

'After what's happened . . .'

'Yes.'

'I'm sorry . . .'

'It's all right, boss. No need. I agree. We can't continue to work together. I've just accepted a job on another force.'

'I am sorry, Sarah. Really I am. You are a fine detective.'

He offered his hand. She shook it.

'Do you mind, Jim, if I take this as a rest day?'

'No, no. No. Go ahead.'

She took her coat and made her way towards the lift. It might not always be a happy one, but the Met was still her family.

Many years previously she had interviewed Kieran Shaw under caution. The words he had said to her didn't hurt at the time. *I don't know how you can live with yourself.* They had been almost a joke to her, emblematic of everything that was wrong with the man. She had been so certain, so sure she was right.

12

At four in the morning Cuts was shouting. Can you help me? Will you help me? Can you unlock? The landing stirred in protest. Raised voices told him to shut the fuck up. The footsteps of the screw moved along the landing. Ryan rolled onto his back. He'd tried sleeping facing the door, but that was worse. He didn't want his back turned if they moved into the room with him, so he lay with his head towards the door and faced the window.

Beyond the bars the moon was full.

Ryan couldn't see them but he knew they were there, the Walkers, outside in the black night at the edges of the window. Holding on to the walls maybe, crouching there. If only he had curtains to draw against them. But would that make it better, or would they be able to come closer?

It was good to have a job outside. Less time on the landing. The landing and the showers and the kitchens: these were the places where shit went down. Ryan had protection, but still he was wary. He found it hard to make friends or form alliances. KJ was on another wing. Shakiel's reach was long, but as well as Bluds there were Soldiers in Dartmoor.

Quint, he seemed to float above it all. Perhaps because he was so old. He could have been sixty. Nothing to take from him, nothing to offer. Maybe it was because of the fish. Everyone liked the fish. When the pump broke they all had a whip-round and got a new one. The screws brought it in.

When they unlocked at last, and before Lily came to take

him out to the garden, Ryan stood and watched the tank. In a couple of moments Quint was on his shoulder.

'Is it true,' Ryan said, 'that in the wild there's no limit to how big they can grow?'

'No, but it's true the size of the tank limits them. Have to be careful. Like those red fish – you probably think they're goldfish?'

'They're not?'

'They're rosy barbs. Like to be in a little shoal, so I have to have, like, minimum five. Because on their own they get aggressive. Very aggressive fish, in the wrong situation.'

'You don't have any of them stripy fish.'

'The ones with the long fins?'

'Yep, them.'

'Angel fish. I'd like some, but they're tropical. All the fish in this tank are cold water. You got to make a choice: hot or cold. The tank, it's a world. Got to get it right. Introduce a new fish, all the others get upset for a bit. And the aggressive fish? Put a mirror in and they'll fight their own reflection.'

'Prison fish, innit?' Ryan smiled. 'Mad.' There was a short silence. 'What kind of fish are you, then?'

Quint put his finger against a little dark fish, swimming on its own right down the bottom. 'Bristlenose pleco. Shy little fish. Keeps out of the way.'

'Used to be a piranha is what I heard.'

'No, son. I was always a bristlenose pleco. I just didn't know it.'

Maybe Quint preferred it on G Wing to the crazy world he had lived in beyond the walls. What had he done to be in here for so long? It must be murder. Or worse. Now here he was, obsessed with a load of fish.

When Lily walked him over to the garden Ryan asked what Quint was in for and she said, 'If he didn't tell you then I'm not going to.'

It was a bright spring day, for once with no mist. Blue sky. Cold in the shadows, hot in the sun. He worked down the row, weeding. Behind him, hiding in the dark lee of the wall, was one of the Walkers.

He thought of that little fatherless boy somewhere out there. He must be, what? Four maybe? You weren't allowed to write to your victim, but you could ask the system to contact them. Maybe he'd ask Colette about that.

13

There were stone-carved lintels over the school gates that had once marked the separate entrances for the girls and boys. The headmistress was waiting to greet them and the new parents were ushered inside and led through. The classroom had a parquet floor and arched windows, the wooden frames thick with years of gloss paint. Connor hung his coat and bag on the peg, next to the others. It was a new coat; soft yellow fleece with a patterned lining and an embroidered patch on the breast: *Born to be wild*. He was still young enough to wear the sweetest things without protest. 'Got to look smart for school, heh?' Kieran's mother, Isobel, had said, handing it over wrapped in tissue paper. There was a new haircut, too, because Isobel had insisted; Kieran would have wanted that, she said. Connor's blond curls fell like soft snow on the floor of the barber's shop. Lizzie picked one of them up and curled it round her finger. She shouldn't always do what she was told. She considered popping the curl in her purse. Then she remembered seeing once a lock of Winston Churchill's baby hair and how it had aged, lost its colour and grown brittle. She dropped the curl and let it lie with the others to be swept away.

Connor was standing beside her, waiting. In the shelter of the coats was one last moment of privacy. Lizzie knelt and kissed him on the forehead. 'Going to be all right, little man?'

He pushed her back with his hand and looked around him.

'Mu-um.'

Already old enough not to want to look like a mummy's boy. Still, she thought with a squeeze of tenderness, those elephants lined up on the shelf above his bed.

The teacher was rounding up the new children and Connor joined them without a backward glance.

She hadn't anticipated the pang she would feel watching him gather with the others. Steve, her mum, Kieran's mum, they'd all offered to help her develop her career. But it wasn't possible. Connor didn't have a dad. He needed her to be there for him. But seeing him, standing with the other children, she could see that very soon he wouldn't. Not really. She was giving her life over to him but he was already beginning to grow up and walk away from her, as he should. And she would have to let him. What would remain for her?

Moving out, through the hallway. A picture of an aggressively smiling bee: manners matter in the playground! Out on the pavement, beyond the school's heavy metal gate, the other parents were making first contacts. There were a lot of couples, Lizzie noticed, dropping off their child together on the first day. One of the dads was in leather trousers and had a blond quiff. 'Joining us for a coffee?' he said, big confident smile. Good white teeth. Some kind of rock-star dad.

'Thanks, but I've got to get to work.'

He smiled with what Lizzie estimated was his habitual twinkle.

'Can't be an hour late on your boy's first day?'

Wasn't he cock of the walk?

She shrugged. She should have thought of this, instead of agreeing a meeting with one of the relief skippers who wanted to see her. Probably important to get to know the other parents: got to think of Connor.

The man winked and said, 'And what is it you do that's so vitally important?'

'I work for the government.'

He raised his eyes in mock astonishment. 'The government?'

'Oh fuck right off,' she said, but luckily not out loud.

Instead, she managed a thin smile and said, 'Another day would be great. I'll give you my number.'

Sergeant Pierson was waiting for her when she arrived in the office. There was a takeaway coffee on the desk and two sugar sachets.

'Didn't know how you like it,' Pierson said.

'Yeah, thanks.'

She threw her bag on the floor and searched for the offending file among the pile on her desk.

Sergeant Pierson said, 'It's the third time you've sent it back.'

'If the case papers are not up to scratch, then the job gets dropped. If the officer . . .' Lizzie checked the front of a case file. 'If PC Nolan—'

Pierson interrupted. 'Jackie.'

'If Jackie wants to come in and talk it through with me, I'm always here.'

Pierson sat, legs wide apart. He put his cap on the desk.

'She was in tears. She's on the point of packing it in. Do you have any idea how it is for the new girls and boys? Not like it was in our day.'

Our day, Lizzie thought. How had that happened? Girls

and boys, she thought. Honestly. Her phone was ringing. She picked it up and glanced at the screen. Elaine. Probably wanting to congratulate her on Connor's first day. That woman was steadfast, but Lizzie couldn't face it. She rejected the call.

She looked back at Pierson. He was smartly turned out, old school – shoes polished, Parker biro neatly tucked into the pocket of his Met vest – but he also had the worn look of someone who had seen a fair bit of service. He had his tried and tested ways of getting things done, of winning people round. That cup of coffee. All very gentle and persuasive, but.

'I can't send the case file back to Clown Prosecution Service until it's right,' she said. 'And I can't solve the problems of the criminal justice system either, because it's fucked.'

He frowned. He had expected her to sort it for him and for the keen girl, whatever her name was. Jackie. Lizzie could teach Jackie a thing or two about crying. And about not crying, too, come to think of it.

She turned back to her computer screen and read the sergeant's details on the case file. He had one of the older warrant numbers, still in the early twenty thousands. So it went, the machine, gobbling up its own people, without a second glance. Everyone thinks they're so important, caught up in all that drama, power of arrest and all that. And then they're gone. The system just cranks on. Leaving little Connor in his yellow coat standing without his father on his first day at school.

'Looks like you'll be out of here soon,' she said. 'Old pension? Lucky you.'

He scratched the back of his neck. 'Come on, Lizzie. Help

the girl out. She's a good officer. We've got to hang on to youngsters like Jackie.'

'How do you suggest I do that? I'm just the monkey who supervises the case papers.'

Over his shoulder Lizzie saw Elaine step into the room. So it wasn't just a catch-up call. Not just a 'send me a pic', and replying with a heart emoji next to the photo of Connor in his yellow coat and his short hair. There must be some new development. That was the thing. It never ended.

She turned back to Pierson. 'On her arresting statement Jackie needs to say what she arrested for. How difficult can it be? Send her over to me and I'll talk her through the disclosure forms.'

'No. Just, no.'

Elaine nodded. 'I thought that's what you'd say.'

They were sitting in a little café, a short walk from the nick. It was all pink and chintz and they could absolutely count on no one from the nick coming in. The coffee was like dishwater.

'I don't blame you,' Elaine said. 'But I had to tell you Ryan had made the request and I didn't want to do it over the phone.' She took a slow sip of her hot chocolate. 'How are you doing? Apart from me telling you that, I mean.'

'Yeah. You know.'

Elaine held one hand in the other. She wasn't eating the Danish pastry.

'What about yourself?' Lizzie said.

'Same old, same old. Kids are getting older. Husband's getting fatter. The job's still fucked. Oh, and Sarah Collins has left the Met, did you hear?'

Lizzie shook her head. 'Why's that then? On promotion?'

'The inquest, I think. Have you read the report?'

'Came out smelling of roses, didn't she?'

'Not sure that's entirely fair.'

'You know what I think.' A brief pause. 'But she's your friend, I guess.'

'Lizzie—'

'Whatever it is you're going to say, Elaine, maybe don't say it?'

'You're right. I'm shutting up.'

'You're not eating your pastry.'

'Losing weight, aren't I? Weight Watchers. Can't you tell?'

Lizzie smiled.

'I'd lose it quicker only I don't think I could stand all the applause.'

'Elaine!'

'While you're laughing, I'm going to slip it in. Forgiveness, you know, all that—'

Lizzie put her hand up. 'Stop there.'

'No, it's my bloody duty. Forgiveness. Like the poet says—'

'Poetry? For God's sake, what are you thinking?'

'OK, all right, no fucking poetry. But still.' She reached over and took Lizzie's hand. 'It's not about *him*. It's about you, Lizzie. You: moving on. You have to make a start, while you're still young enough.'

Lizzie caught the waiter's eye and motioned for the bill.

Elaine took her hand away and leaned back. 'Ah, come on. I'm sorry. My bad. The boy's a total cunt. Stupid of me.'

'Don't think that. I just have to get back to the office. One of the new PCs needs a lesson in disclosure. I appreciate it. I appreciate *you*. You're very kind. You're always kind.'

'And Connor, he's good, yes? First day today? I always hated them myself. Bloody children: growing up. The bastards.'

Lizzie pushed her phone across and showed the photo.

Elaine nodded. 'Grandma's coat, I'm guessing?' She wiped the corner of her eye. 'I'll write to the prison, then. Let them know you're not interested.'

'No, I'll do it. I'll let him know.'

A flicker of doubt passed across Elaine's face. 'If you're sure?'

Connor was asleep and the house was silent. Lizzie sat at her computer, scrolling through. She watched the clips of the various interviewers and then typed into the search engine for the contact details. There was a popular morning show, female presenter. That should do the trick.

14

Colette warned Ryan not to watch it. She told him, just because Lizzie Griffiths did that it doesn't mean, what you've done, the thinking that you've been doing, Ryan, it's still valuable . . . and I'll be writing to the parole board to say that.

But that night he found it easily enough. It was on catch-up. He lay on his bed with his headphones on. Lizzie Griffiths was still pretty and slim. In that respect she was as he remembered her. Sharp little dark trouser suit. Flowery shirt. High heels. Hair cut long and shiny. But there was something different. Her face had become hard.

She'd gone for a morning show. Millions of viewers. The interviewer was sympathetic.

Lots of it he couldn't really hear because he was so angry, but he caught snatches.

The jury's decision is for them . . . but my son is still without his father . . . He hasn't said sorry. I'm not interested in talking to someone who hasn't admitted any responsibility. I'm not interested in making him feel better. I don't feel better. Why should he?

He played it again, more than once.

The absolute cunt. The cunt.

He couldn't sleep. Hadn't she understood? He'd been found not guilty! He didn't even *need* to say sorry.

The White Walkers were at the window all night. A swarm of them. Chattering away but not so he could make out their words. Tapping on the window and pointing their thin white fingers.

In the morning when he went to get his food the guys were all at it, like it was the funniest thing ever. Heard you were on the telly. Cuts, that total loser who cried out in the middle of the night, singing, 'Sorry Seems to Be the Hardest Word'. The whole landing was laughing.

As he walked past the tank on his way back to his cell, Quint said, 'You all right?'

Fuck Lizzie Griffiths and her little boy. Poor little baby. He wasn't the only one who'd had to make it without a dad.

That boy: he had the whole world looking out for him. Probably got a police uniform already, little baby fed. And what did he have? His mum, Loretta on the juice. And Shakiel. Yeah, he had had Shakiel, showing him how things are. Turned up one day with a newspaper in his hand and his mum had shouted at him afterwards.

'I don't want you talking to him. I don't want you seeing him. I don't want you taking his presents or riding in his stupid car. Don't be admiring him. Stay away from him.'

But who was it had sorted out the little smart Alec at school that had dissed her, called her a crack whore? The little shit hadn't looked so full of himself after Shakiel had had a word. And who was it had avenged his dad? That newspaper with its headline: he'd fished it out the bin and sat on the stairs reading it. *Rapper stabbed to death*. Shakiel had done that. Him and his dad had run and Shakiel had done what was necessary. It's not that stupid woman telling you that there's hope for you coz you feel bad. The reality is what Shakiel said. There are things that have to be done and you do them. Then you don't think about them no more. That's how it goes. That's real life. You want that thing, you got to step up.

He's not going to have all those wastemen laughing at him.

He has a speaker in his room, a good one. His sister gave it him. Bose. Pretty heavy, too. The guys were all hanging out on the landing. He picked it up and tucked it by his side. Just needed to get away with carrying it that short distance, and then not fuck up.

He walked past them all, not really hearing the words. One of them said something to him and he said, 'Yeah.'

As he got nearer, he broke his step. Lily shouted – no running on the landing – but too late. He swung his hand holding the speaker out behind him. He put his whole force behind it, swinging his body into the blow. The alarm was already going. Lily must have hit it.

The glass smashed. The water burst out, like a solid mass, and then, gone. The guys were running. There were fish everywhere, flopping about on the floor, gasping for air. He could see the rosy barbs. And the little brown fish. The bristlenose pleco, flapping about. The guys were trying to scoop them all up, trying to get them into what was left of the water.

Ryan sat on the bed in his cell. They'd take the speaker off him. He'd lose some of his privileges, maybe they'd even delay his release, but it was worth it. Man can't live without respect. He was nearly there: a year, maybe eighteen months to go. Easy. Colette said he'd probably be housed outside London as part of his probation. It was an opportunity.

PART FOUR

GOING OT

MONDAY NIGHT

15

The night Leif went missing Asha waited until after midnight before she called the police. After the call she made sure the kitchen was tidy. There was one cupboard that had been bothering her. She took everything out and cleaned inside.

She stood at the sink. Perhaps she should call her older sister? But Bip would tell her off. She made herself a cup of tea and sat on the sofa.

She had been so busy; working, taking Ari to breakfast club, trying to get Leif back into school. She had found alcohol in his room, and a weed crusher. He had a new pair of trainers. Where was the money coming from? Maybe it didn't matter. Boys that age; lots of them get into trouble. They grow out of it, don't they? The tightness in her chest had been telling her something else but the problem was that the people she wanted to talk to were also the people she needed to persuade to let him back into school. So she kept it to all to herself.

Leif had been in the bath and his phone was on the table ringing, over and over. She took a photo of the number. He got out the bath and went into his room. When he came out, he was wearing a new black hoodie and the flash trainers.

'I'm going gym.'

'Where are you really going?'

He shrugged.

'You can tell me, Leif. I'm your mum.'

'I'm Going To The Gym.'

'At least put a coat on.'

And that was it: he went out the front door and disappeared.

She'd called 999 but still they didn't come. She dialled 101 and waited for thirty minutes in the queue. The voice at the other end of the line said, 'They're on their way. We've been busy.'

She didn't like to call again but she couldn't sit still. She emptied out one of her drawers and ironed some things she hadn't worn in a while. She poured herself a glass of wine. When she heard the knock at the door, she tipped what was left of it down the sink and shut the glass away in a cupboard.

Two officers were at the door: an Asian woman and a white man, both in uniform. A police car was parked on the kerb and that worried her because if Leif came home and saw it, he might not come in.

She said, 'I'm sorry to bother you. It's probably nothing.'

She wished she hadn't said that. She had dialled 999 but it had taken them two hours to get here. They were clearly in no rush. She needed them to take her seriously, not to be told it was nothing.

The man said, 'That's all right, that's what we're here for. Can we come in?'

He was already stepping inside the small hallway. She offered to make them a cup of tea but they both said, No. Thank you.

They sat at her table, and although they weren't especially big, they seemed somehow huge in their uniforms and boots. Ari was asleep in his room and she hoped their radios wouldn't wake him.

The woman took the report. Asha didn't like to tell her

everything. Not about the trainers or the hoodie. Not about the weed crusher. She didn't want to get Leif in trouble. They asked if she had any numbers for Leif's friends and she said, No. That was a lie. His friends might not talk to her if she gave their numbers to police.

When the report was finished the man stood up and said, 'Try not to worry. He'll be back in a couple of days. That's what they normally do.'

Asha stood up too. 'What will you do to find him?'

The man shrugged. 'CID will review it after we put the report on. Thing is, he's not really missing yet, is he? He's fifteen. You said he's unpredictable. He could easily just be at a friend's.'

She had the number of one of Leif's old school friends, and she WhatsApped him.

Hi Mahdi, know anything bout where Leif is?

She could see the two ticks, so she knew he'd read it, but he didn't answer.

She texted her sister. Can you take Ari to breakfast club tomorrow?

16

The team were staying overnight in a fake Elizabethan pile. Steve nabbed a table in a corner of the bar set against the back wall, where he could take in the room easily. Craig, heavy-set and slow-moving, had the seat beside him. Kiyana, the new girl, was working on not seeming excited. She'd done secret squirrel stuff before, but this was different. Carrying covertly outside the Met. The dealers called it OT – Out There – and that's what it felt like.

Craig and Steve were happy to sit back and let Kiyana shoulder the burden of conversation. She talked quietly but enthusiastically about one of their jobs that was due for sentencing. Craig and Steve agreed whenever necessary. Around them the room hummed with conversation. There was an abundance of men in V-neck pullovers and women with liver-spotted hands, nails shellacked in bracing colours. The place seemed to Steve both fancy and desolate.

Marilyn, the detective sergeant, walked quickly across the bar. She must have squeezed herself into the tiny basement swimming pool, because she brought with her a strong waft of chlorine. She glanced at Steve and Craig's seats and reluctantly took the one opposite, with her back to the room. She read the menu in an instant and chose the burger. Just a quick drink, everyone, and off to bed.

Kiyana was quick to get the round in. 'All set then?' she said on her return, throwing four packets of crisps on the table.

Steve tuned Kiyana out.

But for the absence of the hum of engines it could be a lounge on a cruise ship. Everything here for the stress-free enjoyment of a comfortable retirement. But there were a couple of guests, also sitting at a table against the wall, who drew Steve's attention. From time to time they glanced at the two men and two women who had arrived late in a single powerful car. The couple were both mid-fifties. The woman was large-breasted with blonde highlights and, unusually for this place, wore jeans and flat shoes. Even sitting you could see the man was tall. He had a head like a potato, wore chinos and a checked shirt, and had glasses on the top of his King Edward. The dog was the clincher – a big slightly overweight wolf of a thing that snoozed at their feet. Partly as a little joke to himself Steve offered to get a last round in. As he moved towards the bar, the man in the chinos stood. Six foot three, Steve guessed. The man left his table with a conspicuously unhurried air, moved over to the bar and offered his hand.

'What will you and your friends be drinking?'

'Thanks very much, but we'll be turning in for the night after this one.'

'Well, good luck with whatever it is you're up to,' the man said with a wink and a smile: a last-ditch attempt to force his own experience on him.

Carrying the tray back to the table Steve glanced at the wife and the dog. She met his eyes and gave him the look. He had reckoned this place would be unlikely to be frequented by drug dealers, but he should have anticipated that retired Old Bill would choose it for a weekend break.

*

99

The curtains in his room were the same colour as the walls. At the foot of the bed was a pull-out stool to lay his suitcase. In the bathroom: a bevelled mirror, a pile of towels, little bottles of soap and moisturiser and a shower cap. He showered and got into bed but sleep did not come.

He thought of the man and his wife in the bar. Would he be like that, he wondered, spotting signs of activity, hankering after the old days of the warrant card in his pocket and the power of arrest? Craving the excitement and the power, like a junkie chasing the first hit. It started as a spotty youth nabbing a shoplifter and worked its way up to murderers.

Steve's mother had been a district nurse. Once, when he was eight or nine, he was too sick for school and his mum, who had no one to help her with childcare, bundled him into the back of her Volkswagen Polo with a duvet and a pillow while she made her rounds. Late morning, they drove up to an old timbered gatehouse and his mother told him to get out of the car. 'You should see this,' she said. It was dark inside and there was a smell unlike anything he had ever encountered. Not dirty, but utterly foreign: soil and woodsmoke and game. A couple of birds were hanging on the wall, head to head like lovers, the cord tight round their necks. Later his mother told him that the couple had lived in the gatehouse rent free as guests of the estate ever since the accident. The wife was cooking over a range. The patient – her husband – had been bed bound for years. He'd been a farrier. A horse had caught him off guard and kicked him in the chest. He'd never really got up from that kick.

If Steve had to describe how it was after he saw Kieran shot, that was the nearest he could come to it: being kicked in the chest by a horse and afterwards not being able to get back on your feet.

His sleep was disturbed. He woke and remembered the days when his children were young and he and his wife took them on holiday in a rented VW camper. He flicked on the bedside light. In a drawer by the bed was a Gideon's Bible but also the Book of Mormon. He picked it up: something to distract him. So many possible faiths in the world. What did these particular nutcases believe?

We believe in being honest, true, chaste, benevolent, virtuous, and in doing good to all men . . . We believe all things, we hope all things, we have endured many things, and hope to be able to endure all things.

He put the book beside him on the bed and stared at the ceiling. He too would like to be able to endure all things. He got up and drew the curtains. The moon was rising over the empty golf course. It was moving away from the earth, apparently, and who could blame it.

TUESDAY

17

Light was barely visible in the sky when Ryan set off. As he cycled with his hands in his pockets, enjoying the balance and his confidence, the dawn began to open. He turned right and then left onto a lane that swept down through a tunnel of hedgerows and trees.

It was a lifetime ago that he noticed the bike from the traffic-clogged main road – propped against the wall inside the lobby of a red-brick student block. He walked it out by its saddle. You could tell it wanted to be with him by the way it ran so easily under his hand. The guy had his back turned at the desk but he spotted Ryan at the last minute and shouted, 'That's my bike!'

Already through the doors and on the saddle, he'd laughed and said, 'Mine now.'

For anyone who knew bikes it did draw attention to itself and Spence thought Ryan should cut his losses and get rid of it on eBay. You'd get a few bills for that, Spence said. But Ryan liked the bike. Why did you have to get rid of everything you liked?

That was something Spencer never understood: bikes. The night he was stabbed they'd been on foot coz Spence had a puncture.

He had been riding the bike on his last day of freedom. He locked it in a side street by the undercover cop's flat never thinking he was about to be swept away from everything he had ever known and that the bike would be left there.

In custody, in that white paper suit, he begged his mum to go and get it before someone nicked all the parts. And she said, 'Ry, I can't. I got to stay here with you.' But he couldn't stop fretting about that bike locked up on its own, a prey to anyone who wanted to help themselves. He thought of those dismembered bikes: just the frame tied up and everything else gone. In the end his mum called his sister, Tia, and Tia, who had always called him a loser, understood how important it was. She got it back to the Deakin, though she was no cyclist. It waited for him all those years in the shed – like him, locked away and longing to get out.

His mum had brought the bike on the train. The station at Middleton was two tracks side by side nearly four hours west of London, a journey that included a long wait at draughty Alnbridge for the branch-line train that was in no hurry on its way to and from nowhere. The nose of the locomotive edged slowly round the bend. Loretta lifted the bike down onto the platform and a sudden longing for what was past ran through Ryan like a gulp of iced water.

Loretta's hair was run through with grey and her spotty woollen dress hung off her. How far they both were from home. He tried to cover the disaster that had happened to her.

He said, 'Mum, what's going on? You look like one of them aunties from church.'

She wagged her finger and he took hold of the saddle and smiled at her.

'I've been dreamin' of my bike.'

And he had been dreaming of it. When the doors were locked and the window was so high you had to stand on a chair to look out, he lay on his bed and listed its parts: steel frame, Shimano drive chain, disc brakes. He closed his eyes and threw his leg over the crossbar. He freewheeled away from the estate and across the park. He took the turn away from his ends and down to the city, over the Thames and along the river. Sometimes the thought of it kept the White Walkers away. When he got out, he would cycle and cycle and cycle.

After Loretta left, he stood and looked out the window of the hostel and saw the supermarket and the car park. The local youth were hanging out, like they always did. Fuck all else to do in this town. He sat on the bed and rolled a few joints.

He ran his hand over the frame.

'I'll take you out tomorrow. Promise.'

He went down to the car park. Lit the spliff before he walked over. It was a smell you never smelt round here. They were all hiding in the woods, and that. He said, 'You want a zoot?' And that was how he started. It hadn't taken much to get the line up and running.

He fitted tubeless cyclo-cross tyres on the bike. He cycled for miles, following his nose. Flowers on the banks and birds flying out of the hedgerows. Who'd have thought this world possible with its dips and rises, little bridges over rivers? It gave him energy. And strangely the joy of it took him back to jumping kerbs and bunny-hopping down the steps of the underpass back home.

There was a white gatehouse, set back from the road. A sign: *Private Road*. He turned down there.

First the path was two lines of worn concrete with a stripe of grass running down the centre, then it was gravelled down to a bridge over a river.

Not a soul for miles but lots of scared stupid birds jumping out of the undergrowth and clucking, and running away. He stopped and watched the water. Held back by a sort of embankment, it seemed solid, like fluted glass. In the spill beneath were fish, holding still in the current.

Behind him a step on the gravel.

He turned and saw an old man in a green jacket with red cheeks and a red nose. Three dogs were running around, disappearing into the undergrowth and reappearing, their tails wagging constantly. A shotgun was slung over the man's shoulder by a leather strap. Ryan saw that and considered it. The man was looking at him and Ryan could feel it like a curtain thrown between them: the man baffled by his blackness.

The man said, 'Are you lost?'

Ryan had seen these men out in their green jackets, on their little quad bikes, rattling over the fields and alongside the woods. Sometimes trailers of men towed by tractors, sitting facing each other on benches, lines of shotguns pointing down. But he'd never seen a man with a gun on his own before.

Ryan said, 'I'm OK.'

The man said, 'You need to turn your bicycle around and cycle up the hill to get back on the road.'

'I reckon this is a cut-through to where I'm going.'

'I'm sorry, son. It's not a right of way. But you can get back on to the road. It loops round the estate.'

Ryan smiled. 'Oh, is it?'

The man smiled too. 'If I can explain?'

'Yeah, why don't you?'

The man narrowed his eyes.

'This is a pristine environment. One of the cleanest rivers in England. It's a triple SI.'

'But I'm not making it dirty, am I? The black, it don't wash off.'

The man cleared his throat. 'It's *people*, you see.'

'Oh, *people*, is it?'

The man rubbed the end of his nose. He spoke slowly, as if Ryan was struggling to follow.

'If there are a lot of people down here it scares away the otters.'

Ryan laughed. 'The otters!'

The man's face clouded. 'That's right. The otters.'

Ryan leaned against the bridge's stone parapet. 'But I'm not a lot of people, am I? I'm just one.'

'You're trespassing.'

There was a sensation like a rope tightening between them.

The man said, 'There's a stand of guns down here sometimes, along the riverbank.'

Ryan looked around him at the tall trees that reached up from the river and threw moving shadows over them both. His gaze travelled over the man with his gun in its sling.

'Not many people here now, though.'

The man reached into his capacious jacket and took out his phone.

Ryan said, 'You frightened of me?'

'Not at all.'

'Coz I wouldn't blame you, if you were. If I were you, I probably would be.'

'You just don't seem willing to go.'

'You got a signal here?'

The man blushed: red splotches on his neck, his cheeks even redder. Even his ears looked red. The gun, well it probably wasn't loaded and even if it was, he'd struggle to get it off his shoulder quickly enough. Ryan took hold of the bike and threw his leg over the crossbar. He paused, as if he was thinking it over.

'I'll go the way I was going.'

'OK. But don't come down here again. It's private.'

There had been a kind of peace in the landscape. It had astonished Ryan. Colette had been wrong. For long periods of time he discovered that his mind was at last empty of anything but the ease or the effort of cycling. The long falls down the swooping twisting hills, the steady climbs, seeing as he stood on the pedals, over the line of hedges toppled barns and ponds and ghost trees stripped down to grey skeletons. But as he pushed up the hill towards the road the peace had gone.

It was hard being spoken to like that.

It was harder, too, climbing from the river along the now gravelled path. He was soon hot. His clothes became damp. Sweat formed into droplets that ran from his temples down his face. He could not climb quickly. Although the land was deserted, he anticipated someone else stepping out and challenging him, or turning a bend in the road to see a group of them waiting for him beside a quad bike, summoned by the red-faced man with his mobile phone.

Ryan stood over the crossbar, and took a gulp from his water bottle.

His blackness made him remarkable here, but a long trial for murder had taught him about evidence and proof. One thing to have a suspect, another to prove it was him. He needed to get back, pick up the car, sort out the new boy, but he still had time. He turned the bike and scooted down the hill, depressing and releasing the brakes carefully to stop the bike skidding on the loose stones. Shade and light splashed over him. The sweat on his chest became cold. Over the river and up, back in the direction he had come. The gravel path climbed, switched to concrete with the strip of grass running down the centre. The man had been on foot and alone. He must be near by. To the left were two houses, set into the hill. The man was through a gate, walking towards a green front door. He heard or sensed Ryan and turned to look. Ryan waved.

18

They met at the car. Steve drove, taking the country lanes towards the ring road. They picked up the Transit that they had left in the overnight park and ride. Steve gave Craig and Marilyn a ten-minute head start. Within twenty minutes they reached the turning. There was only one way out and in: bad skills there from George and Linton. They passed some wide flat ground and something that might be a grain silo. This terrain seemed connected to nothing and no past: chain-link fences, tall lampposts that cast pools of white light over the flat space. They passed a breeze-block health club with a huge empty car park. A large grey Chinese supermarket. A Kentucky Fried Chicken with another huge car park. The Transit was parked up with its lights off. At the edge of the car park was the big yellow box for road salt that the boys used as the drop. Steve swung the car round the roundabout that led nowhere, and headed back out.

Kiyana got out of the car and opened the gate to the enclosure with the silo. Steve pulled in, turned the car in the lee of the building and switched off the engine. Kiyana walked over and got back in.

'It's like Chernobyl,' she said.

'Not quite.'

'Such beautiful countryside and they choose to come here.'

Steve got out and stood by the wall. They were early and it was still dark. The moon lit the dusty precinct and cast long shadows. Steve lit a cigarette and waited for the county's firearms unit. They needed to be quick to tuck in behind the building, as they had planned. It would be safest to do the stop here on this isolated service road.

Kiyana had dozed off but she woke as soon as Steve opened the car door.

He slid the seat back and pulled his flask out of his bag.

'Coffee?'

'Go on then. Thanks.' Kiyana pulled herself upright in her seat and rubbed her eyes. 'I guess they're not interested in seeing the cathedral, then.'

Steve wondered whether Kiyana had been inside the cathedral herself. Steve stood inside it on his visit to the town, gazed up at the tall stained-glass windows, examined the dark carved misericords: did it all, just as the guidebook instructed him.

'I guess not,' he said, handing Kiyana her coffee. He was taking a tin mug out of his bag for himself when his phone rang. Harry Miller on the screen: the local tactical firearms commander. Steve passed the mug for Kiyana to pour his coffee, and took the call.

'I understand. Don't worry. Unavoidable. Thank you. Can you get someone to ring me? I better free up my phone.'

A silver Kia saloon swung by, the tyres singing a high note on the tarmac. Steve took a gulp of coffee, plugged his own phone into the hands-free set on the car. He called Marilyn on Kiyana's phone on speakerphone. She answered after one ring.

'Yep?'

'Sounds like them. On their way to you.'

'They're early. We got back-up?'

'They got called out last night—'

'What does that mean?'

'It means they've got a couple of regular firearms cars running to us on blues but they're fifty miles away on country roads.'

'What the fuck—'

'It was a domestic with a shotgun. Imminent threat to life. Takes precedence over drug dealers. What could they do?'

'They were supposed to drop us a local radio.'

'Least of our worries. We can run it all on phones.'

'Bloody hell. Leave the call open.'

Another car swung past – a blue Honda Civic, travelling fast.

Steve spoke into Kiyana's phone, 'Car two on its way.'

'Received.'

Kiyana felt under her left arm.

'Still there, is it?' Steve said, opening his door and throwing what remained of his coffee onto the ground.

Kiyana laughed, but she also cleared her throat.

Steve handed her phone back. He said, 'We might be busy in a moment.'

Kiyana necked her coffee and gave Steve the cup. Steve screwed it back on to the flask and returned the flask and the spare cup to the bag. He put the bag on the back seat, threading the safety belt through its handle. He slid his seat forward and put his seat belt back on.

Marilyn was on speakerphone. 'First lot coming back your way. Drugs have been handed over. We're in position. The local lads have given our fellas a head start. About to go ahead and nick them.'

'Did you see who's in the first car?'

'Linton and George.'

'OK.'

Steve's phone rang: the local operation room. Two cars were running but they reckoned fifteen to twenty minutes.

Steve left the call open. The comms were a mess, but what could you do?

He said to Kiyana, 'Tuck yourself in low at the side of the building with a view of the road. Once they've turned off, run to the gate and open it. I'll pick you up.'

Steve waited. The Honda swung past back towards the main road. Steve updated the operation room and started the engine. Kiyana ran towards the gate. Steve accelerated forward, then stopped for Kiyana, who jumped in and pulled the door shut quickly.

'Left left,' Kiyana said.

Steve accelerated towards the junction. Kiyana was reaching across and strapping herself in. 'What's the plan?'

'Tail them till the locals get here. Your job to let the ops room know direction of travel.'

As they turned onto the dual carriageway the road bent ahead and the Honda was out of sight. Kiyana gave a commentary into the hands-free. *Lane one of two . . . clear and dry.* Steve decelerated before he hit the bend. As they completed the turn the Honda was in view, travelling within the speed limit. Steve maintained the gap. Two law-abiding early-morning drivers.

'Receiving Met police?'

'Go ahead.'

'How long before your units get here.'

'Five or ten. Hoping to use the next roundabout as a stopping point but the cars are still the wrong side of the city.

Helicopter's on its way.'

The Honda was slowing, doing thirty now on a delimit road. Steve maintained his speed, and soon he had to overtake. He kept his gaze forward, but even with his eyes on the road he could feel Linton and George checking the car out. No way round it: they would look like cops.

Kiyana said, 'We could block them before the roundabout. Stop them ourselves.'

'On our own and unauthorised?'

Steve looked in the rear-view mirror. The Honda was accelerating and the gap closing. The Audi was more powerful but Steve allowed them to overtake, maintaining the same constant speed.

'You letting them go?' Kiyana said.

'Keeping as close as I can without confirming we're Old Bill.'

Silence in the car. Linton and George pulling away.

Steve said, 'They've got about ten grand in the car and intelligence suggests they've got a firearm. They are not going to want to get caught.'

'All the more reason to stop them.'

'This was a hard stop for a reason. We can't do that on our own.'

'We're armed too.'

'The county boys aren't far.'

'We've been tailing these guys for weeks.'

'They're doing about ninety. We accelerate? They're going to be doing the tonne. How fast we going to go? What if they hit and kill someone? None of it would be authorised.'

'We're hitting an intersection in about five miles.'

'Kiyana—'

116

'We won't know where they've gone.'

'The helicopter will find the car.'

'What if they abandon it?'

'I need to concentrate.'

The road ahead turned to the right and the Honda was soon out of sight.

Kiyana said, 'If they don't go straight through the round-about the firearms units won't be in position.'

'It's not a threat to life. They'll come again.'

Kiyana updated the operations unit. Steve accelerated round the turn. The car was out of sight.

'Fucking carrots,' Kiyana said.

'Not their fault.'

'I can't fucking believe it.'

Dawn was breaking. Rabbits were jumping about in a field to the left.

19

Eight in the morning and Asha stood in the shade of a big London plane tree waiting for Mahdi to leave for school. The boy stepped out of the block onto the path. He had big earphones on, and a heavy-looking school bag. He was a good boy, Mahdi. Wanted to be a doctor.

She didn't have to say anything. She could see he knew stuff, that he was uncomfortable.

He said, 'I don't know where he is, but I heard he's gone cunch.'

'Gone cunch?' It sounded silly. 'What's that, then?'

'Gone up country, you know?' And, when she didn't reply, he said, 'OT. Out there. Selling drugs. County lines.'

County lines? She'd heard about it but not really paid attention: those bits on ITV London where someone talks for ten minutes and you don't really listen.

She had never thought of herself as naïve. She was a single mother raising two boys in London! But now she felt like a little girl, and like Mahdi was the adult. He understood stuff she didn't.

'How do you know that?' she said.

'Here.' He got his phone out of his pocket, opened Snapchat. She looked at the conversation.

Heard about Leif?

Yeah, I heard he gone cunch.

Loser.

How'd you hear that?

Mo.

'How would Leif do that?' she said. 'How would he even know how to do that?'

'One of the guys at school, I think. I don't really know them, but, well, you know, we sort of know what they're up to. Lots of cash.'

'So?'

'He introduced him.'

'Introduced him? What does that mean? I feel sick.'

'Look honest, Mrs Abad I'm sorry. I don't know them.'

'This Mo? Who is he?'

'I don't know. There's a flat. I can give you the address. They call it cuckooing?'

'Give me the address.'

Asha handed over her phone and Mahdi typed an address into the Notes app. 'This guy, Mo, you should know. He's an addict. You shouldn't go there on your own.'

She was angry now.

'You didn't tell me.'

'I'm sorry, Mrs Abad. Me and Leif, you know we haven't really been hanging for a while. There's a lot going on. I can't . . .'

'You can't what?'

'Interfere.'

'Why not?'

'Because it's dangerous.'

Before she even took her coat off, she googled it.

First thing up was the *National Crime Agency. County Lines is where illegal drugs are transported from one area to another . . . usually by children or vulnerable people . . .* Next thing down was a headline from Wessex Online. Her eyes scanned through quickly. *Officers found a machete, lock knife, a pistol and £28,000 worth of heroin and crack cocaine.* Her heart was beating, but no way. No way! This kind of thing had nothing to do with Leif. It sounded like something from a TV show. It wasn't true. Further down was the Children's Society. *County lines is a form of criminal exploitation. It is when criminals befriend children and manipulate them into drug dealing.*

She stood in Leif's room. Everything was there. His stuffed dragon. A jar of coins. His Arsenal scarf. His can of Nivea deodorant for men and the razor that he barely needed. She opened the drawers. All the trousers and shirts and pants and socks: all there. Nothing missing. How could he have gone away if he hadn't taken anything? She pressed her fingers hard against her temples. In the kitchen she dialled the number she had photographed when Leif was in the bath.

It answered after a couple of rings.

'Yeah. Whassup?'

'I want to know where my son is.'

'I don't know what you're talking bout.'

'You were ringing my son, Leif. Before he disappeared.'

'I don't know no Leif.'

The phone went dead.

She pressed her fingers against her temples again. There was a buzzing inside her head, like an electric current meeting up against resistance. She took her coat off the hook and called an Uber.

20

Two outfits waited on the backs of chairs in the kitchen. The first was a red tricorn hat with black feathers, a red coat with gold military trim and big white lacy cuffs, red wellies and a plastic hook. The other was a shiny white nightie, a silver cape and some fairy wings.

Connor was eating his Coco Pops in his elephant pyjamas.

Lizzie said, 'Ever considered going as a pirate?'

Connor shook his head. Lizzie glanced at her watch and finished her coffee.

'Pirates are a lot of fun.'

'Maybe. But EVERYONE knows Tinkerbell is the star.'

'Lots of the boys will be pirates. They'll be a big gang. And you'll be the leader! Captain Hook!'

'No, Mum. I've already told you. Captain Hook is boring. Everyone knows that.'

So many things that EVERYONE knew, that Lizzie apparently didn't. She looked over at the framed picture of Kieran with Connor.

Well? she said in her head. *What the fuck do you think I should do?*

'Come on,' she said out loud. 'Hurry up. If it's Tinkerbell get your costume on. I'm going to be late for the boss.'

And she had to admit that Connor looked adorable as he ran to the car in the shiny nightie and, on his feet, his chunky blue Velcro Start-Rites. Her heart broke at the sight of it. Main thing was to support him. Kieran wasn't right about everything. In fact, he was wrong about most things.

'You look great,' she said. 'Fantastic.'

She opened the passenger door. He jumped in and she bent down and kissed him on his soft brow.

'But take the wings off for now, Con. You can't really wear them in the car.'

21

'Is my son with you?'

The guy at the door was skinny. A stale smell came from him, and from the flat. Asha pinched her fourth finger tightly between the thumb and index finger of her other hand. Now she was here, she was afraid.

'No one's here.'

She tried to see behind him but there was no way of knowing whether he was telling the truth.

'My son is Leif. He's small. Fifteen.'

He nodded.

'Is he here?'

He shook his head.

'Can I come in?'

He stepped back and opened his left arm to her. 'Be my guest.'

She had to swallow against the smell of the place. The floor was actually sticky. Like in a cartoon she felt like she had to pull her feet free every step.

'Thank you for letting me in. Are you Mo?'

He wiped his finger under his nose. 'Do you want to sit down?'

She looked at the sofa. She guessed it had once been white. The glass in the windows was stained yellow. If you ran your nails down the panes whatever was coating them would probably peel away.

'I'm all right standing. Thanks, though.' Asha cleared her

throat. 'You got any idea where my son is?'

He scratched the back of his neck.

'Do you know who he's with? Any names?'

'I wasn't here when he was being interviewed.'

'Interviewed?'

'That's what they call it.'

She thought maybe she would have to sit down but then she glanced again at the sofa. It wasn't an option. And that set up another question in her mind. A stupid question, and probably trivial, but one that troubled her nevertheless because how had her son become someone who could spend time in a place as dirty as this?

Mo rubbed the bottom of his nose. 'Can you help me out?'

'What?'

He rubbed his nose again. 'You know, twenty quid. Just something to get me going.' He was reaching into his back pocket and he produced a worn black Nokia. She understood what he meant now. He started to scroll through it. 'I can give you the number of the guy who deals with the children. Jaydn.'

She fumbled in her purse. Luckily, she had twenty quid cash. He handed her the phone. 'Don't tell him I gave it to you.'

She recognised the number. It was the same one she had photographed when Leif was in the bath.

22

In the middle of the night Leif had got up from the sofa and fiddled with the heating controls, but it had made no difference. The air from the blower was cold. It was like trying to sleep in a fridge.

He was in a little caravan chalet thingy, somewhere off a main road and down a track towards a river that moved fast and brown. The sliding doors at the end of the caravan had no curtains and the bike he saw framed against the dark night reminded him of the white bikes of dead people tied to the metal barriers on London's roads. His mum had been right: he should have worn a coat.

The girl, Shell, had bagsied the double bed and had a duvet. Still, she was sleeping in her clothes. He walked over and stood next to the bed and said, 'Can I get in with you?'

She rolled over in her sleep and groaned. 'No, you fucking can't.'

He lay back down on the sofa, struggling in a half-sleep to get his whole body under the thin little blanket he had found in the back of a cupboard. Finally, a pale light seeped through the windows and he woke completely, rigid with a coldness that had settled into his bones.

He went and stood on the step. It was the first time he'd seen the place in daylight.

There were lots of caravans – standing on precarious stilts in rows, dirty white with washes of green mildew down the sides. This caravan seemed to be the only one with anyone living in it. He considered taking a piss round the back but NK, the guy who had met him at the station, had told him he had to use the toilet: 'Don't want to draw attention.' Leif felt a flicker of rebellion. There was absolutely no one here to see him because no one else was mad enough to live here. This was the kind of place where the zombie apocalypse broke out.

He moved back inside. The girl was still in the bed, hidden beneath her duvet.

A skylight in the sitting area had a bucket underneath it. There was a brown carpet and orange lozenge-patterned curtains that didn't close properly. The sofa had purple flowery covers with fringes and flounces that went to the floor.

He wanted a hot shower, wanted his bedroom, wanted a change of clothes, wanted breakfast, wanted a toothbrush and toothpaste. He wanted to be warm. He wanted to go home. He wanted to phone his mum, but NK had taken his phone.

'If your mum goes to the police,' he said when he dropped him off, 'they'll cell site you.'

NK hadn't said anything about when he would give the phone back or how long Leif was supposed to stay here.

Leif held his breath and went into the toilet cubicle. He pulled his sweatshirt sleeve down over his hand before he lifted the lid.

He stepped back inside the main space of the caravan. The girl was moving around in the kitchen area. 'What is this place?' he said, sitting at the little circular table.

'It's a holiday thing.'

126

'Who'd have a holiday here?'

'Don't ask me.'

'NK, what's his story?'

'Who knows?' She put hot chocolate and toast on the table.

Turned out she had a hot-water bottle and she filled it and sat with it on her lap. She rolled a joint and they passed it between them. 'Takes the edge off,' Shell said. She had long, straight brown hair, was bone thin and wore fingerless gloves. The phone was on the table and it started buzzing.

Shell stood up and held out her hot-water bottle. 'You can have it till I get back.'

'Thanks.'

Shell fiddled around in one of the cupboards and pulled out a set of scales, a bag of rocks and some empty baggies.

'While I'm out you better get on with bagging up.'

'But I never done it before.'

She showed him how to do it and told him to keep his in a separate pile. 'Coz I'm not taking the rap if you do it wrong.'

Then she knelt and opened a different door. Leif watched her lifting the bottom of the cupboard and reaching in so far that all he could see was her thin little bum and the soles of her trainers. 'Portal to another world?' he said, but she didn't reply and he felt stupid. She closed everything and stood, holding some prepared baggies. 'Look away,' she said.

'What?'

'I'm not going into that filthy bog just to pack. Look away.'

Leif put his hands over his eyes and waited for permission to remove them. There was a cold draught and he took his hands from his face. The sliding windows were open and Shell was dragging the bike across the decking. Leif walked over and stepped outside.

'When's he coming?' he asked.

'He doesn't tell us nothing.'

As she got on the bike, she gave a little wave.

23

'Sorry, I'm late, sir. Peter Pan day at Connor's school.'

The detective chief superintendent smiled. 'Ah, Captain Hook, is he?'

Lizzie fudged with a smile. 'You wanted to see me?'

The desk was big, but DCS Trask was more than a match for it, especially in his huge jacket with its broad chalk stripes. Everyone on the borough called him KK: King Kong. Trask might be his name, but nobody used it.

'Never complain, never explain. Ever heard that, Lizzie?'

'I'm guessing this is about the television interview?'

'Churchill was fond of the saying, I believe. And Her Majesty.'

He reached inside his drawer and took out a box of chocolates. 'Time was it would have been whisky,' he said. 'Imagine that, whisky! That's within living memory! Feels as far off as ploughing with horses. Tess of the bloody D'Urbervilles, that's me. Do you know what I am?'

'A dinosaur, boss?'

He laughed. 'Correct. Which one?'

'Tyrannosaurus wrecked?'

'Very good. Ha ha.' He pushed the box towards Lizzie. 'Want one?'

'No thanks.'

He popped two into his mouth.

'That interview . . .'

'I didn't ask permission. Sorry.'

'That's not why you're here.' He held a chocolate between thumb and forefinger. It looked tiny and she imagined it quaking just like Ann Darrow in the palm of the giant ape. He thought better of the chocolate and relegated it to the bin.

'Still, I watched the interview and all I got out of it was, Whatever is she thinking?'

'OK.'

'Never complain, never explain. If it's good enough for Churchill, it's good enough for me.'

'Right.'

'Hold on to your dignity, and keep your mouth shut. Best advice I can give you.'

He seemed to expect some kind of response so Lizzie said, 'I see.'

He watched her, as though there was something more he expected. When she didn't speak, he said, 'I've done thirty-two years. Why do you think I've stayed on?'

'I don't know.'

'Because I love it. That's why. Best job in the world.'

There was a silence.

Trask said, 'There have been complaints. That's why you're here.'

Lizzie ran her hand through her hair.

'Does that surprise you?'

'Not really.'

He leaned back in his chair. The chocolates looked a bit out of place on the desk now.

'More than one skipper's come to me. You're rude. You're negative. You're cynical. I hate cynicism! You make the new officers cry.'

130

'PC Nolan?'

'Skipper says she's good.'

'It's only a case file. I told her to come and see me if she didn't understand what she has to do.'

'Well.' He shrugged, puffed out his cheeks. Scratched the back of his neck. 'Sounds like a cry-baby. She'll have to toughen up. Still. What does this say about you?'

'That I won't be seeing out my thirty years. Although it's not thirty any more, is it? With the new pensions, I mean? It's more like one hundred and twenty. Or does it just *feel* like that? I dunno, I can't keep up.'

'Having the father of your child murdered doesn't give you a free pass to say whatever comes into your head, you know?'

Lizzie waited. Trask passed his huge hand in front of his face.

'What you've been through, *you're* allowed to cry, Lizzie, but you don't. Maybe that's the problem.'

'Thought you were old school?'

He tutted. 'I feel sorry for you, of course I do. Everyone does.'

What did he want from her? She said, 'I'm all right.'

He waved his arm impatiently through the air as though he were batting away a particularly vexing fly.

'But you're really not, are you?'

Funny, Lizzie thought, that my not being all right makes him angry. Beneath the sympathy the anger always seemed to be lurking.

He put his elbows on the desk and leaned towards her. 'What's to be done, Lizzie? That's what I've asked myself and that's what you've got to ask yourself. Being a misery guts in some back-office role? Is that how you're going to see out your service? I still love this job. I love policing.'

'I don't, but I'm doing the best I can.'

He pushed the box of chocolates towards her again and she shook her head. He said, 'Do you know what, you're right. They're getting on my nerves.' He threw them in the bin. 'Are you aware of the College of Police's core values, Lizzie?'

She laughed out loud.

'I take your point, but let's not be unkind.' He cleared his throat. 'After all, it's only putting into words what we've always been doing. Take emotionally aware, for example.'

'Yes?'

'Turns out I've always been rather ahead of the curve on that one. I know that some – and it pains me to say this – but that some *emotionally unaware* people may have called me after a certain outsized gorilla, but I have to remind you that King Kong was actually a very emotional guy. So, I watched you on the telly and, emotionally aware as I am, I thought, That girl has' – and here his face clouded over like thunder – 'completely bloody lost it.'

Lizzie stood up. 'Perhaps you could tell me what this meeting is actually about, sir?'

'We're getting there.' His face was without expression. 'You're not Jewish, by any chance?'

'No, sir. Utterly bewildered, but not Jewish.'

'Me too. On both counts. Still, old proverb apparently. Heard it the other day. Took my fancy. Boat full of people. One of them starts drilling a hole. Other guys: What the hell? Guy with the drill: Why are you bothering me? It's only *my bit of the boat*.'

KK looked at Lizzie and blinked slowly.

She raised her eyebrows. 'I'm the guy with the drill?'

He tutted. 'I can see how you might draw that conclusion, but when I heard it, I thought, The guys on that boat had it easy. Just the one guy with one drill? Our boat – it's hard to find someone without a bloody drill. Guys inside the boat, guys outside the boat, guys who have fuck all to do with the damn boat. They've all got drills. How can they even be bothered? And yet, they can. But, Lizzie, however many leaks we've sprung, I am not bloody letting this ship go down on my watch.

'All that complicated stuff about policing, it just goes right over my head. Every ten years they reinvent the wheel and we all have to step up and pretend we've seen the light. Total policing! Ha. That was a good one. Problem as I see it is actually pretty simple: too much work, not enough good people. Some mornings we're parading a third of our minimum strength. You want to convict rapists, you need feet on the ground.

'I had one of my favourite detective sergeants up here this morning. Richard Page, Misper Unit. Needs someone good. I'm giving you to him. I can get some retired old fart to supervise case papers. I need you operational. One good officer can make quite a difference. You've got a nose. Go and use it.'

She wanted to cry. She wanted to say, You may still love the job, but I don't. She wanted to say, I just can't. But Trask had that look about him: he had a plan for her, and he was going to see it through. How had he made it through more than thirty years with this much enthusiasm? And with that thought she remembered how keen she had once been.

Hungry to make a good impression on him when he sent her off to work on Perseus. So excited, so hungry to do *good work*, confident then that she knew what that was.

She said, 'I'm grateful to you for looking out for me, sir. I really am. But I have responsibilities. I need to work flexi-time. I've got Connor.'

'The move isn't negotiable. It's a lawful order, and I'm posting you. Sort your hours with Page. I've talked to him. He'll be sympathetic to your circumstances.'

Lizzie looked around at the trappings of Trask's service. Commendations. Shields and pennants from foreign police forces. A picture of him sailing, a colourful spinnaker filling out before the bows. His arm round his three adult children in their various academic gowns. Trask followed her eye-line. It was as if he was reading her mind.

He said, 'I'm so sorry for what happened. That hasn't changed.' He put his large hands flat on the desk. 'Think of this as tough love.'

24

A car pulled up outside the caravan. NK stepped in and put a Happy Meal on the table. Leif ate. NK stood at the table checking the packaging.

Leif said, 'Could I sit in the car? Just for a bit. To warm up.'

'No, you can't. Where's Shell?'

'I dunno.'

The guy carried on checking the baggies. Weighing the odd one. After a bit he said, 'You didn't bring a coat, then?'

Leif shook his head.

'Why not? You knew you was going cunch. It's always cold out here.'

The door opened but Shell didn't step in. She stood on the grass outside.

'Whassup?'

She didn't speak for a second but her face had that crumpled look. She was trying not to cry.

'I got robbed.'

The guy pulled her inside. He slapped her. 'What d'you mean, you got robbed?'

'They had a dirty needle.'

'How much did they take?'

'All of it. And the bike.'

'Give me your jacket.'

She took it off and passed it to him. He checked the pockets. Then he felt under her T-shirt and round her waistband. 'Get your kit off.'

'I'm not lying.'

He slapped her again.

She pulled her jeans and pants down and NK put his hands between her legs. Leif was so shocked he didn't look away quickly enough and he glimpsed her narrow white hips, the crest of her pelvis, the little triangle of black.

'If I find you've stashed it somewhere I will kill you.'

'You know I wouldn't.'

Shell pulled up her jeans. NK washed his hands at the sink. He stepped back towards her and hit her with the side of his fist on the temple. It was so fast Leif barely saw the blow. Shell lost her balance and fell.

'If they took everything how come you're so late back?'

'Fuck's sake. They took the bike.' She got up, holding the side of her head. 'I had to take the bus. Takes for ever.'

'What they look like?'

'One's fat with blond hair and a checked jacket. The other's got brown hair. Spotty.'

'That's a debt now, mind,' NK said. 'You'll have to pay back. Come on, Leif.'

'What?'

'You're going to get to sit in the car after all.'

NK turned the heating up but Leif's body held on to the cold. It was foggy and there were sheep just wandering around over the rough ground like . . . Like . . . like what? Fuck knows. Like sheep, he supposed. He'd never thought they did that. Just wander about. Nothing between them and the road. Had these people not heard of fences?

NK pulled over. Leif watched him walking to a falling-down brick building without a roof. He disappeared inside. When he came back into the car, he handed Leif a knife.

It was small with commando written down the jagged blade.

'Stick that in the back of your trousers. Don't say a word and try not to look like a baby.'

They pulled into the outskirts of the town. Allotments. Some cabbages outside for sale in a box. Big houses with conservatories. A sign. *Slow. Hedgehogs*. They took a road to the right that snaked round a hill and soon there were rougher houses with pebbledash walls. A fish and chip shop and some kids sitting on the road smoking. NK pulled the car over. He got out and Leif followed. The kids looked at them but said nothing. They took a little cut-through and the bike was leaning against a wall. NK ignored it and walked on through. Over his shoulder Leif could see some garages. The two boys were there, eating a bag of chips. NK walked straight at them. He flattened the smaller one in an instant: just a swift hard punch to the face, and the boy was on the floor. A blade was suddenly in NK's hand. It looked evil, a long, jagged blade. The boy in the checked jacket started running. NK turned to Leif.

'Stand over that one.'

NK was running after the boy. He'd got him by the end of the garages and Leif saw the knife cut through the air and down the back of the boy's leg. There was a cry and the boy put his hand towards his backside. His jeans were soaked and he left a trail of blood. NK dragged him back by his collar. Leif heard him say, 'You're lucky I only wet you.'

The boy who'd been punched was getting up. Leif got the knife out and tried not to be a baby.

'You wanna get wetted like your mate?'

The boy shook his head.

'Don't move then.'

Blood was splatting onto the ground. The other boy was fumbling in his pocket with one hand and holding his backside with the other.

'I need an ambulance.'

'Later.'

There were notes falling on the floor and baggies. Some of the notes had blood on them.

'Where's your dirty needle now? Pick them up.'

The boy was on his knees gathering up the baggies and the cash.

NK nodded to Leif to take them from him and he stepped forward. He could feel the warmth of the boy's hand and smell the vinegar from the chips. But there was blood, too, and that smelt strangely – like rusty metal. There was lots of money. A few hundred. Maybe more. Leif stuffed it into his pockets.

NK said, 'Take your jacket off.'

The boy hesitated and then did as he was told. He looked like he might cry. Leif took the jacket from him and held it over his arm as if he was a shop assistant.

'Now your shirt.'

The boy's chest was white with little man breasts. Leif took the shirt, too. He didn't like to hold it, still warm as it was, and smelling of the boy.

NK stepped back.

'That's your schooling for today. You're not about that life. You tell anyone who did this and I'll come after you. It's a small town. I'll find you.'

He walked away and Leif followed, holding the jacket over his arm and the shirt in his hand.

NK told Leif to get the bike. He wheeled it along the cut-through towards the car. The kids who had been smoking were all gone.

'Ain't we in a hurry?' Leif said.

'Those wastemen won't call the feds. Anyhow, it takes them about an hour to get here. This ain't London.'

The car chirruped and the lights flashed but NK waited for Leif to open the passenger door.

'There's wipes in the glove compartment and a plastic bag. Wipe everything down and put the shirt in the bag.'

They wiped down their hands, and the knife. They put the dirty wipes in the bag with the shirt.

'Put it in the footwell. We'll get rid in a minute.'

NK put the back seats down and they pulled the bike into the back. He pinged out the moulding above the radio and slipped the knives inside.

'You from my ends?' Leif said. 'You Bluds?'

'Not your business.'

NK turned the key in the ignition and pulled away. Leif looked out the window so that his expression wasn't visible.

NK said, 'Don't you worry about a thing. You'll be making bread. Won't take you long to learn.'

On the way out of town they got stuck behind a refuse truck.

'Oh look,' NK said, 'it's bin day.'

Leif turned the jacket over in his hands. There was some blood at the back, inside on the fleece lining. NK overtook the truck. Two streets along he pulled over and dumped the plastic bag in someone's wheelie bin.

'There you go,' he said, shutting the door and turning the music on. 'You've got a jacket now. Sorted.'

25

The Missing Persons Unit was tucked away along a long corridor on the second floor. On the door was a black-and-white photograph of a caddish-looking man with a moustache, and scrawled beside it, *We haven't given up!* Lizzie knocked and pushed the door open. There were six black desks in a bank but only one person in the room: a stocky man with a big head. He was talking on the phone while scrolling through whatever was on his screen.

'Yes,' he said, 'I'll get back to you.'

He put the phone down, leaned back in his chair and smiled. 'You're Lizzie.'

'Yep.'

'Richard.'

'Where is everyone?'

'Everyone!' He laughed. Then he laughed again. 'Every-one!' He stood up and grabbed his jacket from the back of his chair. 'You've seen *Toy Story*?'

'Only about two hundred times.'

He pulled on his jacket. 'Well, think of this bit of the Met as Sid's bedroom. Lot of broken toys. Some of them I never even see. Probably hiding under the bed. But I've got one on duty, come with me.'

Lizzie followed Page a few steps along the corridor and left onto the stairwell. There was another door here and he knocked once and opened it. It took Lizzie a moment to realise that this was a cleaning cupboard. Inside was a desk, shelves, a special chair with arm supports and a tilting head rest. The desk had an ergonomic mouse and wide moulded keyboard with raised pads for the wrists and elbows. Seated at the chair was a red-haired man in a blue shirt and knitted tank top. He had ear buds in and Richard gestured for him to remove them.

'Rhydian, this is the new girl, Lizzie.'

Rhydian looked at her. It isn't exactly the cleaning cupboard, Lizzie thought, it's the fact that he sits in it with the door shut.

Richard was speaking. 'I've just been speaking to social services about that missing boy, Leif Abad. I told you to speak to the mother and find out what's happening. What did she say?'

Rhydian opened in his arms in frustration at the sorry state of affairs. 'It's the equipment, Richard. I just can't get anything done.'

Lizzie had to put her hand over her mouth to hide her smile. Richard pressed on.

'Lizzie here will take him off you. And a couple of others. But you crack on with the rest. No excuses.'

Then they were walking briskly back along the corridor to the office. Richard ushered Lizzie in and switched the kettle on.

'I've got one guy I've never actually seen. Then there's Ian. Got a plate in his head. Or something. God knows. Tells me he's affected by the weather. I've actually caught him carpet cleaning.'

'What?'

'Exactly. Got a thing about hygiene. Didn't know where he was. Found him in one of the meeting rooms. He'd hired a carpet cleaner.'

Lizzie looked around her. 'It does seem surprisingly clean in here. For a police building, I mean.'

'That's the upside. The downside is that any one of the missing persons we're supposed to be locating could be dead.'

'You're selling this to me.'

'Typical routine police work. Too much volume for us to give each one the attention it needs. But mostly it doesn't matter because mainly they find themselves. Kids bunk off. Turn up again in a day or so. An old boy with dementia. TFL give us a ring. He's been sitting on the Circle Line for eight hours. So we limp on. But the odd one might be in real danger. Some of those are easy to spot. They go straight to better resourced units than us grunts. But there are others, buried like landmines among the hundreds of reports. Young people are our main risk. Some of them are just bunking off. Some of them are deep into some serious shit. With our workload how can we be sure to spot the one that's going to go wrong? And if it does—'

He stopped himself. Maybe he'd remembered who she was.

'Upside again, however: I've got a decent coffee machine. And proper biscuits.'

She sat down at the computer and opened her work file. Eleven missing persons. She clicked on the first one. Leif Abad: fifteen years old. One of the possible landmines.

26

Sarah's office was way bigger than anything a DI would have in the Met. It was not only spacious, but also clean. The window looked out over the car park. Beyond that was a view of hills. London ran twenty-four standing MIT teams. Here the force area had on average three homicides a year and no dedicated murder teams. This had been what she wanted, Sarah reminded herself: more downtime and less worry to take home.

She took a photo out of the window and WhatsApped it to her girlfriend, Meghan, with a message.

Not tempted to join me?

There was a tap at the door.

'Come in.'

It was Tom, one of the new direct-entry detectives. Never worn a police uniform in his life. Good degree from Exeter, and a line of ear piercings.

'I didn't get on very well. Sorry.'

'Wouldn't talk to you?'

'Not even that. He'd discharged himself. Told the nurses that he didn't want to hear from police.'

Sarah reached into her drawer and grabbed her radio and covert utility harness. 'Come on. I could do with getting out of the office.'

27

Leif and Shell were on the decking eating Pot Noodles. Shell was very thin and her nails were bitten down to the quick, but she was sexy somehow: her narrow face, and the way she scratched her back, bending her arm up right between her shoulder blades. That broken thing, too – it made Leif want to protect her, which he knew was dumb. Earlier she'd been crying in bed with the duvet over her head but now she was stony-faced. He would have loved to put his arm round her.

Shell pushed the Pot Noodle away. 'You got a debt?'

'Uh-huh.'

'How much?'

'Nearly two grand.'

'You was robbed?'

Leif nodded.

'And you're sure *they* didn't rob you?'

'What d'you mean?'

'NK's lot. The Bluds.'

Two boys had stopped him when he was crossing the park. Took his phone and the bag he'd been carrying. Jaydn was pissed but Mo said, No, calm down, man. Leif could pay it back easy. A week or so OT would do it. Easy money.

It had been like an adventure, getting on the train with the stuff.

Jaydn said, 'You'll get your bread, you'll get your respect, what everyone has dreamed of, you'll get from simply pushing dem packs.'

A cat was moving slowly through the long grass. You could really only see the flick of its tail.

The idea flipped over inside Leif that this had all been a set-up. What kind of money was he making? So far he'd seen nothing. And not allowed a phone. Nowhere near clearing his debt. It was a deep ache inside, the thought that this might all be a trick.

'I don't think it was them,' he said. 'No.'

'What d'you mean, you don't *think* so? You make it sound like it was.'

The cat had disappeared but now it trotted out carrying something small twitching in its mouth.

Leif had seen a picture of a heart once in school. Massive. A big lump of muscle, like something in the butcher's you'd never want to eat. He could feel now that he had one of those inside him. He wanted to call his mum. There was the drugs phone, but NK had taken that. He'd returned, opened the back of the car and lifted out another bike. Leif was to go out with Shell later on when she made deliveries. Take the blade with you, NK said. Don't be a pussy.

Leif didn't want to think about it.

'How far is it?' he said. 'Into town?'

Shell said, 'Why? What you thinking about?'

'Nothing.'

'You do a runner. It's not funny. They'll hurt your family.'

He thought of his kid brother Ari and there was that heart inside him again, a great big muscly weight.

'Is it just us, though? Here, I mean. I mean, if it's just us and there's going to be a fight.'

'Course it's not just us, stupid,' Shell said. 'Who do you think's got the phone right now?'

He might cry and that would be the worst thing to do. And it was so boring here, too. So frightening, and yet still so boring.

He said, 'What do you think of Pot Noodles, then?'

Shell laughed. 'What d'you think?'

'How many you ate?'

'Three hundred thousand.'

'I'm going to cycle into town and get us some chips.'

Shell shook her head.

Leif said, 'He won't even know.'

'What do you think he'll do if he finds out?'

And Leif thought of that boy with his shirt off and his fleshy white moobs. Saying, I need an ambulance. NK hadn't hesitated to cut him.

Shell said, 'He killed someone.'

'What you saying?'

'NK. He was in prison for it. That's what he's doing out here. Killed a fed. He doesn't give a fuck.'

'How d'you know that?'

'What worries me,' Shell said, 'is that you're supposed to be protection. But you don't know nothing. What they think bringing you out here? Honestly. You better fucking step up.'

28

Middleton was cut off from the main landmass of the constabulary by the river. Even with no traffic, it was a good hour's drive. They queued in Alnbridge's one-way system, turned right by the cathedral, snaked over the bridge and then they were out of the town, climbing a single-carriage road behind a struggling lorry. To the right the ground fell away to views of green fields, trees circled with fences, a herd of deer grazing.

'Stabbing or slashing the backside, it's usually a punishment kind of a thing,' Sarah said. 'Violence. Shame. Humiliation. All that. I don't know whether they do it here. We used to come across it a lot in London. That's what worries me.'

The house was part of a line of pebbledash semis in a small estate, tucked up behind the town and hemmed in by the ring road. There was no answer at the front door. The curtains of the living room were closed. As Sarah moved towards the front window, she heard the television. She went round the side and Tom trailed a couple of steps behind her. Sarah tapped at the back door: no reply. She pushed the door slightly open and stepped in.

'Hello? Police?'

Tom didn't follow.

The kitchen window was dirty and too small for the room. A dog bed stood in the corner; there was a strong smell of dog and the smell of weed, too. The washing machine was running. From beyond the door came the sound of the television.

Sarah looked at Tom, who had remained standing outside. He looked as if he was in physical pain and Sarah smiled at that, and said, 'It's fine.'

'You're trespassing,' Tom hissed.

Sarah almost laughed.

'The house is unlocked. One of the occupants of this house has recently been seriously assaulted. The television's on. The washing machine's running. But no one's answering the door, or responding to me, not even to tell us to eff off. You not worried at all?'

'This is Section Seventeen?'

Sarah opened her hands, as if she was stretching out elastic. 'It is, but mainly it's our job. I'm a police officer and a detective – so are you, by the way.'

Tom gathered himself together with an offended inhalation and followed Sarah into the kitchen.

Sarah said loudly, 'Police. Anyone home?'

She moved towards the frosted-glass internal door, tapped on it, then pushed it open. In afternoon quiz-land two teams were lined up facing each other on the TV screen. On the low table was an ashtray with burnt-out roaches, a pack of Rizlas and a small bag of weed. A fat old brindled dog that had been asleep on the sofa jumped down and waddled towards her, swinging its bum and wagging its tail slowly. Sarah offered it her hand and it pressed its head against her.

'What kind of a guard dog are you?' Sarah said, scratching behind its clipped right ear.

The duvet moved, and the person who had been sharing

the sofa with the dog emerged. He moved his hand across his face. 'What's going on?' He was round-cheeked, with blond eyelashes.

'Carl, sorry to surprise you.' There was no reply. 'The door was unlocked . . .'

He pulled himself to sitting, glanced at the ashtray with its bag of weed, and then tried not to look at it again.

'They gave me some powerful shit in the hospital.'

The childishness of the attempt to hide how stoned he was made her smile.

'You've been stabbed. I wanted to talk to you about that.'

'Told them at the clinic already. I'm not interested.'

'Is this the end of it, then? Do you think?'

He shrugged.

'I'd like some reassurance,' Sarah said. 'Wouldn't want the next time I visit you for it to be inside a morgue.'

A flicker passed over Carl's face. Sarah had run him through the Police National Computer; never even been arrested, so he was new to this. Whatever happened must have been pretty frightening.

'Those injuries of yours look rather practised. I'm guessing the guy who used the knife knew what he was about. I used to work murder for the Met. Seen too many people your age standing in the dock. And too many on the slab.'

Carl didn't answer. Sarah rubbed her temple. 'I just want to stop people getting hurt. That's all.'

Silence.

'It doesn't have to be official. Do you understand that?'

His eyes flicked towards the drawn curtains. 'You here in a police car?'

'It's not marked. No one saw us. You don't need to worry

149

about that. We can meet you somewhere if you'd feel safer.'

'So long as you piss off, I'll be safe enough.'

'If you change your mind . . .' Sarah took a notebook out of her coat. She scribbled her number and passed it to Carl. 'Put that in your phone under some name that doesn't sound like police.'

He looked at it. 'I might.'

'Do it now if you're going to do it. I'll be taking the number with me. I don't want to leave you with something that could make you look like a snitch. You're in a dangerous game. Oh, and sorry, we'll have to take that bag of weed. It looks like personal use, so just a warning this time. Tom, can you do the honours?'

29

At two o'clock they were on the bikes, cycling side by side. The road rose and fell. There was a tremendous view over the land. Slate rooves rising from little dips. Round balloons of trees. Lines of hedgerows falling away to the right.

'This where Postman Pat lives?' Leif said.

Shell laughed and she laughed again when Leif asked her about the fences and the sheep.

'Common land, isn't it?' she said.

'That's just random.'

She laughed again.

NK had given them £10 for food and Shell took them to a tiny shop that was just shutting up. Meat and onions and mustard in a bap. They sat in a back alley behind the church eating.

Shell said, 'Can't believe you're hungry.'

Leif said, 'It's so good.'

It could work out all right. He would pay off his debt and get home.

But Shell only picked at her food. She took some cigarettes out of her back pocket.

Leif said, 'You not finishing that?'

She handed what was left across to him.

'But you need to eat. You're way too thin.'

She lit her cigarette. 'You have it.'

With the warmth of the meat in his stomach, optimism

flooded through him. He said, 'You don't need to worry. We'll pay off our debts.'

She shrugged. She was unreachable, somehow. He said, 'I'll look after you, I promise. Those boys, they were shitting themselves. No way they're going to come back.'

She said, 'You're the one from London. You're not s'posed to be so fucking green.'

30

Children's drawings covered the walls. A couple of them – a pirate ship, a fox – were framed. Part of the wall had been painted over with a stripe of blackboard paint and was covered in chalk drawings. Lots of cats and houses with pitched rooves and lollipop trees. Asha was a neatly turned-out woman but her clothes were cheap. She had thick dark hair and was plump. There was another boy, younger: Ari. He was at school but Lizzie had read about him on the misper report. Leif had been in trouble for shoplifting about a month previously. Apart from that no one in this house had any criminal record or had come to police notice before.

Asha said, 'Have you checked Leif's gym pass?'

'No.'

'Only I checked it on the computer and it's been activated. I called down to the station to let them know. Did they tell you?'

'I'll go down there, check out if there's any CCTV.'

'When?'

'Tomorrow. I have to go off duty now.'

'My boy is missing.'

'And my boy needs me to pick him up from school.'

'You've got a boy?'

'Yes.'

'Then you should understand how I feel.'

'Leif is currently assessed at only low to medium risk. I have ten other missing people on my list. Should I not go home until they are all found? What do you suggest?'

Asha's face went stiff. 'Why are you bothering me with your personal circumstances? If you're not able to do your job you shouldn't be a police officer. My boy is missing.'

Lizzie picked up one of the posters that lay in a pile on the table. Leif, in his school uniform, smiled out broadly from a photo. She didn't want to think about the possible risk. Leif was fifteen and no one had any idea where he was?

'Where are you intending to leave these?'

'Here and there. Around the neighbourhood.'

'If you have any information – that would help us. Any reason we should bump Leif up our list of priorities. Anything you're not telling us? A lead I can follow? That's what I need.'

Asha pressed her lips into a thin white line. 'Your list of priorities? You should be ashamed.'

31

Tom was a bit fidgety about working overtime. He had been planning to meet friends for a drink. Sarah suppressed her irritation. She'd never forgotten the talking-to Elaine gave her when they first worked together. *Mostly I find that the people who stay late working on their own haven't got much to go home to.* And she did have someone to go home to, that was the thing, but, possessed by some madness, she'd decided to leave London and her girl. Home was now the isolated barn conversion she was renting, only ten miles from the Welsh border.

'Just one last quick thing,' she promised. 'Then we'll head back.'

In the local nick, in a back room, was a uniformed officer having a cuppa. A small man with cropped grey hair and a toughness about him. Apart from that, the station was deserted. What on earth did they do here when things got tasty? Sarah dropped a fiver in the kitty and made herself and Tom a cup of tea. From her bag she produced a tube of chocolate digestives and emptied them onto a plate: a trick she'd picked up from Elaine.

The constable said thank you and helped himself.

'I'm guessing you're the new DI?' he said. 'Heard about you.'

'That's right. This is my opo – Tom.'

He looked at Tom and smiled. 'Direct entry?'

Tom blushed. 'Yep.'

'God save us.' He offered Tom his hand. 'Mark Harris.

Uniformed constable for twenty years. Don't let the boss be teaching you her Met ways.'

Sarah stifled the urge to sigh and said, 'So is this all we've got west of the river until morning?'

'We've got one more single-crewed out Digby way. Patricia. Twenty-three years old. Draws her eyebrows on with a pencil before a shift and gets to work. Hard as nails.'

'Fair play to you both.'

'Bit different from the fackin Met, heh?'

'In so many ways.' She thought of that boy on the sofa. Was London bringing its ways here without any particular help from the Met? she wondered. 'Have you come across Carl Turner at all?'

Carl, Harris said, was a nobody, but he went to school with Joseph Cooper who, as anyone could tell you, was one of the Coopers.

'They run a nice little family business. Bit of thieving. Red diesel. Local drugs for local people. Violence where necessary, or sometimes for the fun because why not and there's not a lot to do round here unless you're in to cycling or, if you're posh or rich, fox hunting. Massive pub fight a year ago. They've got a few big houses, and land.'

'Anyone else got a foothold?'

'They seem to have seen off any competition, so far, and they keep things reasonably quiet.'

'Saving the pub fight, obviously.'

'Yes, but I attended that and they didn't thump me. Someone paid for the damage. Let me arrest one of the boys for ABH. He accepted a caution. No hard feelings.'

'They're not serious?'

'What's your definition? We had a nasty GBH about three

years ago. Hit the victim in the face with the round end of a scaffolding bar. Broken cheek, lost some teeth and the sight in his right eye. It might seem small beer by your London standards but you don't want to mess with them. This land is their land.'

'Carl got stabbed today.'

'He did?'

'In the arse. Looked like punishment to me.'

'Damn. Who's he pissed off?'

'Won't say. You got anyone will talk to you?'

'The Coopers don't talk to anyone. There's a hay wain went missing in eighteen thirty-four. Could never get to the bottom of that one either.'

'Local drug users?'

'Got a couple who speak to me. I'll pay a call. If there's a war on they'll be shitting themselves, though.'

'Thanks. Where do the Coopers get their supply?'

'Search me. You're the detective.'

'OK.'

Sarah scribbled her mobile number on a piece of paper and passed it to Harris. He said he'd give her his number by a dropped call and offered his hand. 'At least you knew to come and ask the feet on the ground.'

Sarah took his hand and smiled. 'Not so different after all.'

'What?'

'Coppering.'

'Big difference, though, is that if we do have a war on our army's mightily outnumbered with a terrible supply line that's a good thirty minutes away even on blues and twos. Me and Eyebrows Patty with an asp and a can of gas. I don't much fancy that.'

32

Lizzie was taking a risk leaving the car on a double yellow, but she didn't want Connor to be waiting. How could KK have landed her with a job that cried out for focus and long hours and definitely not for looking after your own child?

The approach to the school was thick with chatting mums and kids with school bags. There were plenty of pirates. Some mermaids. A few Lost Boys. More than one Peter Pan. Lizzie hurried to the playground. Connor stood alone, clutching his folded wings to his chest. It felt like looking at a long-shot of pain. Lizzie broke her step. She wanted to hug him but Connor said tightly, 'Don't, Mum,' and she guessed that he was right; a hug would tip him over into the hot tears that were threatening in the fierceness of his expression.

The teacher was standing in the playground watching over the last of her charges as they departed. Lizzie looked at her and suddenly what had probably been going on all day seemed to dawn on the teacher. Lizzie took Connor by the hand and walked over.

'Didn't you see?'

The teacher shook her head.

'You're responsible for him. Didn't you see? Didn't you see? You should have looked after him. Bloody hell. What kind of a teacher are you?'

The teacher looked like she might cry too and Lizzie

thought suddenly of Leif, somewhere, and his mother telling her she should be ashamed. Oh, Christ.

Connor tugged Lizzie's hand and she looked down at him. He was holding it back, but only just.

33

Kiyana started the drive back to London while Steve dozed. Then, at a service station, they swapped and Steve drove the last stretch. Kiyana was awake. Usually you couldn't shut her up, but she was silent.

'Not happy?' Steve asked as they pulled off the motorway.

'It worked out.'

'You would have stopped them?'

'I guess.'

He followed the feeder lane round a roundabout and under a low concrete bridge. They pulled onto a dual carriageway, heavy with goods traffic in both directions.

Steve said, 'Seeing one officer shot dead is enough for me.'

Kiyana didn't reply. Then she said, 'You've got more experience than me. You know what you're doing.'

He wasn't fooled by the soft soap. He said, 'When your blood's up it's hard to believe in the lawyers and the courtrooms.'

The city had wrapped itself around them, making it hard to believe in fields and uninterrupted skylines. The sky glowed orange with the sheen of London's lights. They pulled up outside Kiyana's place: a top-floor one-bedroom flat in a 1930s semi in Kingsbury, handy for Hendon.

She got her bag from the boot and leaned into the car. 'Hope there's no bad feelings?'

'Why would there be?'

'About the stop?'

'Forgot it already.'

'I just wanted to get them.'

'Course you did. But we're still watching them. Patience: hardest lesson to learn.'

Steve put his hands on the steering wheel: time to go.

But Kiyana couldn't leave it. 'Linton and George. They're nasty pieces of work.'

'Yeah. It's a special calling and it never leaves you.'

'It is. It is.'

Steve raised a hand and pulled away. He thought, Hard-working motivated young woman like that, she could be earning a lot more, owning not renting and having a much easier life. And what about later? Didn't she want a relationship? Family? No point raising that though, especially not nowadays with a beautiful woman. She'd get the right hump. Still, he shouldn't have given in to his impulse to make her feel better. He had this way of saying the thing that people wanted to hear. It had made him a good undercover officer once, but he needed to stop that nonsense now.

He spoke to himself quietly, 'Yes, Linton and George. Nasty pieces of work and as soon as we nick them someone else will step in to take their place. And not a single one of them worth dying for.'

He dropped the car in the underground car park at Hendon, and took the lift up to the offices. He logged on, checked out Ryan's prisoner records.

Out, on probation. Served less than five years.

Steve didn't know the town but he pulled it up on Google Maps: a small place, with a river. Then he checked the intelligence systems – just a quick look to see if the locals had put on anything tasty recently.

34

The doctor had given Asha diazepam. She felt as if she had a layer of plastic film between her and her fear.

Asha's sister, Bip, came round. She said, 'I know that someone's mum got kidnapped. And another boy went missing. He ended up dead.'

Asha said, 'Shut up, Bip.'

She poured herself a glass of red wine.

Bip said, 'You shouldn't be drinking and taking those pills.'

'I know that.'

Asha tiptoed into the hall and glanced into her youngest's room. Ari was sleeping on his back with his arms and legs spread wide as if he'd been thrown there. The room smelt of sleeping child, and she felt suddenly as if she was one of those statues with big holes in them you see in public places and that the wind was blowing straight through her.

She stood in the kitchen and rubbed her hands together as if she was trying to light a fire. Then she picked up her phone from the table and dialled the number Mo had given her. Jaydn.

'Wagwan?'

'If you put the phone down, I'm going to give this number to the police.'

Silence.

'I'm Leif's mum.'

'Who gave you this number?'

'You rang him before he left. I took a photo of it.'

Silence.

'You want to tell me where he is?'

Silence.

'You're Jaydn, right? You're the boy what makes the introductions.'

Silence.

'Look, you get him back to me. I won't say anything. I'll throw this number away. But I want him back.'

'He'll be all right. You stressed him out about his GCSEs. That's all.'

'I want to know where he is.'

Silence.

Asha started shouting. 'That's it! I've had enough. I'm going to the police. I bet they know who you are.'

The phone went dead.

Bip said, 'What you going to do now? You going to go to the police?'

'I don't know.' Asha pressed her thumbnail hard against her index finger. The phone rang.

'Yes?'

'I'm his sister.'

'OK. Where is he?'

'Look, miss. My brother doesn't want to be involved in this. He's been in it since he was fourteen. This is going to be the last time he does it.'

'I don't care about any of that. Just tell me where Leif is.'

'All right, but keep my brother out of this.'

'OK.'

'If you care about your son you don't want to get the police involved. Do you understand what I'm saying?'

'I want Leif back. I don't care about anything else. I get him back that's the end of it.'

'He's in Middleton.'

'Middleton? Where's that?'

'Little town with a river somewhere out west. Don't call this number again.'

35

Shell got the text for the last drop at about nine. They were tired and it was dark. She texted NK.

We've been out nearly all day. Can someone else do it?

He messaged back: Who is it for?

Shell read the text and said, 'Oh shit. He's gonna make us because it's fucking Wendy.'

'Who's Wendy?' Leif said.

'One of our regulars.'

The drop-off was up by the garages. It took them a bit to get there, and then Wendy was late. They waited round the back with the bikes. Shell stamped her feet against the cold. She looked at the phone. It was nearly ten. She said, 'Let's fuck off. Tell him she didn't show up.'

'I dunno.'

They stood, hesitating.

There was the sound of quick footsteps. Wendy was standing in front of the garages, all thin and straggly. Leif stayed behind and Shell walked out and gave her the drugs and took the money. The way Wendy hurried off, Leif could feel it. The car was there before he'd even lost sight of her. There were four inside and Leif knew that the knife he had meant nothing. And that Shell was right about him. He was no use.

Three of them got out and Leif could see immediately they weren't local. Two of them were black, but it wasn't just that. It was their clothes, and like NK they moved without hesitation. Shell was reaching in her jacket pocket, offering them the money. The taller one slapped her across the face, as if the money was an insult. He said, 'Where's the phone?'

Leif looked at the car they had got out of and he could see the fat white boy was sitting in the back. This was a war, then. London had arrived. Maybe it was already there when Shell got robbed the first time.

The tall boy had Shell against one of the garage doors. He was pulling at her jeans and she was struggling. She said, 'I haven't got any left. That was my last.'

He said, 'Hand over the phone and I'll leave you both alone.'

Leif put the knife down on the ground and stepped out from behind the garage. He said, 'Here's the phone. I've got the phone.'

The taller boy turned to him and Leif saw that he had a narrow face and a little goatee.

The other two boys came over. One of them took the phone. The other one put his hand round Leif's neck, thumb and forefinger against the two pressure points. He squeezed hard. He pushed Leif back against the garage and took out a knife. It was an evil-looking blade, curved like a scimitar and with a jagged edge. He laughed. 'You the muscle?'

The boy with Shell said to Leif, 'Pay attention. Tell your man, this is our strip now.'

Shell fought like a cat, but they raped her anyway. Leif looked and didn't look. He liked her. He had fancied her. He'd imagined kissing her. Now this. He was a fool. Once he tried to move forward but the boy raised the knife. The fat

166

boy carried on sitting in the car, watching. Leif was wearing his jacket. They were both bystanders. He thought of the knife NK had given him lying there where he had left it behind the garages.

36

Sarah parked at the bottom of the field and opened the back door of the car. Poppy jumped down and ran free, sending up a hare that zigzagged away across the field.

'Somebody likes it here,' Sarah said.

She took the takeaway curry from the back seat. By the time she clocked off the station had become silent. She missed the busy dirty old Met where no police building was ever empty and the officers squeezed onto shared desks and had nowhere to park. There were only two takeaways still open in the town. Rubbish Indian or rubbish fish and chips. Where were the bagel bakeries? The Turkish shops? Shoreditch's all-night food market? Smithfield, where the uniformed relief used to drop by at 4 a.m. to pick up their orders of meat. Where was the hub, the buzz, the city?

As she climbed towards the little barn millions of stars were puncturing the darkness with tiny bright spots. To her right the cloud of the Milky Way was washed across the sky. You'd never see that in London: only a big orange dome. She'd light a fire, FaceTime Meghan. She fished her phone out of her bag and saw two dropped calls from an unknown number. As she slipped her key in the lock she tapped on the missed call.

'Sarah.'

The voice was instantly familiar. She pushed open the door and dumped her bag and the takeaway on the table. The stone room was freezing.

'It's Steve. Steve Bradshaw.'

'Hang on a moment.' She stepped out onto the threshold and whistled for Poppy to come. The dog bounded towards her. She ushered it in and shut the door, turning the lock. 'Can I put you on speaker? I just got home.'

'Sure.'

She propped the phone on the top of the stove, opened the door and lit a match.

'You changed your number.'

'Journos got hold of it.'

'OK.'

The fire began to lick through the prepared paper and kindling. She shut the door, opened the damper to let the oxygen flow through. Behind the glass the stove filled with smoke and fire.

'He's in your force area.'

'What?'

'He's in your force area. Middleton. Part of his release conditions.'

She didn't say anything.

'Ryan Kennedy.'

'I'd guessed.'

She opened the stove door, placed a couple of small logs on the blaze. She moved towards the work surface and flipped the switch on the kettle. 'How've you been?'

'I still don't understand how the actual person who got the gun and pulled the trigger doesn't bear any responsibility at all.'

'Hmm.'

'Anyway, I saw the report you put on earlier.'

'That was quick.'

'You've got some beef going on over there. A new line, perhaps?'

She lifted Poppy's bowl from the floor. The dog sat watching her, wagging its tail furiously.

'Steve . . .'

She spooned food into the bowl and placed it on the floor.

'I'm working on a dedicated unit, Sarah. That's what we do.'

She picked up the phone and switched it off speaker. 'No.'

'What?'

'I don't want you getting involved.'

'We have no evidence that Ryan's part of it. It'll be fun for us to work together again.'

She sat down in the winged chair in front of the stove. The room was as cold as stone. 'I'd love to work with you again, but not on this.'

The line was silent.

Sarah said, 'It was hard on you. And unfair. I'm sorry how things went down.'

'It's not unfair. It's a joke.'

'OK.'

'He killed Kieran. I was there. Kieran was being kind to him.'

'It was terrible. It is terrible.'

Steve said, 'Everything he did – the drug dealing, the robberies, the gun – poor lad, he didn't really know what he was doing. Only people responsible for what happened are the police officers. I'm responsible.'

'It's not fair.'

'Except you, of course. You're not responsible. The judge says so.'

'I feel responsible.'

'I didn't mean that, Sarah. You're not responsible.'

'What did you mean?'

There was a silence.

Steve said, 'Don't you want to get him?'

The fire had petered out. She'd just make a hot-water bottle and go to bed. Back home in London she'd installed an intelligent system she could operate from her phone. The house would have already been warm when she got in. How long was she going to live like this? She needed to get her act together; sell the London place, stop hedging her bets.

She said, 'I'm sorry, I've got to go. I haven't eaten and I'm exhausted. I moved here to get away from it all. I want some peace. That's the truth.'

'Is it? You put that intelligence on at nine this evening.'

'I didn't even know Ryan was living here.'

'You didn't?'

'Please, Steve. Don't come here. Don't get involved. Get someone else in your unit to deal. Do what you should do; recuse yourself.'

'Recuse? I don't even know what that word means.'

'Come on. We go way back. It's good to hear your voice. I hope you're doing well.'

'Seriously.'

'How are the kids? One of them was off to uni—'

'Seriously. Recuse. What does it mean?'

'You're serious?'

'I'm serious.'

'It means . . . You know what it means.'

'Go on.'

'It means declare yourself unfit to participate, unable to judge—'

'But I'm not. I'm not unfit to participate. I'm not unable to judge. Others might not be able to judge. Others might not be able to participate. But I can. I've got the balls to do it. I judge, Sarah. I judge. I judge him. Don't you?'

37

Shell was kind of rolling around in the dirt and a shame descended on Leif that he knew would never lift. He said, 'Do you want to go to the police?'

Shell groaned. Then he made out the words she was saying. 'You fucking idiot.'

In the street light he could see that her face was bruised. There was blood on her jeans.

Leif said, 'Yes, OK, I'm a fucking idiot. I don't know nothing. But something like this? We gotta go to the police. We gotta get you out of this. I saw, there's a station in town. I dunno, talk to them at least. Get you home.'

'If we go to the feds, NK will kill us.'

Shell couldn't cycle. They walked the bikes. It took them ages. The police station was a small red-brick building on the edge of town. There was a car park next to it, and recycling bins. The station door was locked. Leif peered through the glass. The light was on but there was no one inside. Leif's confidence was ebbing away. This didn't look like a place that could help them. It was tiny and the doors were locked. He hadn't seen a single cop car since he'd been here. Shell was right. NK would kill them. They needed a huge police station and bright lights and streets full of people if they were going to get any sort of protection. Maybe it was for the best the station was shut.

Shell had started shaking. She said, 'What we gonna do?

I can't cycle. It's miles to walk and there's no bus this late.'

Leif said, 'Maybe there's a hospital?'

'There's *nothing* in this fucking town.'

A man was walking down the street and Leif thought maybe to ask him, but the man was wearing wellies and his trousers were held up by string.

What would his mum tell him to do?

A little red car was coming down the road and Leif stepped into the road and waved his arms. The car swerved to avoid him and drove past, but the second car stopped. It was a little blue car, size of a toy.

The woman wasn't English but she spoke English very well. She had brown curly hair and wore a big checked shirt. She took one look at Shell and told them to get in the car. They sat next to each other in the back, a sack of chicken feed by their feet.

Leif said, 'My friend needs to go to hospital.'

'What's wrong with her?'

'I can't say.'

The woman looked between the seats at them. Then she said, 'There's a minor injuries unit. I'll take you there.'

The engine was running, but before she drove off, she got her mobile phone out.

Leif said, 'What are you doing?'

The woman said, 'You need police.'

'No,' Shell said. 'No police.'

By nine thirty Leif and Shell should have checked in. NK called the phone from his burner.

He didn't know the voice, but he knew it was pagans.

'Wagwan?'

174

NK didn't answer.

'Soldiers have arrived. Better get out of Dodge.'

He waited to hear what else they had to say, and sure enough they couldn't resist it.

'Gave your girl a good time.'

He closed the call. Don't let them even hear your voice. He'd chuck the burner in the river. The White Walkers were at the edges, muttering and whispering and pointing their fingers. The war was on.

It was a tiny place with a big notice outside telling you to dial 999 if it was an emergency, which didn't make any sense, because this place was called a hospital and there didn't seem to be anywhere else to go. Leif sat in the waiting area. Two rows of chairs faced each other, and there was another row against the wall. The big woman with the accent went with Shell to the desk. A nurse came out and took Shell away into a room. The woman at the desk looked over at Leif and gave him a sort of smile, which he couldn't read: like she herself couldn't decide what kind of smile to make.

In London this place would be packed with people. All sorts; different colours and ages, more people than you could take in or remember. But some would stick out. A bearded guy in a skullcap maybe waiting with an old woman in a wheelchair. And a woman in a headscarf with a hundred kids. Police hanging around looking like shit with lots of bags and radios chattering. And a drunk guy shouting fuck a lot and everyone just ignoring him. But here just one man was waiting. He looked about fifty, in a denim shirt with blood down the front, and a tea towel wrapped round his hand. He'd been there when they arrived and Shell had gone in before him. He wasn't kicking up a fuss about it. He seemed willing to sit there and wait for ever.

The woman at the desk was on the phone. Leif thought maybe he could go up to her and ask to ring his mum. But then Shell came out.

'What's happening?'

'The doctor told me to wait but let's go.'

'You sure?'

She sighed. Yeah, he got it: he was a baby. As they passed, the woman at the desk said, 'Just wait here for a minute.'

Shell said, 'I'm going out for a smoke.'

NK had driven first to the garages, thinking that maybe they'd have the sense to wait. But, no. Idiots. He drove past the police station. No sign of any activity there. Then, on to the hospital. They called it a hospital anyway, a *community* hospital, but it looked way too small to be one. He knew what a hospital looked like. This place was smaller than a decent Tesco Express. What did they do here if someone really needed help?

As he drove up, he saw them together, pushing the bikes. He pulled over, and got out. He told Shell to wait in the car while he and Leif locked the bikes. He didn't speak until they were driving away. Then he asked if the boys had taken all the money and how much. What had they said and who was in the car. He wanted to know, too, which of them had handed over the phone.

Shell said, 'It wasn't the drugs phone anyway. It was just a burner.'

NK slowed the car and pulled over. He put the handbrake on and waited.

'Me,' Leif said. 'I gave it to them. They said they wouldn't hurt Shell if we handed it over.'

'Make any difference, did it?' NK said.

He drove them back to the caravan park and told them to get out. This wasn't the end of it, he said. They'd hit back. Wendy would be first. And Leif and Shell would pay back the money that had been stolen. He would add it to their debts.

38

Leif lay on the sofa under the blanket and wearing the boy's jacket. He was so stoned he couldn't move and, in his stoned state, his physical state revealed itself to him. He could feel the dirt under his nails, the dirt in his mouth. His bathroom with his toothbrush in the glass standing next to his mum's and his brother's came to him like an apparition, and it was just the loneliest saddest thing. He wanted to get up and go out of the caravan where he could make a noise and Shell wouldn't hear him. He imagined that dark field, the grass wet underfoot, the empty caravans and that river rushing by, so wide and brown. Leif started crying. Once he started, he couldn't stop. It kept piling on top of him, all the miserable facts, one after another. Pathetic little facts. He was cold. He didn't know where he was. He owed a huge debt and he could never pay it off. He missed his toothbrush. He'd stood by while Shell was raped. He was a baby, and knowing that made it worse. He tried to cry quietly but he had those awful juddery shaky things.

Shell was stirring. He took an inhalation and held his breath to cover the sound, as if he had hiccups. He put his hand over his mouth. But he heard the duvet being thrown off and her feet padding across the floor. Shell's thin figure was standing beside him in her hoodie and jeans.

She said, 'Here.'

He reached out. It was her hot-water bottle.

'Don't you need it?'

'It doesn't matter.'

He wished he wasn't so stoned. He said, 'You keep the hot-water bottle. I'm OK.'

'No, you're all right. You keep it. I don't need it.'

She opened the caravan door and he could see the moon. He said, 'What are you doing?'

She pulled her jacket around her. 'Going for a walk.'

'You want me to come with you?'

'No, but thanks anyway.'

39

Lizzie was swept by a powerful current into the undertow. Although she was surrounded by ocean the water here was shallow. The shingle slipped painfully beneath her and she couldn't stand. She was cold. Her skin was stripped raw by the rush of stones. She was on a rise in the ocean and the shore was out of sight. Only then she remembered she'd been swimming with Connor. Where was he? With sudden panic she realised she couldn't see him. Had he slipped beneath the waves? Had she not been paying attention? The rope holding her reached its limit and jerked her back. Street light fell across her bed. She flicked on the bedroom light and with her breath coming in deep gasps as if she had been running, she padded to Connor's room. She stood watching him, the soft fall and rise of his breath. She thought of that boy, out there, somewhere.

WEDNESDAY

40

It was still dark and spots of rain were falling. The morning was cold, and as he cycled he blew on his gloved hands. The town was quiet and the roads empty of traffic. Pulling out into the country lanes he felt the wind more keenly. A huge white bird emerged from over a hedgerow and flew low overhead. He was clear as water, possessed of calm and certainty. Just before he turned into the private road, he switched off the bicycle's lights. The way was shadowed by trees. He tucked the bike into the lee of a hedge and lifted the black pannier bag off the rack.

He had his story ready, but as he slipped the gate and walked up the pathway it was clear it would not be necessary. There were no dogs barking or running, no tails wagging through the collapsed autumn grass. There-Are-Otters was not at home. NK pulled latex gloves on over his cycling gloves.

The back door was unlocked.

The kitchen was warm. A musty smell rose that mixed fire and the smell of earth. The room was tidy and ordered. Three dead birds hung on the back of the door he had just passed through. A tea towel hung over the back of the cream enamelled stove. A large steel kettle with a black handle stood on the top. On the draining board a china cup and saucer were drying. A zinc bucket was in the corner by a little door painted in green paint with a latch like a stable door. On the chimney breast a framed photo of a spaniel with a bird in its mouth. In the corner was a large wooden cabinet.

NK moved over and tried the doors. They were locked. He took a metal tyre lever out of his pannier and inserted it between the doors. The wood deformed slightly under the pressure but the door did not give. NK moved over to the shelf above the chimney breast. He reached the photo of the spaniel down from the wall. He lifted the bucket from the floor. He opened the door on the latch and there, in the corner of the stone step that led down into a cold room with a toilet and a small square window, was the key.

Only one shotgun was in the cabinet. The stock rested on the floor and the barrel was held by a grooved bar. There were drawers inside the cabinet. The first held cloths and tins of polish. The next had a box of cartridges, which he put in his pannier. There was a leather shoulder bag too, with little pockets to hold cartridges. He took that too. He lifted the shotgun down and sat at the table with the gun resting across his knees and the pannier beside him. The lever was underneath the forestock, as the YouTube video had suggested it would be, and it moved easily. He put the forestock on the table. Then he pushed the lever on top of the stock and the barrel dropped out onto his knees. He went to the bathroom and got the two towels to wrap the three pieces.

He cycled fast but in no hurry along the muddy uneven track by the river. The gun was heavy in the pannier. Once the tyres slipped sideways on the wet leaves but he kept his balance. The sun was rising through the trees, and he inhaled the smell of rain and undergrowth.

He turned out of the trackway and, against a wide

landscape of fields and woods, saw the deserted barns and farm machinery. He unclipped his left pedal, slipped the latch on the galvanised metal gate and cycled inside across the pitted concrete. The barn was dark wood with a weathered corrugated roof. The door was open and he took the bike inside. A beam of pale light fell down into the barn and, looking to his right, he saw a ladder up to a loft area. He climbed with the pannier slung over his shoulder. He liked the small hidden space at the top of the ladder, with the small window overlooking the wide flat area before the gate.

He loaded the leather shoulder bag with cartridges. Then he lifted the towels out of the pannier and unwrapped the shotgun parts, turning each in his hands before he placed them beside him. The shiny silver plates on the lock were engraved with twirls and flourishes. Colours ran through the polished dark wooden stock like marble and the double trigger with its shaped guard was delicate and elegant. Compared to all this prettiness, the dark metal barrels had a pleasing seriousness about them. The weight and balance were satisfying in his hands and they slotted into the stock with a convincing click. The third part – carved wood with a silver end – fitted easily back below the barrels and into the stock. For all its fanciness it was a simple machine. He balanced the shotgun between his hands, remembering with a smile the weapon Shakiel had given him: a dirty little revolver with tape round the handle. This shotgun belonged to a life where such things were elegant and revered, and now it belonged to him.

The light was opening in the sky.

He slotted the cartridges into the leather bag and slung it over his shoulder. Carrying the gun tucked between his arm and his chest, he moved quickly down the ladder, out from the shelter of the barn and away from the road. The White Walkers were moving through the woods opposite. His heart was loud in his chest but he felt no anxiety. The sound of shots was common here – until the alarm was raised they would disturb no one – and the shotgun invited him. He slipped the lever at the top of the action and the barrel dropped to reveal its two perfectly round tubes. It made him smile to take the cartridges out of their stitched leather pockets and drop them into the barrels. No teeth hidden in socks for these guys. He held the gun tight against his shoulder. As he released the first shot a wave of birds flew out of the trees, squawking and flapping. His finger moved to the second trigger and he caught one in flight. It skated across as if thrown from a sling before it plummeted.

It was only as he took the bike out of the barn that he realised he had a puncture. It must have been a thorn on the trackway from the estate. No matter. The tyres were tubeless and quickly fixed.

41

Sarah reached out from the warmth of the bed to her ringing phone.

'No problem. I'll go straight there. Can you send me the postcode?'

She let Poppy out of the back door, and was struck once again by the stars. Would she ever get used to these skies? She made herself a quick coffee. Poppy was still hurling herself around the field but Sarah called her back. She tempted her into the back of the car with a treat and turned left out of the drive towards the river.

Her thoughts were with Steve. How years ago, when they worked together in the Directorate of Specialist Investigations, they shared cigarettes on the roof of Jubilee House with a half-tame crow, called Sid. Neither of them had a partner to go home to and she had thought of their friendship as an uncommon thing. Detective love, she named it secretly. It was a variation, she had imagined, on the kind of recognition that Volkswagen Beetle drivers experience when they flash their headlights at each other. But then she'd spotted him standing on the bridge over the Thames deep in conversation with the just released Lizzie Griffiths, who had been a suspect in their investigation. Like the lever on a clock escapement clicking into place, something had moved inside her and she knew he had deceived her. When she challenged him, he gave her both barrels. He told her that her zeal was misplaced, and, while he was at it, he told her to get a life too.

Fog hung across the winding roads. The track was churned by vehicles. Water pooled brown in the ruts, and ran down towards the river. As the car wobbled and bounced around the bend she saw the way ahead closed with crime tape. A young police constable, Thermos mug in her hands, sat in a marked car securing the scene, her engine running against the cold. Sarah parked in the lay-by and showed her warrant card.

'Got to leave the dog in the car. Didn't have time to drop her at the minder. OK?'

The constable began writing Sarah's details in the crime log. 'Yeah, fine. I'll keep an eye.'

Sarah reached into her pocket and handed over a set of car keys.

'These are my spare set. Will you hand them over if you get relieved?'

Sarah took her scene bag from the car and threw it over her shoulder. Even from here she could hear the constant flow of water.

42

An alarming sense that something was wrong woke Leif. He opened his eyes wide.

The caravan was already light and the hot-water bottle he held against his stomach was still warm. It was too quiet and he knew he was alone but he still said, 'Shell?' and waited hopefully for her to tell him off.

He threw the blanket off, stepped out into the cold air, and walked over to the bed. It was empty, the duvet still thrown back from the night before.

How could he have just carried on sleeping when she didn't return from her walk?

He slipped his trainers on and ran down the caravan steps. The bikes lay side by side on the decking. He looked up towards the entrance to the caravan park. There were no recent tyre tracks but she could have walked out to the road. There were buses after all. But not at night, he remembered. He hesitated, then ran across the grass and down towards the river, muttering to himself about what an idiot he was.

The river was brown and angry. A tree had fallen across and got pinned. One of the branches tapped repeatedly on the surface of the water.

He wasn't supposed to draw attention, but he shouted Shell's name anyway. His voice was no more than a piece of straw snatched away by the river's constant roar. It was like you were nothing. Shell was nothing. None of this river and trees and birds and stuff cared about anything.

He moved along the bank following the direction of the river's flow. It was muddy and slippery. He could see no footprints. The ground began to climb steeply away from the river. The descent on his right was tree-lined and he couldn't see down to the water but he could hear its continuous roar. There was a fence, with a five-bar gate, which he climbed into a ploughed field. Walking was difficult. The clay clung to his trainers and made them heavy and clumsy. He began to wonder what was the point of this, and to consider turning back. He called Shell's name again and moved on. The land flattened out and then descended. There was a barbed-wire fence at the end of the field and he crawled through it, snagging the boy's jacket. He was on a level again with the river. Broad trees stood along the bank and leaves floated downstream. A stone bridge was ahead and a police officer was standing on it.

Leif clenched his hands into two fists and stood. His heart was thumping and something was going on inside his head that he couldn't understand, as if it had been scraped out with a knife and emptied of all words.

43

Sarah turned out of the trees and saw the weir, and, a little further upstream, an old stone bridge. The river swept past, brown at its banks, and at the centre grey as lead.

Four vehicles were parked up. Right up on the bank two rescue four-by-fours and an ambulance. Nearer the track a marked police car. The paramedics sat chatting in their cab. A group of men in bright yellow dry suits and orange helmets were working on the bank. Two were inflating a small boat. The others were checking each other's kit.

A uniformed police sergeant walked towards her and offered his hand. A big fellow. 'Graham Barnes.'

'Sarah Collins. Pleased to meet you.'

'You're ex-Met, I heard.'

'News travels fast round here.' She laughed uncomfortably and took a Decision Log out of her bag. 'What have we got?'

He gestured towards the bridge. 'It's a busy spot for walkers so the body probably would have been spotted if it was in yesterday. Dog walker out early before work: stops on the bridge to look at the river.'

'We're sure it's a body?'

'Fraid so. From the bridge we can see a hand. They're about to go in. Because it's cold they'll try for a resus but – just being realistic, now – it's nearly an hour since the body was spotted.'

'Feel for them.'

'Yes, and not an easy retrieval. The river's practically in spate.'

'I'll go and say hello. We don't have any intelligence. No misper report?'

'No.'

'I'll go over. Don't want to hold them up.'

The body retrieval was an all-man team. They were volunteers from the local rescue association. The water was flowing fast and she didn't envy them the difficulty of handling the sodden body in the strong current. Only one of them looked like he'd made forty, but this man at least was convincingly grizzly.

'Robert Helms. Team leader.'

'Appropriate name.'

He smiled.

'And I'm guessing I'm not the first person to have said that?' She offered her hand. 'Detective Inspector Sarah Collins. Thanks for doing this.'

One of the young rescue association fellows spoke up. 'It's what we train for.' He had a wide mouth and blue eyes. Blond hair bushed out from beneath his helmet. 'We had a sheep caught in the weir in the town centre a few weeks ago,' he added gamely. 'Good practice.'

Robert met her eyes briefly and Sarah wondered whether, for all his training, this was the young man's first retrieval of a human.

Robert said, 'The boat's a just-in-case thing. This weir shallows just before the drop. I reckon we can walk in on a line and use the basket stretcher.'

'And you'll lay a plastic sheet on the stretcher? I'm

thinking of trying to hold on to anything that might be dislodged.'

The blond man said, 'What's that, body parts?'

Robert said. 'No, Adam. She's thinking about evidence.'

'That's right. And will you be videoing?'

Robert nodded.

'I'll leave you to crack on then.'

Behind her the sergeant and a PC were putting up the tent. Nothing was easy on the muddy shore. She pulled on a forensic suit. It felt a bit silly – no one else had bothered. Her mind leapt to the things they might say about her and she blushed. Maybe it was over the top. Perhaps after a year or so here, she'd just slip some wellies on.

She walked towards the bridge. The water, sliding rapidly over the weir, looked strangely solid, like a tube of grooved brown plastic but flecked with white where small waves rose quickly, and then submerged back into the rapid flow. The body was on its side, face down in the water, wedged against a small tree that had seeded itself into the river bed. It wasn't possible to see clearly beyond the shape of the jacket and the legs, but it looked small, and probably female. She walked on, under the bridge. The further bank was lined with mature trees that shaded the water, the surface patterned with yellow and orange leaves that skimmed downstream. She looked around but saw nothing – no marks on the bank, no person or object that shouldn't be there. She turned up the steep path to her right. A laminated note was attached to the far side of the wooden kissing gate. *Private. No swimming.*

Before a line of crime scene tape, a uniformed PC stood on

the bridge. A man on a road bike with bulging thighs and all the gear was standing beside him arguing persistently to be let through. 'I can't see what harm it will do!' But the arrival of Sarah – a white plastic spaceman in this bucolic scene – defeated him. He turned the bike and cycled away.

Sarah gave the officer her details and slipped on her overshoes.

She walked looking down, but there was nothing on the bridge. She stood on the parapet. The men were moving steadily along the line of the weir, Robert at the front, waist high. Behind him the big blond lad had hold of the stretcher.

She looked at the body again. From this height she could see the hand, white through the brown water.

Robert had reached the body and he started to pull at it. It didn't move easily. She looked away.

The paramedics were working, bent over the shape on the stretcher.

The blond looked close to tears. 'It's a young woman,' he said. 'Looks like a kid. She's so bashed up.'

Sarah put a hand on his shoulder. 'You've done your best for her. You should be proud of yourself.'

One of the paramedics walked up. A tall woman with long red hair. 'I've had to declare life extinct.'

Sarah caught the police sergeant's eye and he walked with her away from the group.

'Would you mind videoing while I have a quick look?'

'OK.'

'And, I'm sorry to ask. But could you suit up and get a mask.'

*

The clothing was torn where it had snagged but the jacket's hood was still drawn tight around the head. The face was marked with abrasions and pink from hypostasis but it was still identifiably the face of a young woman. Blood-flecked foam was inside her nostrils and at the edges of her mouth. Sarah lifted the right hand. There was no rigor but the skin on the palms of the hands and fingers was thickened and wrinkled. The nails were bitten down. One of the fingers looked broken but that could be from a fall into the water, or after death when the body drifted against stones and debris. The girl was deeply cold to the touch but that gave no information as to time of death and the cold water might also have affected the onset of rigor. But there was no decomposition, no bloating. It seemed a reasonable assumption that the death had probably happened during the night.

The jacket pockets were zipped but there was nothing identifying inside them. No phone. No bank cards, just some coins. A lipstick and some mascara. Sarah felt gently around the head. She unzipped the jacket to look at the torso. Here was the girl's tiny little chest. No bra. Just a torn skimpy blue T-shirt. There was bruising on one of the ribs but no obvious bleeding or deformation. This too could have happened after death. Sarah had seen worse damage on bodies recovered from the Thames.

'How deep's the water upstream?'

'It's deep and wide for about a mile or so and the flow's strong.'

Sarah finished scribbling in her log. She looked up. 'What have we got running? In terms of resources, I mean?'

The sergeant cleared his throat.

'Well, we're a big rural force – in terms of square miles

that is, not in terms of manpower – and we've got a lot of water. We do get this from time to time. Usually it's not even suicide. People just fall in. It's very cold this time of year. Had one last year: man walking his dog. But even the strongest swimmer . . .'

'I understand that.'

'So they won't want to mobilise a big team yet. Not till we've got more of an idea of what we're dealing with.' The sergeant's eyes travelled over Sarah's face, then he said, with an air of encouragement, 'But SOCO's on the way.'

'Thank you. Good job.'

The words 'golden hour' popped into Sarah's head. How long had the body been in the water already? In London the marine support unit would have been tasked with the extraction. She hadn't worked any team that wasn't specialist crime for years.

'Tell me about the witness.'

'Brian Wheeler. Deputy head at the secondary. No criminal record. I took a statement. Didn't make a fuss, but he looked a bit grey. Called his wife, she came and picked him up.'

Sarah glanced back at the body.

The sergeant said, 'What do you reckon?'

'It looks to me like she's drowned but we need to wait for the pathologist. I won't interfere any more. I'll get onto the coroner straight away and run a search for mispers in our area. Sooner we can do the PM the better. We need to identify her urgently and get news to her family.'

The pathologist had been helpful. She'd be ready to start in a couple of hours. Sarah would attend. In the meantime she had time to follow up some other inquiries. The clothing was torn. The face and body had abrasions and bruising consistent with drifting in the water. The girl might have jumped from the bridge, but it seemed more likely that she'd come from somewhere upstream.

Sarah had the Ordnance Survey mapping for the area downloaded on her phone, and she opened it up.

44

The walk back was hard. The wind blew in Leif's face and his shoes were big clumsy blocks of heavy mud. Some crows rose from the field as he crossed it. He saw and heard everything as if in splashes. The trees, the brown eddying surface of the water. The sound of the river's roar, a blast of noise that obliterated thought.

His trainers were so heavy he could hardly walk.

He sat by the water's edge and took them off. He used a stick to scrape off the sticky mud, and then held them in the river flow. The water was painfully cold. It tugged at the shoes, as if it wanted to snatch them away. He was gulping and shaking. He put the trainers back on and they were soaked. So were the bottom of his trousers and his pants. His mouth was open and he pulled his hand across his face to wipe away the tears.

He turned and walked towards the caravan. NK's silver car was parked up, the wheels thick with mud. The back seats were down, he saw. Muddy tracks and skid marks broke up the grass. The caravan door was open. Leif stood still. He needed to do something radical, but he couldn't think what that might be.

Inside, the caravan stank of petrol.

NK, can in hand, was moving through splashing everything. He was dressed all in black and he looked like the devil.

NK said, 'What's happened to you?'

'I don't know what you mean.'

'You're covered in mud. Never mind. Get your stuff.'

'I don't have any stuff.'

'Wait outside then.'

Leif stood on the wet grass. Surely something should have changed inside him. Every time he thought of Shell he wanted to cry but he grasped on to hope. Maybe she was OK. Maybe she'd just run away. If she had then good on her. He wanted to lie down somewhere warm.

NK stepped out of the caravan and got a thick rope out of the back of the car. He said, 'Put the bikes in the back. Then sit inside and wait for me.'

Leif dragged the bikes over, lifted them into the car. Behind him NK was splashing petrol over the decking. Leif got into the front passenger seat and looked over his shoulder. The rope trailed down from the decking and NK was standing back from it. A match flew from his hand with a tiny spark and petered out. NK lit another and threw it. Fire billowed from the ground like shaken cloth. It raced up the rope, and roared.

NK drove carefully navigating the grass, not revving, not spinning the wheels. Moving like there was no hurry. Leif looked over his shoulder. The caravan was a blazing fire. Sparks were jumping off into the air.

Leif said, 'Where's Shell?'

'There were police about a mile further down. I asked a cyclist what was going on and he said there's a body in the river.'

45

Asha waited thirty-seven minutes at Alnbridge for the train to Middleton. Rain dripped onto the station's iron-and-glass roof. Asha got herself a coffee and a flapjack in a plastic wrapper. A mum and dad with red cheeks sat with their daughter in the waiting room. The girl wore a blue checked dress, white woollen tights and patent leather shoes. She held her father's hand. The mother had brought a flask and sandwiches. They ate silently. They'd been on the London train too and now they must be heading home.

Before Asha left London Bip said, 'What are you going to do when you get there?' And Asha said, 'I'm going to look for him. I'm going to put up posters and people will talk to me.'

It was more than another hour to Middleton from Alnbridge. Every ten minutes or so the train stopped at a small town or at even smaller brick stations with short platforms and single signs. The countryside rose and fell. Horses stood stoically together in fields, curling their back hooves underneath in the rain. A stream moved alongside and travelled with them before veering out of sight. Twice they went over a river, brown and fast. Geese moved around a field that was lined with little triangular wooden houses. If Leif and Ari had been there, they'd have joked about the geese living in fancy ski chalets. Then she remembered how Leif had stopped talking to her. The train nosed round the bend and under the station overpass.

On the opposite platform a group of boys with rucksacks

were waiting: off on some wholesome expedition, she imagined. In the little steel-and-glass platform shelter was a wooden bookcase with paperbacks and a glass jar to leave a pound for the Middleton Hospice.

There were no taxis. The road curved down towards a supermarket. On the right was a terrace of houses and a dressmaker's. Beyond the line of houses lay hills and fields. A wave of embarrassment passed through Asha. What on earth had she thought she was going to achieve by coming here?

The rain was constant.

The supermarket took a poster and so did the church – a big and ancient place with a nice old lady in a headscarf who greeted her at the door. There was a tiny shop that sold meat and onions in a bap. Asha asked if she could put a poster up and they said, sure. They had a little noticeboard and she pinned Leif on there, next to the knife sharpener and the pest control guy: *Wasps and Bees; Mice and Rats*. There was a shoe repair shop further down but he said no to the poster.

She walked along the high street and down to the river. She stood on the stone bridge. A big branch was sweeping down. On the other side of the bridge the town was already fading into countryside. A single-lane road with allotments ran parallel to the river. In the shade of tall trees was a dark little house. Trying to smile, she took a selfie and sent it to Ari.

Found where Hansel and Gretel live! Back soon!

Her black pumps were soaked. It only took about twenty minutes to walk the whole of the town centre.

She went into a Costa and asked to put one of the posters up. She sat and had a Coke. The only other person in there was a man with two collie dogs. He nodded at her and returning his smile felt to Asha like trying to catch the heat from a small fire.

She said, 'Do you mind if I ask?'

'What?'

'I mean, why are all the shops closed? Where is everyone?'

'It's Wednesday.'

'It's Wednesday?' Asha shifted inside her wet coat and smiled. 'What does that even mean?'

The man smiled back. 'No market on a Wednesday.'

'Oh.'

He looked at the poster. 'That your son?'

She nodded.

'Why do you think he's here?'

She shrugged. What should she say? County lines.

She said, 'Could you tell me where the rough estates are around here?'

'There's only really one,' he said.

The man drove her. The car smelt of wet dog but she didn't mind. He dropped her at the turn to the estate, on the outskirts of town, tucked just inside the ring road. He said, 'Good luck.'

It was still pissing down and there was no one around There was a community centre but it was closed. Behind it were some lock-up garages. She went into a fish and chip shop and got one of the posters out of her bag and showed it to the Asian man behind the counter.

'You seen him at all?'

The man shook his head.

'Can I put the poster up?'

'There isn't really anywhere to put it.'

It was a twenty-minute walk back into town through rain that fell so hard it stung. She sat at a bus stop and took a diazepam. She got her phone out and called the number. It was a woman who answered, probably the sister again.

Asha started shouting. 'I've had enough. I'm going to the police.'

'You call police your boy will end up dead, your whole family is going to end up dead.'

'I don't care.'

'It's not a joke. The guy in charge killed a fed.'

Asha googled Middleton police station and began walking. Her phone was ringing.

The woman said, 'Don't go to the police. Be calm. Your son's going back to London.'

Asha ran to the station but there was no train for forty-five minutes.

She phoned her sister. 'Leif's on his way home. Can you get there? Just in case he's there before I am.'

46

The rain had finally stopped but the sky was heavy with the possibility of another downpour. The caravan was gutted, the steel frame exposed. Sarah watched the SOCO, suited up, moving inside what remained of the structure. It was hard to see what forensic opportunities there could be. The ground was too churned to get any useful tyre impressions. The SOCO had taken some samples from inside the ruts. Who knows, they might get lucky if they stopped a muddy car. But every car was muddy in this county.

The site owner stood beside her, rocking on his heels. He was cloth-capped, in wellies, old brown corduroys and a waxed jacket.

No one else was staying on the site, he said. Hard to get people during the winter. During the summer, too, for that matter. The site was being sold. It was going to be a riverside development. Different-sized houses, all with their own garages. Looked nice on the drawings.

He didn't know much about the rental, he said. Some thin girl.

'How did she pay?'

'Cash every month.'

'You didn't think something was up?'

'Not my business, was it?'

Sarah pulled over to let Poppy have a run around. She didn't have enough time before the post-mortem to turn round and drop the dog with the minder. The spaniel bounded about, sniffing at the tussocks and wagging her tail. Sarah leaned against the car and took in the view, down across the hills towards the town. It lay like Camelot in the distant valley, its tall Norman church tower rising through the low-lying fog.

The mortuary was a small modern building a forty-minute drive north of Middleton on country roads. The route was through a gently rising and falling plain: single houses and farms dotted among the curves of hedges; a level crossing where the cars patiently queued as the local train hurried through, beeping its horn; a stream winding alongside the road, leaving and rejoining.

Nearly two hours from Alnbridge, this was the furthest end of the constabulary.

Sarah had asked the sergeant at the scene if he could organise an officer to assist at the PM as exhibits officer and PC Simon Landry was waiting for her in the car park. He was tall and athletic, late twenties probably, with a serious air. She guessed she'd been lucky to get him. They moved through into the building and in the waiting room she talked him quickly through the routine. They wrote up some of the labels together and jotted the bag numbers down in the exhibits book.

'If you don't know what to do, ask me.'

'Of course.'

I must be getting old, Sarah thought: Dr Julia Houghton, the pathologist, seemed unbelievably young. She had long wavy hair with blonde highlights, wore bright red lipstick and had a toughness about her that inspired confidence.

Houghton broke the ID tag and unzipped the bag.

The girl lay, nameless, in the cool mortuary light. She had long brown hair that was thick with river mud. Her clothes were torn and stained by mud too: tight-fitting jeans, a T-shirt, a once blue puffer jacket and black New Balance trainers with what had once been pink laces. The mortuary assistant cut the clothes off and Landry put them into unsealed plastic exhibits bags then in brown paper bags for the drying room. The girl was stick thin. Her ribs and the twin crests of her pelvis protruded. Now that she was naked the damage to the body seemed worse than it had at the scene. Down one side was a livid bruise. Her right forearm and her right shin were fractured. The tibia of her right leg poked through the torn skin.

'Any idea if that's all after death?' Sarah asked.

'It's consistent with her going into the river upstream and travelling on the current before she's snagged by the weir. But I can't tell you what's *post-mortem*. If she went into the water alive, she could have broken those bones while she was still living, just by hitting a rock. The current is very strong and there are always submerged obstacles. Injuries like that would have contributed to her drowning. Or they could have happened after death.' Dr Houghton sighed. 'I'm sorry I can't be more definitive. Bodies in water are notoriously difficult. She could also have been thrown into the river already injured. Perhaps there was a fight or even an accident and she fell in as a result of that. They don't look to me like defence injuries. I'll swab under her nails but everything's going to be contaminated by river water. It's a difficult post-mortem: so many unknowns. But as you already mentioned, the bloodstained froth at the mouth and in the nose strongly suggests drowning.'

Dr Houghton surprised Sarah; she gently stroked her hand down the dead right arm as if offering comfort.

The skin of the forearms was marked with multiple white lines, the scars of self-harming, and by recent incisions that had not yet healed. On the inside of her upper left arm was a tiny black ink tattoo of a swallow and some words. The skin was swollen from immersion and discoloured by bruises.

Dr Houghton looked closely and said, 'I can't make it out.' Sarah leaned in but she couldn't read it either. 'Simon? You want to try?'

He pinched his nose for a second and then looked.

'I think it says, Sad birds still fly.'

'We can run it through PNC. We might get a quick ID.'

There were bruises around the thighs, too.

Dr Houghton parted the girl's legs and began the vaginal examination. She said, 'There are deep internal injuries here. I can't see how they would have been done by the river.'

Simon and Sarah stood outside in the shelter of a small plastic bicycle store in the mortuary car park. Rain poured down its sides. Simon had asked the mortuary attendant if he could spare a couple of cigarettes.

'I wouldn't have made you as a smoker,' Sarah said.

'I'm not,' Simon said, holding the lighter to Sarah's cigarette.

'I've given up myself,' Sarah said. She inhaled. 'Was that your first PM?'

'Uh-huh.'

'I'm sorry.'

'It's OK. Got to learn.'

'I've probably done about fifty.'

'Does it get easier?'

'Just different. There was something about her not being identified. And the tattoo.'

'Yeah.' Simon threw his cigarette on the ground. 'I'm a runner,' he said. 'Long distance. Can't be smoking. I better toughen up.'

Outside, Poppy, a smudged and bleary shape through the rain-streaked plastic, raced around.

Sarah called Tom back in Alnbridge.

'Search the crime reporting system for any rapes over the past five days. Middleton is the obvious location but do a force-wide search. Call me if you get anything.'

As soon as she closed the call her phone rang.

It was the Middleton station office. An angry member of the public was at the front counter. His shotgun had been burgled from his gun safe in the early hours and he wanted to speak to someone senior.

'James Halford,' the station officer said. 'Used to manage Lord Wentworth's estate. Can you talk to him?'

Sarah looked at her watch. 'Request his postcode. If it's on my way back I'll pop in on him.'

47

Lizzie was late and Richard was in the office eating his way through a packet of biscuits as he supervised the missing persons reports. He looked up from his computer.

'Oh dear,' he said, 'someone hasn't had a good morning.'

'I can't hack this level of risk.'

Richard stood up and stretched. 'Sounds like you need one of my famous coffees.'

'You know that one report that might be hiding away like a landmine? I've got one of them.'

'How do you like your coffee?'

'Leif Abad. He needs more than one part-time officer. He needs someone out making inquiries but I had to speak to Connor's teacher about an incident yesterday and she wasn't free first thing, so I'm late.'

Richard pushed one of the capsules into the machine. 'I can froth the milk. Would that help?'

'For goodness' sake.'

Richard put the coffee in front of Lizzie. She took a sip.

'Good, heh?'

'I can't be in this kind of role.'

Richard sat. He leaned back in his chair and folded his arms behind his head.

'Tell me about Leif. What makes you think he needs more resources allocated? Is there something specific that bumps him up?'

'He's fifteen, for God's sake! His mother doesn't know where he is.'

'Being fifteen isn't enough. There are thousands of them: thousands of boys and girls who stay away for a night or two. We don't have the resources to make them all high risk. We have to prioritise.'

'OK, being fifteen isn't enough. I get that. London's fucked and the job's fucked. I do get it! But I can't *hack* it, that's the thing. You don't seem to understand. I've had it go wrong once.'

He offered the biscuit tin. She shook her head.

'I could open some Choco Leibniz?'

'It's not funny.'

There was silence. Then Richard said, 'We're all in the same boat. I'm just trying to find our way through this.'

'I had a good job in the CJU driving a desk. The job owes me that after what I've been through.'

'I'm really sorry. KK was adamant.'

48

The seventies office block was scheduled for demolition and most of the floors were empty. Steve had heard on Radio 4 when he was doing the washing-up how buildings like Selborne House had been almost immediately superseded by the realisation that a building should have a narrative, a dramatic progression as you moved through it. A building, apparently, should take you on a journey, atriums open up and lead you on to new and enriching experiences. But didn't Selborne House have a story of a kind? A boring one, admittedly: floor after floor of the same. Large open spaces cut up by the mere humans that needed to work there with hardboard dividers that you could kick over if you had a mind to. That was a story, wasn't it?

You want to keep your firearms ticket you got to keep your fitness up; Steve got out of the lift on the third floor and took the stairs – plastic-looking supposedly marbled treads with blue handrails – for the last six storeys.

The best thing about the building was the glass. It was floor to ceiling, held together by big metal lattices. All that glass made the building cold in the winter and hot in the summer, but climbing the staircase was like moving through London's sky. As was his habit, he walked quickly enough to be out of breath. On the ninth floor he swiped his warrant card at the glass door that had been obscured by taped paper, and tapped in the code.

The offices were largely deserted. Steve's immediate team

had taken the opportunity to have a lie-in after the days away. At Selborne House everyone turned in the hours and no one questioned anyone's timekeeping. If you wanted any kind of home life you didn't work here.

They had neither the resources nor the will to vet cleaners and so, in spite of the complaints and badgering emails from the bosses, empty drink containers and grease-stained take-away boxes stood on the desktops.

Steve threw his jacket on the back of a chair and logged on. There were no updates on Sarah's report so he picked up the phone.

'Yes, hello. It's Steve Bradshaw here from the County Lines taskforce. I wondered if you'd got any update on the report you put on last night regarding the assault in Middleton.'

'DI Collins put that report on. She's not in the office right now. Can I ask her to call you back?'

Steve scratched the corner of his eye. 'No, no. Don't worry about that. Who am I speaking to?'

'DC Tom Edgerton.'

'Hello, Tom. Is DI Collins out on a call right now?'

'She went out first thing this morning to a drowning.'

'In Middleton?'

'Yes.'

'Why's she handling that? Is it suspicious?'

'I don't know, to be honest. It's a young woman. Still unidentified. Sarah's got me doing some intel . . .'

'You sound like you're still new to this?'

'Well, yes.'

'Good for you! We need young people getting involved. I'm not a big fan of all this modern cynicism. Enjoying it?'

'Most of the time.'

'Everyone finds it hard sometimes.'

'Yes.'

Steve looked over his shoulder. His boss, Fedden, was standing behind him tapping his watch. Steve put his fingers up: two minutes.

'Why don't we get you down here to London? You'd love it. I could put a word in.'

'I'm not really a big city person.'

'Don't blame you. Anything else out of the ordinary in Middleton this morning? It's for my boss. He's asked me to update him.'

Fedden shook his head. He leaned over the desk and scribbled on a piece of paper. *You total wanker.*

'Well, Sarah asked me to look into recent crime reports for a rape. And we did have one. Yesterday in Middleton. And we've had a shotgun stolen by burglary.'

'Sounds like it's all kicking off in the sticks!'

'I don't really know, to be honest. Sarah's in Middleton.'

'Any suspect for the shotgun?'

'I've only glanced at the report.'

'Is there a description? Anything?'

'The victim reports seeing a black boy on a bike the previous day.'

'No.'

Fedden was leaning up against the door jamb to his small office, Stoke City mug in his hand, Stoke City scarf round his neck. Outside the rain moved across London in broad stripes of grey.

'Ryan's actually living in the town. It's one of the terms of his probation.'

213

'I want to see the murdering shit get his as much as you do, but at this stage we have to treat Sarah's report only as building intelligence. We're already stretched and, until there's more to get our teeth into, we can't commit to an operation.'

'There's a shotgun been stolen by burglary this morning – by a black boy on a pushbike. Ryan loves his bikes. How many phones did I have off him that he'd snatched on that fancy bike he'd stolen?'

Fedden took a gulp of tea.

'Changing the subject, I was pleased to see you in. Linton and George are not at all happy about the drugs being seized and their country boys getting nicked. We've got a CHIS who's shitting himself. One of those videos has gone up on YouTube. They've shown it to me – all the usual: plastic *Scream* masks, big trainers, moving camera. I don't understand a word but the gist is apparently that there's a grass going to get smoked. They've got money in their pockets and we think they're about to pick up a weapon. I need bodies on surveillance. I've rung Kiyana and she's hot-tailing it in. Can't wait to catch them at it. I know how you love to work with her. What was it you said to that poor DC? We need young people getting involved.'

49

In the dips in the fields mist had settled. The road ran with streams of water. Sarah's phone had lost signal but there was a phone box on the right. A field gate on the opposite side of the road was open and led to a large flat concrete-paved concourse. She drove in. There were three weathered corrugated barns shaped like huge 1940s bomb shelters. A mysterious red machine on two wheels holding a coil of wire stood alone. A brown dark wooden structure, maybe three storeys high, was set back, and behind it, in a field that edged the compound, stood a large herd of deer. Silver light shone through the dark clouds that were racing over. Poppy was whining and Sarah took the opportunity to let her out of the car. The dog darted beyond the barn out across the field towards the woods and the deer scattered. Some crows also rose up, like a black cloud dispersing. She followed quickly, taking Poppy's lead out of her pocket. A dog that wasn't under control could get shot out here.

'Poppy, Poppy!'

At the edge of the field were two spent shotgun cartridges. Perhaps shooters used this as a stand, sending the birds up from the line of trees opposite.

Poppy ran towards her, tail wagging furiously. She had something in her mouth: a dead pheasant.

'Oh God, Poppy, no.'

The bird was fresh. Did that happen? Did all the birds not get collected? On command Poppy dropped it and sat.

'You're a gun dog now, are you?' Sarah said, quickly clipping the lead on and walking her back towards the car.

There was something else, close to the gate: a little red metal cylinder. She bent and picked it up, held it between finger and thumb. It had a crown logo on the side and maker's mark: PEATY'S. Was it part of a gun? Out of force of habit she got a tissue, wrapped it and dropped it in her pocket. Poppy was pulling to be set free.

'Bad dog,' she said, without conviction.

She walked to the phone box. To her amazement it worked and she was able to get through to Halford, who gave her directions.

She drove the car back out onto the main road and, about a mile further on, took the turning to her left, past a white stuccoed and crenellated gatehouse and then, further along, turned right past a *Private Road* sign and downhill. The track was worn concrete with a stripe of grass running down the centre. The house lay in a hollow. There were canes in the front garden tied into two peaked rows and chickens moved around in the long grass. Halford's face appeared almost immediately at the window. The door was open before she had covered the distance from the gate to the green wooden door. Three spaniels raced out. Halford recalled them with a whistle and they instantly bounded back inside, tails wagging. Good thing, she thought, that she had left her own less perfectly behaved dog in the car.

The room was dark, with a waxed wooden table and a chipped cream Rayburn. Three pheasants hung on the back of the door. There was pervasive smell of woodsmoke and of earth and no sense of any other person here. The only sentimental object seemed to be the framed photo of the spaniel. But Sarah thought again. All of this – the pheasants, the gun cabinet, the order of the room – had something of love or pride about it. Halford wore a flat cap and a green tweedy jacket with leather elbow patches. His cheeks were a map of broken blood vessels and of a life spent outdoors. He offered his hand.

'James Halford. Used to be the estate manager on Lord Wentworth's estate.'

'Detective Inspector Sarah Collins.'

'You found it in the end, then?'

'Yes, I was amazed the phone box worked.'

'We've got a few of them round here still. There's no reception for mobiles so they keep them. We're always at least twenty years behind. Good thing too, in my opinion. Tea?'

'No thanks, just had one,' she said, resorting to the old lie.

'It was a Purdey,' he said mournfully.

'I'm sorry, Mr Halford, I don't know much about guns.'

'If you did then you would know it was more than just a *gun*. A work of art, really.' He pulled a chair out from the table for Sarah. 'It was a very generous retirement gift from Lord Wentworth. An absolutely beautiful gun. Scroll engravings on the silver sidelocks. Polished walnut stock.' He shook his head. 'Breaks my heart to think he might saw it down.'

Sarah sat and rested her hands on the table. 'It meant a lot to you.'

'Black boy,' Halford said. 'On a bike. It's got to be him.'

'He was a boy, then?'

'Eighteen, or even in his twenties, maybe.'

'And you met this young man on the Wentworth estate?'

'Young man then, if you must, Detective Inspector.'

'Anything distinguishing about him?'

'He was black.'

'Yes, but anything else distinctive that would help us to identify him—'

'He was cycling through, very early in the morning. It's not public land. I used to be the estate manager.'

He looked at Sarah sharply, as if expecting something, and she took a breath and said, 'Yes, I believe you mentioned that. Lord Wentworth gave you the gun.'

Halford crossed his arms and glared at the hanging pheasants. 'I'm retired now, so it's no skin off my nose.'

'And you spoke with this person, the young man?'

'I explained he was trespassing. Lord Wentworth doesn't want lots of people down there. It's a site of specific scientific interest. I told him that. There are otters.'

'Otters?'

'Yes.' Halford turned to her with a look of complete outrage. 'Otters!'

Heading off the sudden unexpected possibility of laughter, Sarah had to look down.

Perhaps sensing it too, Halford said quickly, 'And he was very aggressive.'

'Physically?'

'Well, not physically.'

'How then?'

'He told me.' Halford cleared his throat. 'He told me his colour wouldn't wash off.'

Sarah pressed her fingers against her mouth.

Halford raised his voice. 'What did he bloody think? Did

he think I was a bloody idiot?' Halford met her eyes. 'He asked me if I was frightened of him.'

Sarah felt a little shock of sympathy. 'And were you?'

'Of course I wasn't!'

But Sarah had glimpsed the shame in Halford's face. He wasn't accustomed to having to back down, but he had been frightened, properly frightened.

'You're not from round here?' he said, his colour rising.

'Why do you ask that?'

'Because you don't seem to be taking what I'm telling you seriously.'

'A firearm has been stolen. I am taking this seriously. How did he get into the gun cabinet?'

'He must have had a skeleton key.'

'Or found a key? Did you leave one in the house?'

Halford blinked slowly, his face stiff. 'It was well hidden.' He cleared his throat. 'I called 999 first thing, soon as I got back to the house. No one's been out to me. That gun was worth about thirty thousand.'

'We had a sudden death this morning. That's why there's been a delay in the forensic examiner getting to you. When was the gun taken?'

'Between five thirty and seven. I always take the dogs down to the river. Luckily, I had the other gun with me. Shame I didn't catch him. He must have been bloody quick. Probably a dab hand at it. Took a couple of towels, too. Probably wrapped it up.'

'How did he get in?'

'Just walked straight in, I suppose.'

'The house wasn't locked?'

'Who locks their doors round here?'

People with firearms, Sarah thought, but she said, 'And when you met this person on the bike yesterday, you had a shotgun with you?'

'Yes, and he cycled off, but then he must have cycled back because just as I was turning into my house he was there on the path. He waved. Finding out where I live, you see.' Halford met Sarah's eyes again but the vulnerability she had glimpsed was gone. 'I want that boy arrested.'

'By your description he's not a boy, he's a young man.'

'For goodness' sake! Whatever he is, he's got my shotgun.'

'We can't be sure of that.'

'If you were from round here you would know how exceptional it is for anyone to see a black boy on Lord Wentworth's estate.'

She looked down at her notebook and read out the description she had scribbled down from the crime report. 'Black boy. Age eighteen to early twenties.'

'That's right.'

'It's not a very distinctive description.'

'It is round here.'

'What about the bike?'

The man shrugged. 'It was a bike.'

'Handlebars?'

'Of course it had handlebars.'

'Dropped or flat?'

'Are you one of those people that insist on being a complete stranger to reality?'

'I'm asking you was there anything distinctive about the bicycle?'

'He's a black boy, for God's sake! It's not like London. There aren't many around here.'

Sarah shut her notebook. 'Thank you, Mr Halford. The scenes of crime officer will be here to look for any forensic opportunities. Your conversation with that young person isn't by itself enough to justify an arrest but I'll look into what you've told me.'

'I'd lay a wager on it being that boy. If you don't arrest him and he kills someone with my shotgun it'll be on your head.'

Sarah turned out of the private road and began the drive back to Middleton. The rain had started again, travelling across in grey curtains.

The thing was, Halford might be right. It might well be the boy he had seen on the bike who had stolen his shotgun, and yet it rankled, the way he had spoken. It was so important to try to keep a clear mind. Was it just that he kept saying black, as if that was proof enough? Or was it the lack of description? He was unable to provide anything identifying that would have distinguished the individual from any of the other brown or black boys in the town. There must be more than one! If he could have described the bike, she could have maybe linked that to a suspect. But he seemed to have been blind to everything but the young man's colour.

Into her mind came a vehicle stop at the start of her career. Two black men in a car. She'd still been in uniform and only just qualified to drive a police car on blue lights. It was night duty, the best duty of them all for a young keen cop, and she was crewed with one of her friends, Nisha Chatterjee, a tiny little thief catcher.

'We're Lipstick One,' Nish said. 'Old school.'

They took the calls, ate the Haribos, shot the breeze about

the rest of the team. Ian, who specialised in farting with the windows shut, was a particular source of conversation.

They had been driving back to their ground after dropping a victim back home. It was one of those cars that, from miles away, draws your attention: a souped-up Ford with tinted rear windows, cruising just below the speed limit.

They draw parallel and the men turned their heads. Sarah overtook and glanced in her rear-view mirror. The car had slowed and was falling behind.

'They doing anything?' Nish said.

'Who knows?'

Just to see what they would do Sarah pulled over and dropped her speed. The car accelerated and overtook, the men looking straight ahead now. Sarah kept up. The car took the slip road with such suddenness that Sarah nearly missed the turn. They took the first exit off the roundabout, down a side street that ran through a neighbourhood of traffic-blighted houses and then came out unexpectedly into an area of lonely playing fields, a jumble of commercial greenhouses and, over a bridge, a decommissioned reservoir. They were out of their ground in one of London's strange isthmuses that had been created by a concatenation of roads and water that cut it off from the city that surrounded it. The Ford pulled over and stopped. Sarah overtook, drove down the road, and then pulled over. Behind them the car's headlights flared brightly and the car pulled out.

Nish said, 'That's got to be a tug.'

Sarah still wasn't sure, not in her bones, but she pulled behind and flashed the blue lights.

She'd never forget the stop. How her heart was beating – she and Nish on their own off their ground in this strangely isolated little spot. The anger of the men and tiny Nish, who wasn't the backing-down kind, standing up to them.

'What were you doing?' she said. 'Speeding up and slowing down and all that?'

'Avoiding you!' said the driver.

'Third time we've been stopped in two days,' said the passenger.

'Can I ask you for some ID?' said Sarah, turning to the driver.

'Why?'

'I don't need a reason. It's Section One Six Four of the Road Traffic Act.'

The driver opened his wallet and offered his driving licence. Nish went back to the car to run the man's details through the data terminal.

'Driving while black,' the driver said.

The two men were tall and Sarah thought that if they really were dangerous, they could have got away by now. There was so much heat. It was hard to think clearly.

'I'm sorry you feel that,' Sarah said.

'Blah blah blah,' the passenger said.

'We're Christians!' the driver said. 'We've been working with a youth group.'

Out of the corner of her eye Sarah could see that Nish was calling up for assistance from the local officers. This was either a really bad stop with no real justification or it was really dangerous and she couldn't tell which. Christians or not, the two men had that vibe, that heat. But if this was the third time they'd been stopped in two days, then no wonder they were angry.

'I'm trying to work it out,' Sarah said, 'whether it's

223

one of those things, where you wind us up and we wind you up.'

By now a second marked car had pulled up and two male officers got out. They nodded at Nish and Sarah and introduced themselves to the driver and his passenger – Pete and Sean. The implication was clear. Man to man Lipstick One were numpties. The dynamic had changed. Nish and Sarah were demoted to bystanders. The local officers took over, searched the boot of the car.

The driver said, 'Just be warned there's a firearm in there,' and the smaller of the two policemen, Sean, said, 'You're joking.'

The driver said, 'It's part of our presentation to the young men. It's a toy.'

And the mood turned again. There was a gun, but it was a little red water pistol.

'Negative search,' Pete said, handing the driver a stop slip. 'Thank you for your patience.'

Sean said, 'Sorry for stopping you.' He offered his hand and it was accepted.

'We don't know these two officers,' Pete said. 'They're not from our ground. We were just called to assist.'

And with that Pete and Sean got back in their car and left Sarah and Nish standing on the road.

The driver looked at them. 'You got anything to say?'

Sarah ran her hand down the side of her face. 'I'm really sorry. Your behaviour, it was—'

'It was what? Two black men in a car got to be suspicious?'

Nish said, 'You were giving it off. It's not like you haven't got convictions. I mean serious convictions.'

The driver said, 'And now I'm a Christian and I'm reformed. Are you never going to leave me alone?'

Sarah said, 'I'm sorry. Thank you for your patience.'

'Yeah. Right.'

The two men got in the car and drove away.

But as Sarah turned and headed back to the slip road Nish said, 'Why did you apologise? He had convictions for firearms, a Section Eighteen GBH. And supply. Our big-boy colleagues, Pete and Sean? Did they do a proper search? They didn't look for voids. Nothing.'

'They'd been giving a talk, Nish. They had a red water pistol!'

But even now Sarah still couldn't decide about the decision to stop the car. For some officers it would be straightforward: good proactive policing, and a chance to take weapons off the streets. If the men had nothing to hide, these people would say, then why the need for aggression? But for others it would be just racism. And Sarah understood that being constantly stopped must make you angry.

Nish was a DCI now. She'd had a good career: Flying Squad, National Crime Agency. She had a good nose and good procedure and she had taken down some proper criminals. And Sarah too, she'd had a good career, but she thought of Baillie in the church and the contempt he'd expressed for her squeamishness. Think you're better than just doing the job well, he'd said. Better than just bringing a job home. Too pure to let a little lie pass, and, because of that, responsible for Kieran Shaw's death.

She turned the car onto the main road to Middleton and her phone picked up reception and pinged with missed calls. She pulled into a lay-by and called Tom.

'What have you got for me?'

'There's a rape reported last night in Middleton at the community hospital. It's a third-party report – from the doctor. The victim left before police arrived.'

'Who attended?'

'The local officer we met, PC Harris. I've texted you the crime reference number.'

'OK.'

'And someone from the County Lines unit in London called. Wanted an update. Said his name was Steve Bradshaw.'

Sarah was furious. Steve had pumped green-as-grass Tom for information and Tom had given it all up. She'd told him to back off.

'Tom.'

'Yes?'

'How did you know the caller was who he said he was?'

'He'd read the report, Sarah. Who else could it be?'

'You don't just give out information over the phone. You should have verified his identity, asked me how much we wanted to share with another force.'

'I'm sorry.'

Sarah's chest tightened. This was the stuff that made her unlikeable. And Tom was young in service; he needed encouragement.

'Just for next time, then. OK?'

She closed the call. Momentarily she lacked the conviction necessary to turn the key in the ignition. A lorry thundered past, shaking the car.

She needed to get a grip on the investigation. The drowned girl, the torched caravan, the rape: they must be linked. But the stabbing of Carl Turner and the theft of the shotgun?

Were they linked too, or just coincidental? She needed a strategy. She needed resources. Who could she even talk it over with? Once, a long time ago, it would have been Steve.

Detective Chief Superintendent John Cheng, the man she would have to take her information to, still felt a stranger to her. He was a small man, smart in a white shirt and houndstooth jacket, with close-cropped hair and a canny look about him. His very tidy office was two floors above hers on the other side of the building, and she hardly saw him.

Sarah parked by the empty market square. Outside the church a man with a collie lying on a blanket beside him was playing a penny whistle. Next to a tweedy outdoors shop was a little takeaway with a big queue that ran down the narrow street. The queue moved quickly and she was soon near the front, stepping into the shop. There was a poster on the wall with a picture of a teenager, and a telephone number. Sarah took her phone out of her pocket and photographed the poster. The two women and the man behind the counter – all wearing blue cotton aprons stretched over ample tummies – were working efficiently, filling baps.

'Mustard? Ketchup?'

You better answer promptly.

'Mustard, please,' Sarah said. 'Lots.'

The woman was wrapping her bap and she nodded towards the poster. 'You seen him, then?'

Sarah shook her head. 'Who gave you the poster?'

'A woman. Indian. Came in here earlier today and asked to leave it. She was soaked through. Not from round here.'

'Do you mean Indian?'

'What else would I mean?'

'Are you talking about how she looked? Was she British born, do you think?'

The woman rolled her eyes.

The man behind Sarah, tanned, tall and strong with an incisor missing, said, 'Come on, love, hurry up. There's a queue.'

Sarah sheltered in a doorway and got out her mobile.

'Elaine? It's Sarah.'

'Sarah! Done anyone for red diesel yet? Issued any Fixed Penalty Notices?'

'Ha ha.'

'How is it?'

'Good.'

'Good? That's very informative. Always nice to chat.'

Sarah said, 'How are the children?'

'Oh, come on!'

'No, I want to know—'

'You're not even remotely interested. What is it you want?'

'I've got a telephone number. Could you run it through IIP?'

'Not sure about that. What's my authority?'

Sarah bit her lip.

'Just joking, you nelly. Stand by.'

50

A tall figure swiped into the gym. His hood was up, his back to the camera. There was a little skeleton dinosaur logo on the back of his bag: Arc'teryx. Hoping that when he exited she'd get a glimpse of his face, Lizzie fast-forwarded the CCTV, but on his way out the man kept his head down and his face angled away from the camera. Still she spotted the MONCLER logo on the tongue of his trainers. The bag and the shoes: unless they were rip-offs that was nearly a thousand quid just there.

It wasn't Leif. This figure was all angles and even in the jerky frame of the CCTV he moved with swagger. Leif was smaller and plumper, and he was still a boy.

Asha didn't answer her phone, but her flat was only five minutes away from the gym by car. Rain was falling. The road was lined with terraces of late-Victorian houses, all with parades of down-at-heel shops. A criminal solicitor's was housed above a barber shop. Outside a little Italian coffee shop a man in a stripy apron stood smoking. The traffic stopped and started behind a slow-moving bus. Inside a launderette a woman was unloading a machine into a blue plastic basket. Beside her a furious toddler strapped into a pram was arching its back and kicking its legs. Boys on bikes loitered. One of them – he only looked about fourteen – did a mighty wheelie past her car. He banged on the bonnet as he passed, looked over his shoulder as his front wheel touched the ground and gave Lizzie the finger before he turned left into a bollarded side street. So that hadn't changed since she'd been away from the streets: the locals knew the unmarked cars.

A few yards up she turned into Asha's street. It lay just outside the Deakin Estate. A little Victorian terrace that had survived the night of heavy bombing that had flattened the land where the Deakin was built in the 1970s. Most of the houses on the terrace had been cleaned up: bought probably under Right to Buy and sold on to pioneers prepared to take a punt on a rough neighbourhood. Some had solid Victorian doors in Farrow & Ball colours, renovated sash windows and burglar alarm boxes beneath the eaves. You might be able to afford a characterful house here, but you didn't want to become a target. But three of the houses had held out against the improving trend and these had the social housing look: UPVC tilt windows, blank-panel front doors in weathered paint and numerous doorbells.

There was no answer from Asha's flat. Lizzie's phone rang.

'Lizzie?'

The voice was familiar, but she couldn't place it quickly. 'Who's speaking?'

'It's Sarah Collins.'

'Sarah.' Lizzie was standing on the steps to Asha's flat. She glanced to her left towards the Deakin. The wind was blowing across. She felt sick. 'Who gave you my private number?'

'Your sergeant.'

'He shouldn't have.'

'You're right. I'm sorry. Call me back when you're ready.'

Lizzie, furious now, was walking back to the car. 'No, go ahead.' She sat in the driver's seat.

Sarah said, 'How have you been?'

'Is that why you're calling?'

'No.'

'Get it over with, then.'

The line was briefly silent.

'OK, so one of your mispers, Leif Abad, is probably in my new force area, in a town called Middleton.'

51

There were plenty of car parking spaces at the community hospital. Sarah turned the engine off and let Poppy out of the back on her lead.

As Poppy sniffed around, the conversation with Lizzie shadowed Sarah with a feeling of shame and uneasiness. She had been right not to tell Lizzie that Ryan was a possible suspect in whatever was occurring in Middleton. Definitely.

She felt impatient, with Poppy and with herself. Never again, she swore; whatever went down, she would always get the dog to the minder before she put herself on duty.

It was unpleasant to feel so unsettled.

She had heard of officers incapacitated at the scene of major incidents, unable to make a decision while everyone waited and precious minutes were lost. Might she be suffering from some version of this? Trust your instincts, they said, but she had always been proud to tend in the opposite direction: to question her instincts. She had never considered that there was a third possibility: that her instincts might entirely desert her.

She walked back to the car and put Poppy in the back, sliding the driving seat back and taking her job laptop out of her bag.

Truth was that Ryan was a good fit for someone stealing a firearm. How many of the relatively few black men in Middleton would also have connections to London street gangs and a conviction for possessing a firearm? And the bike? Ryan had been a robber, jumping the pavement on his bike and having the mobile phone niftily out of the victim's hand.

She sent an email to Ryan's probation officer.

Dr Seidou – dark-skinned with a flawless complexion, her head covered by a silk patterned scarf – was studying her computer screen, which she had turned away from Sarah's line of sight.

'Do you have any images of the dead girl?'

'I could access post-mortem photographs but she's pretty smashed up. She had long brown hair, green eyes. Small – five foot three or so – and thin.'

The doctor's face registered the description but said nothing.

'What can you tell me about her?'

'She didn't want anyone to know what had happened to her. I have to respect her confidentiality, even in death. If it is the same girl.'

'She was a victim of rape.'

'I can't comment.'

'The hospital receptionist called police for assistance. When the officer arrived the patient had already left. Anything would be helpful. Did she tell you anything about her assailant?'

'If people are to trust doctors they must know we don't breach their confidentiality.'

'It's a live investigation. Other people may yet come to harm. That's covered by the GMC guidance: overriding public interest.'

The doctor rolled her chair to face Sarah. 'There is a procedure, as you must know, to apply for the patient's medical records.'

Sarah thought for a moment. 'Can you at least tell me if she was accompanied? If someone was with her, then they weren't your patient.'

The doctor pressed her index finger hard against her lips, almost as if to silence herself. Sarah waited.

'There was a boy with her.'

'Hang on.'

Sarah got her phone out and pulled up her photograph of the missing poster. She screenshotted the image of the boy.

'Could this be him?'

Seidou nodded. Then she stood up and gestured towards the door. 'But for the girl's records, please, make a formal request. I promise to deal with it promptly.'

'The officer who attended – PC Harris – he asked to seize the swabs you used.'

'I couldn't hand them over.'

'But you have kept them?'

'They're bagged up in the fridge. If she came back, if she changed her mind, I wanted her to be able to access them.'

'Please hold on to them until I can get you that request.'

'Of course.'

Sarah offered her hand. 'Thank you, Doctor.'

Sarah sat in the driving seat, checking her emails. The probation officer had got back to her.

Ryan was doing well, settled into his hostel and biding by his conditions. He'd even got a part-time job in a bicycle repair shop. Making a new start, the probation officer wrote. Always attends his appointments.

Sarah stepped out of the car and stood on the drive outside the clinic. The sound of church bells drifted across. She found Harris's dropped call from the previous day.

'Sarah! You were lucky to get reception. I'm ten miles away at a domestic assault.'

'As soon as you're free, then.'

'I've just made an arrest. I won't be free this shift.'

'I'm desperate.'

'Doesn't sound good.'

'A dead girl in the river this morning. A burnt-out caravan. The rape you attended last night. Carl Turner with his sore backside. This morning's stolen shotgun. Leif Abad—'

'Who's Leif Abad?'

'A boy who's reported missing from London. Fifteen years old—'

'If it's county lines beef you're going to need more than me and Eyebrows Patty, tough though she is.'

'I'm in the process of trying to get us a bigger boat.'

'And in the meantime, I'm in the shark cage with a hypodermic?'

'Like the man said, you got any better suggestions?'

52

By the time the train finally pulled in to Paddington, London was in darkness. Everyone waiting on the Circle Line's cold open platform seemed tired. It was an awkward journey from there: a change at King's Cross, and then a further change onto the overground and a walk.

Asha paused at the end of her road.

The Deakin Estate rested, its walkways and windows lit up. It seemed an entire world. She had never given it much thought, had assumed its life without having to imagine it fully. Families with their time-for-beds and their rushed early mornings getting their kids dressed up and out in time for school – No, I don't know where you school bag is – and pushing their toddlers on the swings that lay beyond its ramparts. The newcomers, now that it had become trendy, with their fold-up bikes and personal trainers. The delivery drivers struggling to find the address, shouting on their phones: Where exactly are you? She'd always been aware that other business was conducted there too, but that aspect of the estate – the boys standing on its corners, the passing police cars – had not seemed to have any bearing on her own life. If they wanted to smoke a bit, where was the harm? And they only hurt each other, didn't they?

Asha tripped quickly up the stairs to her flat and let herself in. Leif would be home. Disaster would be avoided. She would move. But Bip came out into the hall and shook her head.

'Sorry.'

The news was crushing. In spite of the anxiety that had welled up on the train and subsided repeatedly like an inner tide, she had believed.

Asha said, 'He hasn't been back? Not at all?' and Bip said, 'Come in. Take your coat off and have a cup of tea. Ari and my lot are watching the telly.'

Asha did not move. Nothing had prepared her for this disappointment. She could just lie down and weep, but she also couldn't. She couldn't take her coat off and relax because she needed to do everything possible for her son. She needed to push herself just one little bit further.

'Could you stay here a bit longer and I'll go back to the train station and look for him?'

Bip said, 'You're acting crazy.'

'I am not acting crazy. I want to get my son home.'

'Yes, you are. Leif can come in on a different platform. He can come by car. You're one little woman. You want people to look out for him, you better call police.'

Asha raised her voice. 'But I can't call police, can I?'

'Don't shout. You'll scare the kids.'

'I told that boy, Jaydn, if we get Leif back that's the end of it. His sister said if I involve police then Leif will end up dead, my whole family is going to end up dead.'

'Don't be a drama queen, Asha. Your whole family is not going to end up dead.'

'You said yourself that one boy ended up dead.'

The door opened and Ari stepped into the hall in his pyjamas rubbing his eyes.

He said, 'Mum, where've you been?' and Asha said, 'On an adventure, but I'm home now. You should be in bed.'

Bip took the bag out of Asha's hand. 'Come through to the kitchen.'

Asha said, 'Just a minute, I should call that other number again.'

Bip gave her a cool stare. 'And say what?'

53

Sarah's laptop rested on the detective chief superintendent's big shiny oval table. The station at Alnbridge was almost silent and the car park nearly empty. Night had fallen, and even here in the town it was blacker than anything London had to offer. The moon was rising, huge, glowing brightly above the darker line of hills.

Her phone rang and a little circular photograph of Meghan appeared on the screen. She rejected the call and turned the phone on its face on the desk.

'Sorry, sir.'

She clicked on the CCTV.

Two figures were leaving the hospital, both in trousers and jackets. They gathered the bicycles that had been tilted against the wall of the clinic and began to wheel them away just as the car pulled up into the access road. The camera was high and distant and the man who stepped out of the car had his hood pulled up. The smaller figure got into the back seat. The other wheeled the two bikes towards a railing. The driver opened the boot and took out a D lock. He secured the bikes while the boy stood by watching. They both got in the car and it pulled away.

Sarah clicked on another thumbnail. 'This is less than two hours later.'

The car was back and the driver stepped out again, hood still up. He lifted the bikes into the back of the car and was gone.

'Good work.'

'It was the local PC, Mark Harris, grabbed the CCTV for me. It was good of him. He'd already got an arrest.'

Detective Chief Superintendent Cheng looked at her. 'That's how it is here. It's not like London, three coppers per square foot.' He looked back at the laptop. 'And is it Kennedy?'

'I can't say,' she said. 'It could be. Harris doesn't like anyone else for it.'

'That's all we've got?'

'So far.'

'Tell me about the car?'

'The VRM's not legible. Can't say much more than it's a silver hatchback but I sent a screenshot to my girlfriend.'

Cheng's eyebrows raised. 'And she is . . .?'

'A traffic skipper, investigates fatals. She reckoned it's a Corsa. Tom checked out ANPR for me. Twenty minutes after the pick-up at the hospital there's a hit on a silver Corsa in Hambridge, which is on the way to the caravan site. It's there again this morning, about forty minutes before I got there. And it's heading back towards Middleton only thirty minutes after it's passed in the outward direction. That Corsa's registered to Wendy Halpin, a local drug user.'

'Have we spoken to her?'

'Tried. Couldn't find her. We're going back to her place early doors.'

'Have we looked at CCTV around Halpin's address?'

'Best we can within our resources. No hits yet.'

'How are we doing on the girl in the river?'

'Pathologist is pretty sure she drowned. No identity yet. Tattoo's not come up on PNC and she's not a local misper.

There are quite a few white girls of the same age on the national database. We've submitted an urgent DNA request.'

'And the misper, what's his name, Leif Abad?'

'The Met officer dealing is calling on mum this evening to see what she can get out of her. We're not going to show our hand because we don't want mum to stop using her phone. And there is a complication there, sir.'

'Go on.'

'The Met officer dealing with the misper – Lizzie Griffiths – she's the mother of Kieran Shaw's son.'

'Bugger. Does she know Kennedy might be in the frame?'

'I haven't told her, but that doesn't mean she won't find out.'

Cheng pinched his chin. 'We'll keep Kennedy's identity on a need-to-know basis. Don't want any red mist prejudicing anyone's actions. Lizzie Griffiths is based in London, so she'll just be dealing with mum and the misper. If we lift her off the job, we'll have to justify why we're doing it and that will send hares running.'

Hares will run anyway, Sarah thought, and remembered Poppy setting one darting across the field the previous night. Out of the big corner windows, the moon was higher already, bright as a lamp, its craters clearly delineated.

She sat down.

Cheng said, 'Are you all right?'

'Yes, sir. Thank you. Long day.'

Sarah thought of the dropped call and Meghan's face on her phone turned down to face the table top. She said, 'Should we be getting a Section Forty-six warrant for the firearm?'

'Would Kennedy be idiot enough to keep a stolen shotgun in his own room?'

241

'He's been a long time in prison, so probably not.'

'We put his door in, he's alerted. We don't and it's in there and he uses it . . .'

'Main problem it seems to me is we've got no intel. If he's at it he's kept under the radar. What about directed surveillance for Kennedy?'

'Have we got enough to justify it?'

Sarah's reservations flashed into her mind: that stop on the lonely road all those years ago and those two angry men. *We're reformed. Are you never going to leave us alone?*

'Threat to life,' she said. 'We've got enough.'

'It's such a bloody small town, that's the problem. The bike shop's out on the Walcot Road, for God's sake. Do you know it? Tiny little country road that leads to other even tinier country roads. Just the odd tractor going up and down. There's absolutely nothing out there. How on earth do we sit up on that undetected with our surveillance resources?' Cheng sighed. 'No, I'm sorry. The London unit will run this from now on, with us providing local support. They'll get Kennedy's mobile from probation and cell site him. And London will develop the boy's mother's phone. You'll be our liaison with them, reporting to me.'

Hares, she remembered, looking again at the huge autumnal moon. She was surprised that she could suddenly feel her heart beating. It was the thought of Steve, of naming him, getting him specifically taken off the case. She said, 'If we're handing the running of it to London there might be issues.'

'Why would there be issues?'

'I know those units, I've worked them. The Met's a big organisation but serious crime's much smaller. There's maybe a few hundred people who work covert operations. It's tight knit. A Home Office funded County Lines unit is very likely to have people who worked with Kieran Shaw, even maybe people who were on the operation that led to his death.'

'Raise your concerns with whoever's running it. They can keep the suspect's identity within a tight group. But to be honest, any Met officer is going to want to nail Kennedy.' He laughed. 'I mean, I can't stand the Met but I'd love to put Ryan Kennedy behind bars where he belongs.'

54

Lizzie pulled into a residents' bay outside Asha's house and put the logbook on the dashboard. She had cause to regret, that was what she thought as she turned the key in the ignition and the engine died. The car's interior lights flared and dimmed. She sat in the dark. Lit up beyond her was the Deakin, the patchwork of lights where Ryan had lived. Perhaps his mother, Loretta, lived there still.

Lizzie had arrested Ryan there once. She had seen the fridge empty of food, the dirty sofa on which he slept.

That day she had caught perhaps the last glimpse of Ryan's childhood. In interview when they'd gone through the process of identifying themselves on the recording – Philip Strong, legal representative, Loretta Swift appropriate adult – he had said, 'Ryan Kennedy, I'm the criminal.'

Loretta and she had laughed out loud.

It had been a glimpse of a childishness that was already almost extinguished. Lizzie didn't know it at the time but Ryan's friend, Spencer Cardoso, had been murdered in front of him the night before, bleeding out on Gallowstree Lane. Ryan's laughter at his own joke in custody had foundered almost instantly. He had seemed, mostly, elsewhere.

After the murder trial Ryan's mum, Loretta, wrote to her. Elaine intercepted the envelope that arrived at the police station and asked her whether she should open it and read it first. All sorts of nonsense had come through the station mail in those days, some of it hateful. But Lizzie had seen

Loretta's hand on the back, with her address, and she knew this envelope was for real. In those days everyone seemed to be watching for her reaction and she wanted to open it in private.

Elaine said, 'You sure?' and Lizzie said, 'Perfectly,' before she remembered to add, 'But thank you.'

The card had been the same colour as the envelope: cream. It had blue flowers on the front and dragonflies. The paper was stiff, textured paper with scalloped edges. Kieran would have loathed it. He despised anything sentimental.

Dear DC Griffiths.

Not her first name then, not Lizzie, though Loretta had used it freely when they were in custody.

I hope you don't mind me writing to you.

We'll see.

I remember so well that day you came and arrested Ryan. You seemed a nice person. It was almost fun doing the interview with you. I remember us laughing. I still can't believe what happened.

She had been running along easily enough through the line of Loretta's banalities when those two words tripped her up.

What happened.

Like someone who must examine the broken paving stone that has caused their fall, she had to pause and turn back. Had Loretta thought at all before she wrote that?

What happened.

The words hardly covered it, or rather they *did* cover it. They were all about covering rather than facing the facts of Kieran's death. The bullet released from the gun held by her son.

However likeable Loretta might have seemed laughing

at her son's jokes, the truth was no mother should have found it in any way funny that her son was comfortable enough in a custody suite to describe himself on tape as a criminal.

Loretta didn't write, as she should have, I am sorry there was no food in the fridge. That I never taught him right from wrong and that he destroyed many lives, including his own, but mainly Kieran Shaw's, the father of your son. I'm sorry I didn't do better.

That would have been a letter Lizzie might have respected.

Plain paper would have been better, too.

But Loretta couldn't even conceive those thoughts. Kieran's death had been something that merely 'happened', as if by magic. No gun in her boy's hand. No gunshot wound to the chest in that meagre flat.

Loretta just couldn't stop herself.

I am so sorry you will have to raise your son without his father. And my poor Ryan is in prison. My heart is broken.

As if their griefs were equal, and shared.

The hideous card, with its vanilla flavour like cheap ice cream, disgusted Lizzie. Loretta probably wanted her to speak up for Ryan at his probation hearings, or to write a letter about compassion and moving forward and closure. But Kieran was dead and she had to raise Connor alone. At least she should be allowed to have a heart of stone.

She thought of Asha, who all this time had been lying and not telling her how much she knew, who only today had been in Middleton putting up posters for her son.

The car's heat had ebbed away and the hard rain was a streaming film on the windscreen.

The children were watching telly in the sitting room when they should have all been tucked up in bed. Asha and her sister, Bip, were drinking wine in the kitchen.

Lizzie stood in her coat. She said, 'Have you heard anything from him?'

Asha shook her head but Bip caught her eye momentarily. Neither of the sisters was any good at dissembling.

Lizzie knew she should be patient. She should build a relationship with Asha. But she said, 'I've stayed on late—'

'You've changed your tune since yesterday. How come you're so concerned suddenly?'

Formality descended on Lizzie.

'It's nearly forty-eight hours since you reported your son missing. The length of time he has been gone elevates his priority.'

Asha glanced at her sister. 'So it isn't because you know something that makes you more worried for him?'

'The longer he's gone the more worried we become. I passed by earlier to talk to you but you weren't here.'

'I was putting up posters.'

Yes, Lizzie thought, in Middleton. She glanced around the kitchen, at the blackboard with its children's chalk drawings of trees and houses. That this woman could withhold what she knew so shamelessly appalled her.

'You didn't answer your phone.'

'I mustn't have heard it. I'm sorry.'

'I'm not with my own son right now because you didn't pick up.'

Asha, with every look of defeat about her, did her best to

fight back. 'If you can't do this job properly then you shouldn't be a police officer.'

'I've got two jobs. The main one is raising my own son. I'm trying to do that properly.'

Asha put her hand over her mouth, and Lizzie felt a stab of remorse for the person she had become.

Bip said, 'Can I make you something to drink, perhaps? Cup of tea. Can I tempt you?' She lifted the lid on a little white cardboard box revealing an incomplete row of plump little gulab jamun sat in their sugary juices. 'I got them a couple of hours ago.'

'No.' A pause. 'But thank you.'

But thank you. But thank you. But thank you. She was so tired of saying that.

Bip said, 'Will you at least sit?'

'I need to get home.'

Asha's long black hair had fallen in strands around her soft face. She had a self-pitying look and it made Lizzie hate her. She had told KK she couldn't do this job. It wasn't fair even to ask her. She said, 'If you know anything, you should tell me.'

'I will.'

With a supreme effort Lizzie summoned her argument.

'Sometimes people don't talk to us. They think they're doing the right thing. They think they can handle things better themselves. I've come across it. And afterwards, when it goes wrong, they regret it.'

'What are you saying?'

'That you should talk to us if you know things. If your son is caught up in gang activity it can be very serious for him.'

Asha looked like she was about to cry. 'You think I don't know that? You think I don't care about him?'

Lizzie closed her hands, interlocking her fingers in front of her chest.

Bip said, 'Thank you for staying on tonight. I appreciate it's difficult, you having a young child too.'

Lizzie said, 'Leif can come to harm.'

Asha said, 'You don't need to make me anxious. I'm anxious enough.'

'Leif can hurt people, too. Do stuff that can't be put right.' Lizzie got a card from her pocket and handed it over. 'That's the duty mobile number. It's manned twenty-four/seven. If Leif comes home, call it.'

55

The two older kids had fallen asleep on the sofa but the three-year-old, Parth, picked up his mum's phone from the table. Bip took it off him firmly and said, 'I've already told you.' He threw one of Asha's pretty cushions at the telly and knocked over a glass of orange juice on the white rug. Bip slapped him on the leg and he started wailing.

Asha said, 'It doesn't matter about the rug, Bip.'

Bip said, 'Don't interfere, Asha. Honestly, you're the last person to tell me how to bring up my children.' She lifted Parth. 'I've told you not to play with my phone.'

In between sobs, he got the words out. 'You're. Mean. Mummy.'

Asha went into the kitchen. After a minute Bip followed her in. 'I'm sorry,' she said. 'I didn't mean what I said. It could happen to anyone.'

'It's OK. Take them home. You've been great. I'll be all right.'

Asha watched them going down the steps. After his tantrum Parth had fallen asleep and Bip carried him over her shoulder. Little Ari was so tired Asha put him almost sleeping into his bed. He had the warm musty smell of child. His pyjamas, that had once been Leif's, were washed to softness and the little foxes had almost faded into the brushed cotton.

She sat on the sofa with a glass of wine. The feeling that she could not keep her boys safe was like a kind of vertigo.

She remembered Leif's little toddler body all red-hot in the bath: his fat little legs and the dimples behind his knees. Asha chose her son's name because it meant loved. Like the song says, all you need is love, and that had been the thing she was most certain of; guided by love, she would know how to raise him.

And at the beginning it felt like she had been right about that. When they finished dinner he would clear the plates away. In fact, sometimes he'd jump up and she'd have to say, Leif, wait a minute, sweetheart, Ari and me are still eating.

Kind and caring. If she had to choose four words about Leif, those were the first two she would have chosen.

But troublesome and naughty: those were the next two words she would use about him.

Little things. She was called in to school. The teacher said, 'He doesn't sit down when it's mat time. He gets up and walks around when it's story time.'

That was the first time she began to feel that maybe she didn't know what the right thing was. She wanted to say, Does it matter, though, that he doesn't sit still? He's five. She drifted on the current of her first uncertainty. This was his teacher, after all, who was trained in these things. And she wanted to be a good mother. She thought, Maybe it does matter. Maybe he should sit still when he's told.

She said to Leif, Promise me you'll be good and sit still.

But maybe she should have gone in and told them not to be ridiculous. She didn't know.

Then there were the stars. Five certificates equalled one star. All sorts of things went towards getting a star, but Leif didn't seem to be good at any of them. And the children who did get stars, they seemed to be good at all of the things. She saw those children in the morning wearing their blue school jumpers with the little gold stars on the shoulder. One of the things that went towards a star was getting twenty out of twenty in the weekly spelling tests. It wasn't getting just the easier first ten words right, but also the more difficult special extra words, and Leif was a slow reader.

They had star assemblies every month where they got their stars. She summoned up the courage and went into his teacher and said, Give Leif a star. Find something he's good at and give him a star.

She went into school that Friday morning to clap him when he went up to get his star.

The children were sitting on little benches on either side of the stage. Jostling together into the hall were lots of the mums who already knew each other. One of them, a small woman with dark curly hair, a denim skirt and lace-up black boots, smiled and said, 'Hello, aren't you Leif's mum? I'm Natasha.'

Asha said, 'I'm Asha. Pleased to meet you.'

Instantly an embarrassment turned over inside her as if she'd eaten something she didn't like by mistake but had to swallow it out of politeness. Natasha was *being kind*. Being Leif's mum, she realised, meant that either the mums would ignore you or you would be an object of their kindness.

The adults took up their places on the rows of chairs. First up was a girl from Leif's class. Julie-Anne was already wearing one big star and one small star and Asha worked out that for the children with multiple stars they had had to put a system in place.

The headteacher said, 'We've never had a child before who's got seven stars. So a big well done to Julie-Anne.'

Asha did the maths quickly: big star equals five stars. Seven stars equals thirty-five certificates: for crying out loud. She applauded, but she had a pain in her throat. She could almost smell the years of children who had played in the hall. She imagined their feet entering and leaving and how their different lives had all begun here.

The head teacher said, 'There are three children here who are getting their first stars and I want you to give them all a big clap.' Leif went up with the other two, who were younger, and the head teacher pinned the star on his jumper and Asha applauded, but a terrible embarrassment was churning inside her like a shoal of vigorous fish.

Leif said, 'The kids with stars, they've all got four or five. I'd rather not have any stars at all than wear one.' She said, 'Come on, Leif,' and pinned it on his jumper, but when he came back from school it was gone.

We believe in the limitless potential of all children.

That was the banner tied outside the gates to the local comprehensive. The John Deakin School was ranked Outstanding by Ofsted. Asha read all about their visions and values on the website.

Children can be knowledgeable, articulate and university ready.

Our teachers know and care about every child. We build positive relationships between school and home.

She got called in the first week. The phone call alone filled her with a dread that she didn't want to face; the uncertainty she already knew might turn out to be only the tributary to a vast ocean.

First Leif was making noises in class. Then he was talking back. When she confronted him, he wouldn't own up to anything. Mostly he wouldn't admit responsibility, but sometimes he came over all remorseful and well behaved. He did the washing-up and told her he loved her. Then the phone would ring again. He had kicked a chair over. He had called one of the teachers stupid.

It was a good school. Parents fought to get their children in to the John Deakin. But when one of the other boys punched him in the face, the teachers didn't do anything. Was there more to it? A reason for that? She didn't know. There seemed to be two mutually exclusive paths. She should be the parent who supports the school. Or she should go the other way and fight. She had heard of mothers single-handedly lifting cars off their children. She thought, If I only knew what to do it would be straightforward. I could do anything, if I knew what it was I should do.

It wasn't just Leif being told off, of course. She understood perfectly the implication that she too was doing something wrong. She was ashamed and angry and nearly always anxious.

The teachers told her there should be consequences for Leif's behaviour so she took his PlayStation off him, and his TV. After that he stopped talking to her.

He got caught shoplifting. As they were leaving the police station, she got a voicemail from social services. They weren't sure why he'd been referred to them and they were closing his case. He was not a child in need. She said, 'But he's just been arrested for stealing.'

The school suspended him. His friends' mothers wouldn't let their sons see him but still he seemed to be out all the time. Ari's dad said he'd seen Leif in the park carrying bags. Bip said, 'Here's what you have to do, you've got to lock him in his room. Don't let him go out.' But he was big now. How was she going to stop him?

She had closed her eyes and fallen asleep on the sofa. When she opened them, she could hear knocking.

She ran to the front door.

'Leif!'

She thought her heart would burst. She hugged him and he smelt awful. As she held him close it came to her how long it was since he had permitted any kind of physical contact. Things must have been very bad to have brought him to this. He stepped back. He had a lonesomeness about him she hadn't seen before. He'd only been away two days but he looked so thin and dirty. His face had black on it and there was dirt under his nails. He was still in the clothes he had left in except he was wearing a strange jacket. It was too big, checked with a corduroy collar.

She wanted to hug him for hours. She wanted him to have a hot bath, too, and put on clean pyjamas and eat some good food. And then she'd hug him some more. She wanted him to be a little boy again, someone she could protect.

The question where he had been popped into her mind, but she didn't ask. Bip would have asked. She was at sea.

'Have you eaten? I'll make you something. What do you fancy?'

'I need a bath.'

'I'll run it.'

She ran the tap hot, put in some of her own bath oil. The room filled with steam and the smell of geranium. She stopped and breathed. This was it at last: safety. They would move away.

In the kitchen, Leif was pacing up and down.

Asha said, 'I reported you missing. I'm sorry, I'll have to call the police. Just to let them know you're home.'

'Can we call them in the morning?'

Asha hesitated. She took the jacket off the back of the chair. Inside on the lining at the back she saw brownish stains that might be blood.

'Where did you get this?'

'It doesn't matter. Just get rid of it.'

'I'll do it now.'

'Call the police in the morning, OK?'

He went into the bathroom.

Asha stood. She remembered Leif jumping off the top bunk bed with his baby brother. It was so sweet. Leif did it even though he was too old for the game already, because he loved little Ari. Should she ask him what the story was with the jacket? Or was it better not to know?

It was like parenting in deep space; as if this man-child who had once been her little boy had passed through an airlock and drifted out into a dark, silent vacuum. She had to go out in one of those huge awkward suits with her visor misting up and try to catch hold of him.

She put on her rubber gloves and stuffed the jacket into a bin bag. She went out of the house and walked a few houses down before she put it in a stranger's bin. She couldn't believe she was doing this. If she had read in the newspaper about a woman doing this for her child she would have been disgusted. But she was afraid.

You call police, your boy will end up dead, your whole family is going to end up dead.

Just two streets away was a lamppost with teddy bears

and wilted flowers and rain-blotted words behind water-soaked cellophane.

She took Lizzie Griffith's card from her pocket and considered it in the street light. She should have asked her, But if I do talk to you will you help me? Will you be able to protect my son?

THURSDAY

56

The lab had come back with a DNA hit for the dead girl. She was Michelle Barnes: sixteen years and five months old at the time of her death. Born in Staffordshire. A May birth: blossom on the trees and the smell of hawthorn.

The constabulary's intelligence unit had put together a short precis of what they could find about Michelle and the most recent custody image was attached. Sitting alone in the back office at Middleton police station, Sarah clicked on it.

How many thousands of these records had she viewed? Against the blistering clamour of today's selfies and TikTok videos, the images remained defiantly a form all their own. The detainees experimented with a multitude of expressions – sad, angry, bored, intimidating – but there was no answer really as to the winning face to pull for the custody camera. In front of the blue-grey blankness of the screen each person was reduced to a catalogue of features: of eyes and nose and mouth, of proportions and size and colour. There was no escaping the camera's indifference. The faces were all a record of failure of one kind or another, and they never held any answers to the questions that bubbled up.

Here was Michelle, aged fifteen at her last arrest, staring at the camera: green eyes lined with a smudge of black kohl, straight brown hair parted in the middle, spots on her chin.

The pathologist's preliminary report confirmed drowning. 'The lungs appeared hyperexpanded with a dough-like texture,' Dr Houghton wrote. 'There was silt and sediment in the airways and stomach.'

Momentarily Sarah closed her eyes.

She remembered the body, held against the small tree just as any debris might be by the force of the current. The knowledge of that figure – the hand washing white in the water – had deepened in stages. (The big blond lad's face white and tearful.) Inside the scene tent, the morning light filtering palely, the hush in spite of the wind flapping the canvas. The girl's hood drawn tightly around her head, like someone who even in death was seeking shelter. The bitten nails. The hands broken and swollen by immersion. The body so deeply cold when anyone would know that this child should be warm, and dry. Later, in the mortuary, the discovery of that tiny black tattoo of a swallow hidden away on the inside of her arm. What was it? Sad birds still fly.

Drowning was the cause of death, but it didn't explain how Michelle had ended up in the river.

She opened Michelle's PNC record. Also known as Shell. First arrested for shoplifting at the age of thirteen in Staffordshire. A youth caution. Another arrest. More shoplifting. Criminal damage: a smashed bus shelter. Reported missing aged fourteen. Arrested in London a few weeks later: possession with intent to supply Class A (crack cocaine). Missing from secure accommodation a couple of weeks later. She was still wanted by police for the possession charge.

A list of offences, of incidents, but no explanation of the intervening spaces, of the steps along the way. Had she sat on a bench with a friend? Gone sledging on a tray down a hill?

Sarah imagined the girl last night, walking down to the riverbank in the rain. Was it no more than a slip of the foot that had taken her from the bank into the fast cold water? She remembered, too, the footage of two young people leaving the community hospital, a car drawing up and the girl stepping into the front seat.

Sarah pulled up the address on Street View where Michelle had resided at the time of her first arrest. It was a large detached house in a village, set back from the road. The Google car had been down on a sunny day and the trees were in full leaf. The house was white and over-exposed in the sunlight, but Sarah could make out a peaked slated roof, a tall dark tree topiaried into waves and curves and, closer to the camera, a small cherry in blossom with gnarled branches and lichen on the trunk.

There would be an inquest. The stages of Michelle's decline would be mapped and the opportunities that had been missed, but there was no sense to be made of the death, not really. It was as brutal as the bird that flies out from the hedgerow into the path of a car. The girl's heart would not beat again. Sarah closed her eyes and her father's preaching supplied the words.

Bodies lie like waste on the fields, like grain left behind by the reapers that no one gathers in.

Local officers had been dispatched to the mother to notify her of her daughter's death. Arrangements would be made.

57

Ari was jumping all over Leif. 'Where've you been? Where've you been?'

Leif picked his brother up and squeezed him to his chest. 'I've been hiding under your bed, stupid.'

Asha, wiping the kitchen surfaces down, said, 'Don't call him stupid, Leif.'

'You haven't!'

'I have, I have.'

Leif started tickling his brother, digging his fingers into his waist.

Ari was laughing and wriggling. 'Stop it, stop it.'

'That's enough now.' Asha tapped the table. 'Come on, Ari. Eat your breakfast. Don't want you late for school.'

Leif put his brother back on the floor.

'But where've you been, Leif? Where've you been?'

'With a friend,' Leif said. He got himself a bowl from the cupboard and sat down. 'Come and sit with me. I'm having my breakfast.'

They had a spelling test at school and Ari was monologuing on about words beginning with B – Billion. B I L L I O N – and catching the opportunity when Asha's back was turned to whisper and giggle.

'Bum. B U M.'

Leif said, 'Bottom,' and Ari nearly wet himself.

Asha glanced at Leif. He had poured some Frosties into a bowl but he wasn't eating. When Asha caught his eye, he remembered himself and grinned at Ari and said, 'Buttocks. BUTTOCKS.' Ari was helpless.

Asha went into Leif's room and looked under the bed. His England football backpack was stuffed at the back towards the wall. She reached it out. Inside was a towel, a change of clothes, his toothbrush, a Nokia phone she had never seen before.

She went back into the kitchen. The boys were playing Candy Crush on Ari's phone. She said, 'Put that down. Brush your teeth and get dressed for school.'

Ari pulled a face.

Leif said, 'Come on, I'll help you.'

'No,' Asha said. 'Stay in here, please.'

Ari looked towards Leif to back him up but Leif said, 'Do as Mum tells you.'

Ari sensed the mood. He put the phone on the table. His walk was all sulk but he left.

When she could hear the sound of Ari's toothbrush Asha said, 'I'll give you money.'

'What are you talking about?'

'I've seen the backpack. I'll give you money. You don't need to go to them for money.'

Leif put his elbows on the table and rested his head in his hands. 'Mum, it's not that any more. There's a thing I have to do.'

'What is it you have to do? You can tell me.'

'No, Mum, I can't.'

'What do you have to do?'

He shook his head.

Asha said, 'You can talk to me.'

'But I can't.'

Asha felt that old flash of anger. Then tears in her eyes. She felt so unable. He was here in front of her, in the same room as her, and yet at some moment – now, or later, what was the difference? – she would have to leave him, and then he would be gone. The thought of it was a huge gap inside her.

Ari was standing in his school uniform, one sock up, one sock down, and with his backpack on.

Leif said, 'Come on, little brother, give me a hug.'

But Ari twisted his body away and ran out into the hallway, out of the front door and down the steps. He turned back, hands on hips. 'Too slow!'

Asha stood next to Leif at the top of the steps. Up the street the Deakin loomed. The boys were out there every night in the playground dealing. They could be here for her son within minutes and it would take her twenty minutes, there and back, to get Ari to school.

She said, 'Leif, I'm begging you.'

'I'm sorry. I've got to go.'

It felt like her whole body was a sob about to break. What could she do? She said, 'I spoke to that boy Jaydn's sister. She said one of them killed a cop.'

'That's not true. He's just bragging.'

'Bragging? Listen to yourself! Bragging? How's that bragging? Who brags about stuff like that?'

Leif put his hand on her shoulder. 'It'll be all right, Mum. I'll do this one thing. Then it will be over.'

Ari was still standing with his hands on his hips. He said, 'Bosoms. B O S O M S.'

Both Asha and Leif laughed. Then Asha put her hand on

her forehead. She said, 'Stop that right now.'

Ari frowned. 'Well, I'm WAITING, aren't I?'

Asha said to Leif quietly, 'I'm not going to take Ari to school. I'm going to call the police and stay with you until they get here.'

Leif said, 'I've got to go, Mum, and you can't stop me. Don't make a scene in front of Ari.'

She belted Ari in to the passenger seat.

'Why are we driving?' he said. 'There's a prize for the kids who walk every day this week! Why are we driving?'

The usual imperative descended on her: to seem as though she knew what she was doing. Even now. How ridiculous!

'Not now, Ari.'

'Why not now? Why won't you tell me? Why are we driving?'

'Do you have to know absolutely everything?'

He slammed his little fists on the dashboard. 'You're a terrible mum!'

Asha's throat tightened. Ari was right. Her eldest son had become a drug dealer, for God's sake. Tears pricked behind her eyes.

She said, 'Ari, please.'

Something about her tone must have stopped him. He looked at her. 'Are you crying, Mum?'

She shook her head.

'Mum, why are you crying?'

She drove round the corner and pulled over.

'I've got to make a phone call.'

She had tried to sound reassuring, as though what was happening was just run-of-the-mill stuff, but Ari had fallen

267

silent. His face was blank with worry. If she ever found herself short of guilt this was another thing she could feel bad about.

She stepped out onto the pavement and called the number on the card that Lizzie had given her. A man identified himself only as night-duty CID. Lizzie wasn't in the office yet.

'But she said any time.'

'I'll look into it. Someone will call you back.'

She looked around her, then swallowed her last iota of pride and called Anjem, her sister's husband. He was a minicab driver. Would he wait outside the house and watch?

'I'm sorry to ask. I know what you think of me.'

'No problem. I'm only five minutes away.'

58

Lizzie was up early, opening the curtains in Connor's room and jostling him out of bed towards breakfast. Her rostered hours were supposed to give her time to take Connor to school, but this was where reality hit the equality-at-work cobblers, as it always did. Leif had made the leap to high risk and Lizzie had been tasked to act as liaison. Her other mispers would be reassigned until the investigation was complete. It wasn't a job you could count on for finishing on time.

Connor moaned and pulled the duvet over his head.

'Chocolate mousse for anyone who's at the table in five,' Lizzie said, thinking there ought to be a reality TV show for parents getting their children to school punctually. Extra points for single mums! Although, of course, in any such show she'd be penalised heavily for the food bribe.

Connor was out of bed, his feet sliding automatically into his dinosaur slippers. She moved through to the kitchen and plonked the chocolate mousse on the table.

'Fill your boots.'

'But, Mum, you'd be ever so cross.'

They both giggled. It was one of their favourite jokes. Lizzie leaned over and gave him a kiss on his brow.

'Oh ugh, Mum! Get off!'

She looked at him. His feet didn't reach the floor yet and he was swinging them under the table.

'If you're not careful I'll hug you as well.'

Maybe she should go all in and give him the iPad but she

decided instead she could manage with a very quick facewash and sent up a prayer of thanks to her mum for the ironed shirts. She raced around: teeth, lipstick, mascara.

The job was tugging on Lizzie. It reminded her a little of how she had been when she started, but it wasn't the same. There was much less excitement and much more anxiety. Sarah had talked her through it – the possibility that this fifteen-year-old boy was caught up in a turf war that had turned very nasty. The boy might have been a witness to a rape. There was a link to firearms.

Policing pulled one way and Connor the other. Whichever way she jumped she felt guilty.

There was the door – Kieran's mother, Isobel. Smartly dressed with full make-up. Leather gloves. How did she do it? She must have been up at five, or even earlier.

'Thanks so much,' Lizzie said, pulling a sheepish face.

'Not a problem!' Isobel said, hanging her woollen coat on a hanger in the hall and kissing Lizzie on the cheek with her dry lips. 'What do they say? It takes a village!'

Lizzie's own mother hadn't been free last night when she'd called for help at short notice. 'I *could*,' she said, 'but I did promise Natty I'd go to Lauren's presentation.' Lizzie had imagined instantly her older sister's habitual annoyance at the short-notice disruptions and her rage: her children coming second again!

'Don't worry, Mum. Honestly. It was just a thought. I'll be fine.'

'It *is* much easier if I can plan. If you're sure, then?'

Plan! That was another thing.

Isobel left her little wheelie bag in the hall and moved through into the kitchen. Lizzie, following her, remembered she hadn't changed the sheets since her own mother had last stayed.

'Always pleased to see little Connor, aren't I?' Isobel said, pinching Connor's cheek. Connor stared at his mother with a face like thunder and Lizzie gave him the strongest *don't-you-dare* look she could muster. Isobel had taken a folded blue cotton apron from her large handbag and started the washing-up, which was stacked on the side.

'You don't have to—' Lizzie said.

'Not a problem!'

Why did a statement so often suggest its own opposite? Or was that just paranoia? Lizzie ran her teeth under a fingernail. So many negative thoughts bursting inside her head.

'There's a dishwasher.'

'Only a few things here! I'll be done in a jiffy.'

Lizzie's phone was ringing with a withheld number. It was night-duty CID. Asha had just rung: she was ready to play ball at last. They were about to go off duty – could Lizzie get in pronto and do the meeting.

Isobel flashed a kindly look at Lizzie. 'Looks like you need to get going, dear.'

Pulling her jacket on and hurrying out of the door, Lizzie felt remorse. Isobel always made the best of it. Maybe she did judge Lizzie but she never said a word of recrimination. Later, just as Lizzie left the tube station, there was a phone call. A tantrum was blowing a force nine in the background.

'Only I said I'd ask you,' Isobel said, sounding strained. 'Connor says you let him take his dad's elephants to school in his bag.'

Lizzie thought of the precious wooden elephants and the possible catastrophe of their loss. 'I'm not sure about that.'

Isobel's voice was muffled: she had taken the phone away from her mouth. 'Mummy says—' A wail of exasperation carried.

'But they're my bloody elephants! Daddy gave them to me!'

Swearing, too. Lizzie would blame the imaginary builders, but no one would believe her. She shouted into the phone.

'Isobel, Isobel!'

Isobel's voice came back to her ear, as exasperated now as Connor. 'Yes?'

'Maybe one,' Lizzie mumbled, thinking of little Connor on his own with his strict grandma, and fully aware, too, that to say no and then change her mind was absolutely the worst kind of parenting. Completely unfair on Isobel, too. The slippery slope and all that.

59

Sarah stood alone at the window of Middleton police station and looked out onto the road. She still had Fedden's private number and she called him. 'Jim.'

'Sarah.'

'Grateful to you for taking on the Middleton job.'

'No problem.'

'It'll be good to work with you again.'

'Thank you. That's mutual.'

Sarah could hear voices in the background and imagined the busy London unit. She remembered her conversation with Elaine, and said, 'How's the family?'

'Good. How's Meghan?'

'Yes, good too.'

Outside two women were walking past, deep in conversation.

Fedden said, 'Why are you ringing, Sarah?'

'Because Ryan Kennedy's a person of interest.'

'I'm aware.'

'This conversation . . . It's not official.'

'That's not like you.'

Sarah put her hand on her forehead. She'd tried to play it his way, but she didn't really know how.

Fedden said, 'Well, spit it out, whatever it is.'

'It's Steve. He called one of my DCs, pumped him for information.'

'I know.'

'He rang me, too, asking to be part of the investigation. He's too emotionally involved. He wants to get Kennedy.'

'Don't we all?'

'I suppose we do, yes. If it is him. But—'

'Let's just stop here. Steve's currently tasked to something different. If I need him to work on the Middleton job you can trust me to supervise him appropriately.'

'Thank you.'

'No problem. Send my love to Meg.'

'Will do. Send my love to—' She stopped because she couldn't for the life of her remember Fedden's wife's name.

'To Jane. I will. Bye now.'

Sarah video-called Meghan. Her girlfriend was by the roadside, wearing her white traffic skipper's hat, and Sarah felt a burst of love and homesickness. She said, 'You busy, love?'

'Yeah, sorry. Not a good moment. Speak later.'

She sat at the table. She wasn't sure she could stand it if something else went wrong on her watch.

If only she had a better grasp of her own investigation. There were a hundred lines of inquiry she would like to follow. Her instinct was to throw a huge net out – delve into the Coopers, request extensive CCTV trawls, deploy surveillance – but she only had Harris in Middleton and Tom back at base to help her. The London unit was running it now, and they didn't much like her.

There had been an actual murder in Alnbridge last night – a street stabbing where no one had seen a thing. Much of the force's specialist investigative capacity was focused on the immediate response to that.

'So far a lot of what we've got is conjecture,' Cheng had

said. 'It's worrying, I agree, and I wish I had more to give you. But it's not a murder.'

Not yet, she thought, remembering the several dead young men she had seen when she worked homicide. David Hendrick, seventeen; Kyle Loughlan, fourteen; Omar Begum, eighteen . . . Spencer Cardoso, fifteen: Ryan's friend. His body had brimmed with the health of boyhood. His muscles as sculpted as an athlete's and his skin without blemish: so perfect but for the single neat wound in the upper thigh.

And Michelle, torn and battered by the river. Michelle hadn't been murdered and yet her death was surely a consequence of whatever was happening in Middleton.

She picked her phone out of her pocket and sent Meghan a text.

Sorry I've been so useless about ringing you. Love you.

She dug her fingers into her scalp and turned her attention to the phone work that Fedden's unit had sent her. Their specialist tecs would have already studied it thoroughly, but she had local knowledge. In the absence of a proper investigative capability and surveillance, the phones might start to piece things together.

The team didn't have much to start from: just Asha's number. But Asha had known where to look for Leif and so her phone was of interest.

Looking at recent traffic, one number in particular – ending in 76 – had drawn the team's attention: this was the number Asha had called from Middleton. There were a few calls between Asha's mobile and –76. Sometimes the call was terminated and redialled. In Middleton the call was finished within a minute but then –76 returned the call.

The number might just be a friend. After all, who wouldn't

turn to a friend at such a time for advice and support? And if it was just a friend then they hit up against the problem of collateral intrusion: invading the privacy of someone who was nothing to do with any criminality. But a few details made –76 promising.

Asha had called the number only after Leif had been reported missing: almost immediately after, in fact. And yesterday, half an hour after the call between Asha's mobile and –76, CCTV showed her at the train station in Middleton. The inference must be that the call had precipitated her journey home. The London unit had used both facts as support for a RIPA application to look further into –76.

The results vindicated the application. The number was pay as you go and unregistered. It had only gone live four days previously. –76 had called Leif's last known number seven times in the day before he disappeared.

Cell siting showed the phone in London. Apart from the calls to and from Leif and Asha, the only other calls made by the mobile had been to and from two payphones in the Middleton area.

If –76 hadn't called Leif's number it might never have looked so interesting. Was this carelessness by whoever held the phone? And did whoever was using the payphones realise that they had been compromised?

Sarah looked through the locations of the payphones. One was on the road out towards the caravan site. Another was from the phone box she had herself used to call Halford, at the edge of the Wentworth estate. The call history seemed to corroborate the idea that whoever had stolen the gun was also linked to Leif Abad. But what more did it give? What did it give that she could action?

If they could verifiably ascribe −76 to a named individual, or identify who had stolen the gun, then this phone work might form part of a detailed jury bundle. With more resources and time, what might she do? In any case, the number had been inactive since the calls made to Asha in Middleton. The SIM was probably broken and lying in a storm drain somewhere.

Her task was to prevent further harm. She had no doubt there was serious beef between the new line and the locals who had previously been running drugs into Middleton, but the gaps in her knowledge remained and so did the biggest difficulty: trying to work out what these people would do next.

60

Lizzie sat at Asha's kitchen table with her laptop open. Her heart was thumping. 'So he's gone already! Why didn't you call the number I gave you sooner? Why didn't you call the moment he got back?'

Asha was slumped in the seat opposite. Her skin was pallid. She spoke quietly and Lizzie had to ask her to speak more loudly.

Asha repeated herself, with just a hint of revived defiance, 'Because they said they'd kill him if I went to the police.'

That gave Lizzie pause. She thought of that gun lying on the floor and Kieran bleeding out. It was a plausible threat after all. 'OK. I get that.'

'Actually,' Asha added, as if it was an afterthought, 'they said they'd kill all of us.' She fumbled in her bag, took out a blister of tablets, glancing at Lizzie with shame as she swallowed one. 'Sorry. It's the only way I've been able to cope.'

It startled Lizzie how her heart suddenly opened.

'God, Asha, I'm so sorry. I should have done a much better job of persuading you to talk to me sooner.'

'Oh, don't worry. I've done everything wrong, from the start. I mean, not just now. Since he was little.'

Lizzie laughed. 'What absolutely everything?' She gestured with her head towards the kids' pictures on the walls, the blackboard wall with the drawings of cats and houses and the lollipop trees. 'Looks like you've been doing OK.'

And then, remembering Connor's grandmother arriving prepared with her very own apron, she laughed again. 'For a start this place is way tidier than my kitchen.'

Asha raised her eyebrows and sighed. Tidiness? What on earth did that matter? She said, 'I've got a phone number for the boy whose been dealing with Leif. His name's Jaydn. It was him told me Leif was in Middleton.'

'How did you get that?'

'I took a photo of it when Leif was in the bath. The night before he left.'

'Have you called it at all?'

'I have.'

So this number would already be known to the unit. No need to ring it through urgently. 'That was resourceful of you. Anything else?'

'When I left this morning to take Ari to school I phoned my brother-in-law to keep an eye on the flat. He's a cabbie. He saw Leif leaving in a little blue Fiat. There were a couple of boys in the car. Anjem did his best to follow them but he missed them at the lights. He got some photos and a registration plate, if that's any help?'

She pushed a piece of paper across the table on which a VRM had been scribbled.

Lizzie said, 'That's brilliant. Well done. What was Leif wearing when he left?'

'Blue puffer jacket. Blue trackies. And he had a backpack.'

'I'm going to go outside and make an urgent phone call, OK?'

Asha nodded.

'Just one thing, before I go, in case it's important. What changed your mind? I mean, was there something that happened that made you suddenly decide to tell us what you know?'

Asha looked like she might cry. Lizzie leaned forward and took her hand.

'Let's try and work on this together now, heh?'

'He said he had to go back. He said there was a thing he had to do and that frightened me.'

'Do you know what that is, that thing he's going to do?'

She shook her head. 'I don't. I said to him that I was frightened and that Jaydn had told me that the guy who's running this – in Middleton – this guy, he killed a fed. I'm sorry, I mean a police officer. He killed a police officer.'

Asha was still talking but Lizzie could barely hear her.

'Leif said, No that's just bragging. And I said, Who brags about something like that?' Asha stopped speaking. 'What's happening?' she said. 'Are you OK?'

61

Kiyana said, 'I'm dying for a wee.'

Steve stretched out in the driver's seat. 'That's another reason why you girls can never do the job. Can't piss in a bottle.'

'Oh, fuck off—'

Steve put his hand up for quiet. The commentary had resumed. The targets had come out of the house and were moving towards their car. It was a positive ID and a description followed. IC1 male, six foot, grey Belier padded jacket. IC3 male, five foot eleven, black puffer. Silver Volvo VRM—'

Steve turned the key in the ignition. He pulled out into the street, following the Volvo at a distance. A silver Ford pulled out from a side road and Steve gave way, happy to let a civilian mask the surveillance. Only a hundred yards away the road ended in a T-junction and he would hand over the targets there. Kiyana commentated the target car taking a left turn and Steve waited for George and Linton to clear. Then, directed by Kiyana, he took side roads to pick them up further on.

It came over the radio: they had pulled over again and got out of the vehicle. They were going into another house.

Kiyana said, 'Oh, for fuck's sake. That's going to be another two hours then, is it?'

Steve pulled over into a residential bay. He reached into the back of the car and got his flask out of his bag.

'You want a coffee?'

'Fuck off.'

'Where's your sense of humour?'

'My bladder's taken it hostage.'

He poured himself a coffee. It was a nice flask: pale green and a good size. His son had got it for him from Fortnum's.

Kiyana said, 'Do you think they've made us?'

Steve shrugged. He was thinking about the flask, festively wrapped under the tree. His ex-wife included him for Christmas lunch nowadays. It was seven years since the divorce and she had remarried. It was all very friendly. The new husband welcomed him with a drink and Steve brought him a large bottle of Jameson's because no hard feelings, plus it was on offer. And he opened the present from his adult son and thought how he knew the perfect gift for a father who spent most of his life at work, waiting for something to happen.

He said, 'After the drugs seizure they must have known we were onto them. They'd have to be idiots to acquire a firearm now. Still mostly they are idiots, so who knows?'

'Is it being cynical that keeps you so young-looking?'

'They'll screw up. Today. Or tomorrow. Or next week. But they will. They always do.'

His mobile was ringing and he fished it out of his pocket. The banner on the screen said Lizzie.

Steve was right-handed but he held his mobile with his left hand to his left ear. It was awkward, but it was unavoidable. Before the shot that killed Kieran, Ryan had discharged a bullet near the right side of his head and he'd lost some hearing.

Lizzie was talking quickly, her voice pressured by distress. 'It's Ryan, Steve. He's running a line out in the sticks.'

'Hang on—'

'The misper I'm looking for – he's been working for a line, out in Middleton. His mum says the guy in charge out there killed a police officer. It must be Ryan.'

The radio began transmitting. Steve said, 'Lizzie, I'm really sorry. I'm on a job—'

She cut him short, her emotions already zipped tightly back up. 'That's all right.'

'I'll call you back.'

But the line was dead. Steve threw the coffee out the window and turned the car on.

Kiyana said, 'The intel on the house has come back. It's known for firearms, has a connection to the Waltham Spartans . . .'

Steve waved his arm impatiently. 'I can't keep up with all their affiliations and I don't give a fuck. We've just got to keep eyes on them until Trojan get here.'

It was coming over the radio: the armed stop was on. The Volvo had taken a turn left onto Kendal Road, running alongside the park. They should stand by to pick up the follow. The streets were a warren of possible twists and turns and George and Linton knew the ground well. The commentary gave a left onto Hamilton Road and Steve made a turn. The sky was Tupperware white. It was 1930s suburbia: pollarded trees, little red-brick houses with wooden balconies and oversized hedges shielding their tiny front gardens. Ahead a Sainsbury's van was parked, hazard lights flashing, obscuring their view. Steve overtook to see the Volvo immediately ahead, pulled over. George was on the pavement shutting the passenger door. Steve overtook as if in no particular hurry. Kiyana transmitted.

'Vehicle has stopped. Hamilton Road. George has left the vehicle. George has left the vehicle.'

Steve said, 'At the T-junction it's Dollis Hill tube station.'

The Volvo was pulling away, but it was George Steve was watching in the rear-view mirror. The target was walking quickly down the road towards the T-junction. Steve pulled the car right. The station entrance was easy to miss, set back from the road with a small sign and with no building visible. George was running lightly across the zebra crossing, and he ducked quickly into the alleyway that led to the trains.

Kiyana said, 'Target vehicle left, left along Burnley Road. Behind us and moving in the opposite direction.'

Steve was thinking it through. They didn't have capacity for a follow on foot through the underground and it was a good station for a get-away with connections both north and south. There were so many possible side roads here, too, for the car to lose surveillance.

Kiyana was transmitting. 'George has entered the tube station. George has entered Dollis Hill tube station.'

The team leader was transmitting.

'Stay with the vehicle. Repeat, stay with the vehicle.'

The inspector was cutting his losses. Surveillance was in place for the vehicle and Trojan were near by for the hard stop. They didn't have the resources to split the team, or to follow on foot. But George had the gun: Steve could sense it. And he was absolutely fucked if he was going to spend more days watching those boys while Ryan was just begging to get nicked out in Middleton.

Steve pulled over and stepped out into the road.

Kiyana followed him. 'What the fuck?'

'Drive the car.'

'I'm not—'

'Drive the car. You need to be part of the vehicle surveillance or we're both in the shit.'

He was running. The entrance to the station was down three or four steps to an alley, with a hedge on the left and green railings on the right. A woman was walking ahead in a red coat, holding an umbrella. He ran past her. The light shone off the wet concrete. He was in a covered walkway with wooden-framed windows on either side and fluorescent light above. At the turning towards the line the tunnel continued giving the option to exit towards Chapter Road. There was a glass-fronted office on Steve's right but it was unmanned. He hesitated before turning left into the station.

The steps to the track were steep. He slowed his pace, taking in the indicators above: two minutes to the next train. Ahead were two wooden benches and a waiting room with multiple metal-framed glass panes that looked all the way through. Standing at the very end of the platform was George. A northbound train was pulling in and, through the curved-glass façade, Steve saw George step towards it.

Steve entered the train just as the doors were closing, moving up the train, opening the doors and stepping between the carriages. The tracks raced beneath him. A woman with a little white dog on her lap looked up and said, 'You can't do that. It's dangerous.' Steve smiled at her, aggressively enough that she looked down. He stopped in the carriage before George's and texted the inspector.

Jubilee Line north bound.

A man was sitting opposite balancing a tennis ball on his

head: begging for likes, as Steve's son would say. A woman sat with two plump children: one boy on the seat beside her and a younger girl, looking boiling hot in a pink patterned coat with a fur-lined hood, strapped into a pushchair. Civilians. People who shouldn't be shot.

George could change onto the Overground at West Hampstead or, worse, go into busy complicated Baker Street. His only mistake so far was that the train was not in a tunnel: there was phone coverage. Steve got another text ready.

The train was slowing, the tone of the brakes climbing to a whistle. On the right they were sweeping past a fake timber-framed building. The recording announced the station. A man with a wheelie bag was waiting by the doors and Steve was able to use him as a shield. Through the windows between the carriages, he saw George.

Steve sent the text. **Willesden Green. Alighting.** He put his phone in his pocket and stood back from the doorway, holding on to the pole, and watching the platform. He thought, George is younger, fitter, stronger.

The mother was approaching the doors, moving past Steve, struggling to get off the train with her two children. He helped her lift the pushchair onto the platform. She thanked him but he barely made eye contact. He was looking over her shoulder. George was ahead and alone, hands in his pockets, moving along the platform towards the exit.

Steve walked briskly. George was climbing the left-hand side of the stairs. They were steep with low risers and metal-edged treads, divided by a handrail. On either side was a green metal lattice through which the wind blew. A woman in a black puffer jacket was descending and the certainty came into Steve's mind that what he was doing was irresponsible. More irresponsible perhaps than Kieran trying to take the gun from Ryan.

There was a bulge in the back of George's waistband under his jacket: the firearm, he was certain of it. Steve began to run up the right-hand side of the steps past the woman, willing her to hurry up and turn onto the platform.

As Steve passed, George glanced to his right. Steve counted on his age, his tired demeanour, the grey in his hair. Nearly at the top, he slowed a little, as if breathless. He held his side, slipping his hand into his jacket under his elbow and leaned a little to his left as if he was in pain. George was catching up. Steve quickened his step again, still leaning to his side but keeping two steps ahead. Late for work! As he reached the top he glanced behind. Praise be: a moment with no civilians. George was beneath him on the stairs and Steve had the advantage of standing on level ground. He turned hard and withdrew his firearm, arms straight, legs well balanced.

'Armed police! Show me your hands.'

George's hand moved as if towards his back.

'Don't make me shoot you! Show me your hands.'

George was hesitating. Steve could hear no sound and see only darkness around the edges of his vision. Then George lifted both hands in front of him, palms up, like in the movies and they were back running the film on normal speed. The tiles in the station were green, Steve noticed.

He said, 'Put your hands on your head. Walk up the steps like that and sit down. Then don't move.'

The woman with the pushchair appeared at the bottom of the stairs. The boy, holding her hand, walked beside her. She flushed with disbelief and pulled the boy closer.

'Step away from the stairs. Use the station intercom. Call for police.'

George said, 'You're going to be so sorry.'

'Not as sorry as I'd be if you shot me. You're detained for a search under Section Forty-seven of the Firearms Act.'

He could hear a descending whine as a train pulled into the station below and a wind travelled up the steps. Thirty seconds later and Kiyana was running up the steps, her Glock in her two hands.

62

Leif got in the back of the car. Jaydn sat up front with another man Leif had never met before.

'Your mum,' Jaydn said. 'Did she talk to the feds?'

'I told her not to.'

Saying that much was too much, but it was too late. Jaydn said, 'She's a fucking liability. You need to manage her.'

Leif shifted his weight. His mum hadn't said anything. How did Jaydn even have an opinion about his mum? They'd never met. Something must have happened.

Jaydn leaned between the front seats into the back of the car. 'You best man up. And if you can't, then think of your little brother.'

Ari! A stab of anxiety went through Leif. The car was moving slowly through heavy traffic and he had an almost desperate urge to leave, but could not. The car pushed its way round the big roundabout and past the magistrates' court on the left. Fat raindrops rolled down the passenger window. The wipers worked steadily.

He thought of Shell, and that walk down the swollen brown river and the policeman standing on the bridge. NK had said there was a body. That was on him too. 'Do this one thing,' NK had said.

Jaydn reached into the back of the car. 'Give me your burner.'

Leif reached into his jeans pocket and handed it over.

Jaydn popped the SIM. He snapped it in two and the

driver pulled the car to a stop. Jaydn got out and bent down by the side of the road in the lee of the car. Leif leaned his head against the window to watch. Jaydn was chucking the SIM in a drain. He got back in and the car pulled away.

'I never even used it,' Leif said.

'Yeah, well.' Jaydn laughed sarcastically. 'Your mum might have.'

Leif felt disorientated, like he'd been smoking too much weed.

Jaydn seemed furious. He said, 'You need to step up.' He reached behind him again and handed Leif another Nokia. 'Never been used. Don't you go using it, neither. It's for us to reach you. You get me?'

'Course I do.'

'Leave it switched on.'

'What's happening now?'

'Wait your time. You'll learn soon enough.'

From then on the boys up front ignored him and talked shit to each other. Leif looked out of the window.

The road ran parallel to a long low line of iron railings that shielded an expanse of grass and autumnal trees. Opposite were little pods for bicycles, a café with tables and street heaters, a florist with buckets of flowers outside, and a book shop with arched windows and green ceramic lamps. They pulled left along the line of the park and then immediately right into the neighbourhood. The houses were big with heavy glossy doors, bay windows and pots in the front gardens. A white Hyundai was parked up and they pulled in a few feet away. Jaydn leaned past the headrest again and looked at Leif.

'Perfect here. No CCTV and them lot are out all day making their money their way. Keep your mouth shut.'

The Hyundai's engine was running. Leif and Jaydn got in the back. There were two men up front but Leif couldn't really see them because they both had their hoods up and they didn't turn.

Jaydn said, 'Whassup?'

The man in the front passenger seat said, 'Yeah, one G, like we said.'

'Calm.' Jaydn reached in his jacket and took out a roll of notes which he held so the man could see them. 'You wanna show it me.'

The passenger pulled some latex gloves from his pocket. He handed a pair to Jaydn and slipped on a pair himself. He popped the front of the dashboard and reached inside. He handed over something wrapped in a blue sock. 'It's a spinner, like we said.' Leif saw the man's face. He had one lazy eye, but the other one fixed him in his gaze. 'You don't know nothing about me.'

'Course.'

The man faced front again but Leif could see him watching them in his rear-view mirror.

Jaydn peeled back the sock and took out a small black revolver with a brown fake wooden handle. It was tiny, almost a toy. Something a gambler would have hidden in his boot in a Western saloon. But Leif had seen the movies and no one laughed when someone pulled those dinky little guns. Leonardo shot by that German fella in *Django* was just as dead as if it was an AK47 and Tarantino was famous for getting that kind of shit right.

The front passenger said, 'Takes a thirty-eight so easy to source. And clean as a whistle.'

Jaydn said, 'You got teeth for me?'

The man put his hand back in the dashboard. He handed over another sock. Jaydn reached inside. He opened his hand and Leif saw a handful of bullets.

The passenger said, 'Give me the strap.'

He leaned between the seats and took the gun in his right hand, tipping it to the side.

'Release is here,' he said. 'Push it forward and tip the cylinder out of the frame, like this. Thread your thumb through to hold it open.'

Leif glanced at Jaydn and saw the concentration on his face.

'So you've loaded it and . . .' The passenger shut the gun and the cylinder locked back into position. He placed his thumb on the hammer. 'You cock it, like this. Then it's armed. Keep firing till you're done.'

63

Steve and Kiyana stood together in the lift.

'So, what changed?' Kiyana said as the narrow box climbed steadily, the floors lighting up on the lift's panel.

'What do you mean?'

'Two days ago you didn't want to risk an unauthorised stop?'

'I'll tell it to the boss, if that's OK by you.'

Kiyana looked at the floor. The lift pinged.

In the middle of the room a cluster of DCs were sat around a clump of eight desks that had been pushed together beneath a pool of fluorescence. Fedden was with them, arse spreading on one of the desks, and holding forth. Seeing Steve and Kiyana he offered a Vulcan salute, stood up, hitching his trousers over his non-existent waist, and gestured with his head for them to follow. Everyone else nodded at them non-committedly as they passed. Steve scratched his eyebrow and then, just as he cleared the desks, gave them the finger. He looked over his shoulder.

'All of you.'

Fedden's so-called office, constructed from wobbly partitions that didn't even make it to the ceiling, was a makeshift space in the far corner of the open-plan floor. He stood behind the desk, his hands resting on his lumbar spine as if it was a source of constant pain. Steve and Kiyana remained standing too, side by side.

'So?'

Steve shrugged.

'Nothing to say for yourself? No explanation of what the fuck you were doing?'

'I should say I'm sorry?'

'That's even a question?'

Kiyana said, 'Can I just say, boss, that Steve's instinct was right. It was George with the firearm.'

Fedden put his hand up. 'Thank you but when I need to hear from you, Kiyana, I'll ask you.'

Steve said. 'Definitely not Kiyana's fault. She tried to stop me leaving the car.'

'Yah dee yah,' Fedden said. 'Genuinely not at all interested in how we all stick together and have each other's backs.'

'I took a loaded firearm off the street at personal risk. So I'm not sure how sorry I should be.'

Kiyana looked at her feet. Steve looked straight ahead.

Fedden said, 'And if it had gone wrong? If you'd shot him? He'd shot you? All of it completely outside operating procedures? Never mind that a civilian could so easily have been killed. Christ.'

'If he had shot me, then I don't think operating procedures would have been uppermost in my mind.'

'What about if he'd killed that baby?'

'That didn't happen because they weren't there when I made the stop. And those things can still happen even when everything's by the book. The SOPs might give you a safety net to defend your actions, but they don't stop shit happening. What can I tell you? Guns: they're just not safe.'

Fedden glanced at Kiyana. 'This was at Steve's initiative. You just decided to follow him?'

Steve interrupted. 'That's right.'

'Kiyana?'

'Yes, sir.'

'Get yourself a coffee – well out of hearing distance, please.'

'Boss.'

Fedden waited for the door to shut. The partitions wobbled. He gestured towards the chair in front of his desk. Steve sat and looked to his right out of the window across the wide view of rooves and train tracks, and rolling clouds. In another open-plan office, below and across a vertiginous gap of air, other people sat working at their desks. What on earth were they doing? Perhaps they oversaw the orbit of the earth. Or maybe they were in marketing.

Fedden said, 'What am I supposed to say to the super-intendent?'

'What he should already know: that not everything falls within standard operating procedures. I had no choice. I honestly believed – and on good grounds – that George was carrying a firearm. It would have been dereliction for me not to follow him, and dereliction not to search him when the opportunity arose. He was a real and present danger. It would have looked far worse if he'd killed our informant.'

'That will all sound good if you have to argue it in front of a board. I'm sure you'll be fine.'

'I'm going to have to defend myself in front of a board for taking a firearm off a criminal? Really?' He glanced at the ceiling as if looking for something he'd maybe left up there. 'Time was it would have been a commendation.'

'Steve, really.' Fedden shook his head. 'This kind of talk.'

'Real world, boss. What can I say? I had to make a snap decision.'

'You're not convincing me you're safe. That's the issue.'

'The job doesn't always provide an easy choice between safe and dangerous.'

There was a brief silence.

Then Steve said, 'OK. I'm sorry. I'm sorry, OK? I know it's a problem for you. I'm sorry for that, but I'm not sorry for taking George's Beretta, and I'll stand by that. I didn't have time to discuss it with the commander. It wasn't ideal, of course not, but my gut told me it was George with the weapon, and it was. No disrespect, but the guvnor made the wrong call. Not his fault. He's only been doing this five minutes. If George and Linton were splitting up, it was because they'd clocked the surveillance team. The firearm was always going to be going into the underground, not staying in the vehicle. It wasn't red mist. It was a judgement, based on a lot of experience, which used to count for something incidentally. Lesser of two big evils, that's how it was. If he'd slipped surveillance and killed our grass? That would have been OK? No consequences? No special inquest for our grass?'

Fedden leaned back against the window. Behind him the city fell away and grey clouds swept across. 'You've been through a lot, Steve. No one would blame you for stepping back for a while.'

'Is this about the Middleton job?'

Fedden sighed.

'The misper's mum got a VRM for the car his handlers are driving. There's an ANPR hit on Paddington station. We've got officers looking at CCTV but we need someone on blues driving to meet any possible train and I have fuck-all surveillance-trained officers available.'

'Except Kiyana and me.'

'That's right. But Sarah called me. She told me how you rang her, all worked up about Ryan.'

Steve's eyes clouded over. He shook his head slowly. 'Seriously?'

'Yes. Seriously! And she's not an idiot. Are you safe, Steve? After all we've been through, I'm asking you to be honest. Can I trust you? Are you safe?'

Steve stood up. He brushed his hands down his trousers. 'I know I'm safe, boss, but at the end of the day, it's your call.'

Fedden pinched his lower lip. He said, 'I don't want to prevent you working on the job. We all want to get him. I need to be sure I can trust you, that's all. That's all. You fuck up, and it's going to be on me. Does that carry any weight with you?'

'It does. One hundred per cent. You can trust me.'

64

Harris knocked once and then opened the door and put a foot in. 'Wendy?' He looked over his shoulder at Sarah. 'We can go in.'

Wendy was sitting, her legs inside a sleeping bag, on a dirty sofa in the corner. Her shoulder-length hair was uniformly blue, and a big flat silver cross on a leather cord rested just below the notch of her collar bone. The little dog, who had been sitting next to her with his head on her lap, jumped down and walked towards them, wagging its tail submissively. It had round brown eyes, a black button nose and cocked ears.

Sarah offered her hand. 'Nice dog. What is he? Bit of terrier?'

'I dunno, do I? Me mum gave him me.'

Sarah thought better of talking more about the dog. She sat at the table and waited. Wendy's skin was sallow and marked by acne. She had green eyes, freckles across her cheeks and on her upper arms, and looked thin enough to fall between the bars of a storm drain. Looking more closely Sarah could see a bruise below Wendy's right eye.

Harris put the two loaves of sliced white bread and the couple of tins of dog food on the kitchen table.

Wendy shifted in her sleeping bag. 'Thank you, love.'

'I wanted to introduce you to a friend of mine—'

'Sorry, Mark, an' thank you for the bread an' all that, but it's not a good time right now.'

Harris moved over to the sink – filthy and full of plates and cups. He began washing a couple of mugs. 'Just a quick cuppa, heh?' He glanced at Sarah and almost winked. 'I think my friend's just had one.'

'Really, Mark, I want you to go. D'you mind? Take the bread with you if it's a problem.'

Mark sat at the table. He picked the dog up and tickled it under its chin. 'That's not like you, Wendy. Something wrong?'

'Nothing's wrong.'

Sarah said quietly, 'That bruise on your face—'

Wendy interrupted. 'You got a car with you?'

Harris shook his head. 'Not one anyone round here would know. I expect that's what's worrying you?'

She scrunched up her face. 'I want you out of my kitchen.'

He put the dog back on the floor and it lay down on its belly next to him. 'Thing is, I've told my friend we can probably just talk to you but if you won't let us then we'll have to arrest you and talk back at the station.'

Her eyes widened with outrage. 'Arrest me? You're joking. What for?'

Harris glanced at Sarah. She said, 'You're on the Enterprise car register. You booked a car out last night. It's in connection with that.'

'Go ahead and arrest me, then. I'll say no comment, and we'll all have wasted our day.'

'Some new people have moved into town . . .'

Wendy searched around in her sleeping bag and pulled her phone out. 'I'm gonna call my lawyer now because I've asked you to go nicely and you haven't left.'

Sarah said quietly, 'The car last night. It's linked to some arson, and to a dead girl.'

Wendy pressed her lips together so hard they went white.

'What dead girl?'

'Long brown hair. Thin. She'd been selling you drugs?'

Wendy looked at Harris. 'Is it true?'

'It is. I'm sorry.'

Sarah said, 'These new people, they're very dangerous.'

Wendy blinked. She said fiercely, 'All the more reason for you to go, then.'

'These people are preying on you, Wendy. I can offer you protection if you're willing to talk.'

'No way.'

'Can you give us the number of the drugs phone at least? No one will know it was you. It could have been any one of thousands of drug users.'

'I don't believe this.'

Wendy wriggled out of her sleeping bag and moved towards the table. She wore a grey T-shirt and men's checked pyjama bottoms that hung down at the waist. She picked up one of the cans of dog food and held it at her shoulder as if she was about to throw it. 'Think I'll sell my soul for some dog food?' she said. 'I don't need any of this shit. You can stick it.'

The threat was a bit ridiculous but Sarah stood up and took a step backwards, because, well you never know, and Wendy had started to look at bit crazy.

Harris said, 'You're frightened.'

Wendy shook her head but the hand holding the can had already lost its conviction.

Harris said, 'Come on. You know you can trust me. Sarah, she's very good, very experienced.'

'No way.'

Harris smiled. 'She's DFL. Fancy that.'

Sarah picked up the prompt, 'DFL?'

'Down from London.'

Wendy sat back down heavily. 'I hate you fucking London people.'

Sarah pulled her own chair back quietly, careful not to disturb the improved mood.

'Me too,' Harris said. 'Loathe them. But it's a sign how dangerous it's getting that they're getting involved.'

Sarah sat. 'If I have to arrest you, then I'll take your phone and get the number anyway. Then they'll know for certain it was you. There's nothing so public as a custody suite.'

Wendy gnawed at her thumbnail. 'If I give you the number will you promise to fuck off?'

Sarah nodded.

Wendy opened her phone and read it out. Sarah wrote it in her day book.

'Thank you.'

Sarah's phone buzzed. She glanced quickly at the banner: Lizzie. She rejected the call and put the phone in her pocket. She said, 'We are worried things are going to escalate. Before I go I'm going to give you my number.'

'I don't want it.'

'I understand that, but if you need me you'll be able to get hold of me.'

Wendy nodded angrily. 'Go on then.'

'Put it in your contacts. Under your mum's name or something.'

Wendy tapped it in.

Sarah said, 'The main guy, have you seen him at all?'

'You said you'd go.'

Sarah stood up. 'We're leaving. But have you maybe got a name for him?'

Wendy looked around the room as if she had lost something. She said, 'I've never seen him, OK, but he calls himself NK.'

'NK? Do you know why?'

She shook her head. 'Please go now.'

Sarah reached out and touched Wendy's arm. 'OK. Thank you. Call me whenever you need to. Day or night.'

Sarah called Lizzie from the car while Harris drove. Lizzie didn't wait for any niceties. 'Did you know the guy who's running the line in Middleton killed a police officer?'

Sarah said, 'Who told you that?'

'Asha, the misper's mum. Did you know?'

'The suspect could have been putting it out about himself to frighten people.'

'Fuck that. Is it him? Is it Ryan running the line?'

'It's feeling more likely.'

'Stop talking like a politician. Did you already suspect it was Kennedy and not tell me?'

'Give me a moment, I'm not free to speak.'

Sarah put her hand up to Harris. He indicated right and pulled into a car park. Sarah got out of the car and walked away. She said, 'Ryan's been a person of interest for a couple of days. He's on probation down here.'

'Why didn't you tell me?'

Sarah closed her eyes. Words did not come to her.

Lizzie said, 'You didn't trust me to be professional. Was that it?'

There was silence. Then Sarah said, 'I think you might credit me with more generous thoughts than that.'

'What then?'

'You know what: the usual stuff. Protecting the investigation . . . but not not trusting you. Not that.'

'You always know best, don't you?'

'God, no.'

A man was approaching Sarah across the car park. He was pushing a pram and leading a small child by the hand. Lizzie was talking in Sarah's ear, quickly. 'You didn't think I had a right to know?' The man said, 'Have you got change for the meter?' Sarah shook her head and turned away. Lizzie was still rattling away angrily. 'That sometimes your scruples might have to come second to being kind?'

Sarah put her hand to her face. 'Would it have been kind to tell you?'

'What's the matter with you? Of course it would have been kind! Better than hearing it like that.'

'You're right. Yes. I should have thought it through.' Sarah held the phone away from her ear for a second and took a breath. Then she said, 'I'm sorry, Lizzie, I'm going to have to call you back. I'm in a car park.'

'Well, I'm with Asha right now. She says she's going to Middleton to look for Leif. I've told her not to but she says I can't stop her. What do you want me to do?'

Sarah glanced towards Harris in the car. She felt like a total fraud. She had no idea what to say, or what decision to make. She said, 'What do you want to do?'

65

Steve and Kiyana drove on blue lights for over two hours and made the local train to Middleton at the first stop just after Alnbridge. Stepping into the carriage smelt to Steve of a different time, like the taste of metal, as he remembered it from licking a scaffolding bar in childhood.

They took table seats, beside the window and opposite each other, and put their bags on the seats beside them. 'Where's a plastic dog turd when you need one?' Steve said.

Kiyana laughed without conviction. Their relationship had shifted.

'How we going to work this?' Kiyana said.

'Walk up the train looking for your friend, "Oh, where is he?" I'll wait here. Text me if you spot the target. I'll change carriage and join you.'

Kiyana took her bag and squeezed out into the aisle.

Another memory from childhood: putting his hand on the glowing red bar of an electric heater. The shock had kicked him across the room. After the fear had subsided, he had been ashamed. Had stopping George been like that? Crazy. Impulsive.

No, it had been exactly what he had said it was: a quick judgement, but a judgement nonetheless. It had not been something entirely different, driven by some motivation that he was hiding even from himself. This was what he did, and he'd been doing it for years. There was no way but to run on instinct, trusting that behind that lay experience and knowledge. It wasn't thoughts, it was more like a state of being, like an athlete might feel about to run a race or a climber determined to summit.

The train passed a line of trees, flushed with late colour. A man in wellingtons with a dog was moving a small herd of sheep across a field towards a gate. The train left them behind, rushing past hedgerows, a little pond on the left, a church.

The time had come. Ryan was offering himself up and Steve needed to be part of that, not sitting on endless surveillance of George and Linton as they picked up and dropped off and picked up and went about whatever other tiresome business they had in their gangster world.

The banks of an embankment rose up and swallowed the view. The engine paused, as if for breath.

His phone vibrated: a text from Kiyana.

Three carriages along, nearest your end of the carriage. Right side. Window seat. On his own.

Steve texted back.

Where are you?

Furthest end of the carriage.

Steve checked the train app.

Next station. Two minutes.

He texted Fedden.

Kiyana thinks she's identified the target. All good for meeting the team at Middleton.

They emerged from the cutting to a low horizon of woods and fields. On the right a timber-framed farm with a low stone stable block. The train blew its horn. Toot toot! As if they were props from a children's programme, cars queued for the little branch-line train as it raced over the level crossing, leaving them almost instantly behind. The train was suddenly slowing, drawing into the station. Along the platform a woman waited with a big grey lurcher on a lead. A group of girls in school uniform waited too. Steve moved towards the doors. The dog strained forward on its lead and the door lights flashed. He stepped down and walked along the platform, looking in the train windows as if searching for his friend.

He saw the boy Kiyana had identified. There was just time to catch a quick glimpse: his face was turned down towards the screen of his phone but the clothes were bang on from the CCTV description. Blue puffer jacket. Backpack on the table with a brown leather patch on the bottom right-hand corner. His EarPods were in.

The guard was standing ready to wave the train off. Steve moved quickly along the platform and took the next set of doors. He raised his hand and beamed at Kiyana: joy and relief that the plan they'd made somewhere else in a made-up life had worked out. She patted the seat beside him. He kissed her on the cheek.

'You made it!' she said.

Steve grabbed a quick look across the carriage. If the weapon was inside the bag, there was no possibility of the target accessing it quickly enough to prevent his own arrest. Steve closed his eyes and leaned his head against the window. Something was troubling him about the identification. The individual in the carriage wasn't a boy, that was it. His demeanour was older. And his clothes. This guy was into his threads, and he had money. Steve opened his own phone and glanced at the photo of Leif the mother had supplied.

He looked at Kiyana.

She said, 'What is it, honey?'

He picked up his phone and texted a message, which he allowed her to read.

Not the misper.

She opened her own phone and flicked through the CCTV images the officers at Paddington had grabbed of the car arriving and dropping off its passenger. There he was entering the station. She stretched the image to show the logo on the puffer jacket: the same Arc'teryx dinosaur the teenager opposite had on his jacket. Seen from behind walking towards the platforms: the same high-top trainers with the black flash on the heel.

Steve stretched and stood up. 'Got to visit the little boys' room.'

66

The phone was plugged into the hands-free set. Lizzie swiped to answer and said immediately, 'Not free to speak. Give me five.'

She closed the call and took the exit lane off the motorway into the services.

'I need to take this call,' she said. 'Do you mind waiting?'

Asha shook her head and Lizzie stepped away from the car. 'Steve, yes?'

'What can you tell me about the boy who groomed your misper?'

'We think it's Jaydn Kelly. Nineteen. Runs with the Bluds. Couple of convictions. ABH, if I remember right. PWITS. He was using the boy's gym card so I saw him on CCTV.'

'Arc'teryx wanker?'

'That's right. And Moncler. He's making money.'

'What's your situation?'

'Driving to Middleton with the mum for when her son's arrested. We're about forty minutes away. I've been told to stay out of the action but I'm allowed to act as her liaison if I keep my distance. Got a referral to occupational health as well to review my involvement, so help me God.'

'It's not the misper on the train. It's Jaydn.'

'Where's Leif?'

'Fuck knows. Try to see if you can get anything out of mum. And, Lizzie, just in case . . .'

'Yes.'

'Think of Connor. If something does crop up, stay well out of it. We've got intel that at least one of them has acquired a firearm.'

Lizzie closed the call and leaned into the car with a smile.

'Shall we grab a quick coffee? There's no rush.'

Asha chose a Gingerbread Frappuccino. Lizzie had a flat white.

Lizzie said, 'That's not really coffee, is it? That's a pudding.'

Asha took a sip and licked away the froth moustache with relish. 'Got to get my kicks where I can.'

Lizzie laughed. 'Maybe I should have got one!'

Asha smiled and said, 'You're a single mum too?'

Lizzie nodded.

'How many children?'

'Just one. A boy.'

'Why are you on your own, if you don't mind me asking?'

'His dad died.'

'Oh God. I'm sorry.' She paused. 'I never even thought of that. That makes me feel worse.'

Lizzie shook her head and smiled. 'Why?'

'Well, Leif's dad, he's still alive. He's just useless.'

'It's not your fault he's useless.'

'Course it is. I chose a useless man.'

Lizzie laughed. 'Actually, I did too.'

Asha's eyes widened. 'How can you say that?'

'He was married. We worked together. He was older than me. I was, I dunno, I was . . .'

Asha laughed kindly. 'Besotted, were you?'

What should she say? That she'd become tingly and excitable in Kieran's presence? That she had looked for excuses to go out on shouts with him, not realising that everyone knew what she was up to. She'd been naïve and unrealistic, and obsessed. She couldn't say no – not to him, nor to herself. And then he was dead and she was on her own to raise Connor. She couldn't make sense of the grief that had emptied her out and which, nearly five years later, still woke her at three in the morning. When would it ever stop? Sometimes there was a terrible fear, too, of the universe in which she and Connor were nothing.

'We had an affair. I got pregnant.'

'Were you together, though, when he died?'

'Kind of, but no, not really. He was living with his wife. We argued a lot about Connor. He suggested—' She stopped herself. *He suggested that he and his wife should adopt Connor.* The memory was like a splash of scalding water. 'Oh, it was awful.'

'Don't tell me if it makes you feel bad.'

Lizzie looked at Asha's face and saw only kindness. A memory expanded inside her of her last hour with Kieran, how they sat in that crummy café pretending to be a married couple out house-hunting. Perhaps because the anxiety was terrible there had been a softening between them, and even laughter. Then he'd walked away and up the stairs into that flat.

She said, 'But before he died, it felt kind of OK.'

Asha was listening with great concentration. She said, 'Can I ask . . .? Do you mind? How did he die?'

'It was cancer.'

'How awful.'

'Yes. It was.'

'But you were able to be with him?'

310

Lizzie picked up the car keys. 'I'm so sorry, Asha. We should get going.'

Asha leapt up, leaving her coffee unfinished.

As she got into the car and swung off back onto the slip road Lizzie realised that she hadn't told Asha that it probably wasn't Leif on the train. The shame of the omission burnt her. They weren't here to talk about her grief. They were here to recover this woman's son.

The satnav told her to take the next exit. Middleton was thirty to forty minutes away over country roads. The car swung up a steep slip road towards traffic lights and paused before a big roundabout. She took the first left, past a 1950s tiled pub that looked way too big for any modern clientele. Beyond that was a side street and she pulled into a cul-de-sac of 1980s houses with red bricks and blank windows. She switched the engine off.

Asha stretched her legs out and Lizzie suddenly imagined her anxiety as if she felt it herself. She said, 'I got a bit lost when we were talking back there.'

'That's OK.'

'But it isn't. That phone call was about Leif. I didn't tell you that we don't think he's on the train.'

Asha clasped her hands together tightly. 'If he's not on the train, where is he?'

'I'm so sorry, we don't know right now.'

A wail escaped Asha. It was almost unbelievable that she could make that sound.

Lizzie said, 'We're putting everything we can into finding him. He's absolutely our priority.'

'I don't know what to do with myself.'

'Is there anything else you can remember that Leif told you?'

'I've told you everything I can think of! Don't you believe me?'

'I do believe you. I do, completely.'

Lizzie turned the key in the ignition. She sat with the engine running, wishing she could find better words, wishing that she could magic Leif to safety.

She said, 'Thing is, I've got to be professional. I shouldn't have talked about my own circumstances.'

'That's all right. I asked.'

Lizzie reached out and squeezed Asha's hand. Asha squeezed back.

Asha said quietly, 'You're doing your best.'

Lizzie took a breath. Now, when she could least afford them, those tears that never came rose inside her. She cleared her throat.

'We better get to Middleton. You can talk to the detective inspector. She's a very good investigator. Exceptional, actually. You couldn't be in better hands. I've known her for a long time.'

They pulled out. The road swept down past a big plant nursery and then fed right onto a ring road.

Asha said, 'Oh, this is Paxton. You can come this way if you take the coach.'

'What?'

'Middleton is awkward to get to by train, and it's really expensive, so I looked at getting a coach. This is the nearest you can get. Then it's another fifty minutes on another local bus. It's much cheaper, but I couldn't make it work. Not with getting enough time in Middleton and being back for Ari.'

'Hang on. I'm going to call that in. In case they haven't thought of it.'

Lizzie pulled left into the car park of a big carpet warehouse. She called Steve, but there was no reply. She tried Sarah.

'I'm in Paxton. Asha says there's a coach station there that you can use to get to Middleton.'

'Did she say Leif had used it?'

'Hang on.'

Lizzie went back to the car. 'Did Leif say how he got to Middleton?'

'No.'

Lizzie went back to the call. 'I've just asked her. He didn't say how he got there.'

'I'll look into it. See if we can get anything off financial. There's not enough time to check CCTV.'

'But wouldn't it be perfect? I mean, trains have BTP. He'd be much more likely to draw attention. Whereas coaches.'

'I hear you, but it's a question of resources. We need more intel than it being a possible route to deploy another firearms team. He's been seen in a car, and we know they're using trains too. There's a limit to how much we can cover.'

'OK.'

Lizzie pulled up the coach timetable on Google. There were only two a day. The second was scheduled to pull up in seven minutes. She got back behind the wheel and tapped the coach station into the satnav.

67

Kiyana was patting Steve's arm as if to wake him. But he wasn't asleep: just avoiding conversation. He opened his eyes. The boy was getting up and squeezing out into the corridor. The train was slowing, running along an embankment, then parallel to a road, dipping under a bridge and pulling in along the platform.

Steve got up too. 'Looks like our stop, honey.' He threw his bag over his shoulder. 'Why don't you text your mates to say we've arrived?'

Kiyana shot him a look. 'I'm sure they'll be there already.'

'We'll see.'

The three of them stood together before the doors. The train stopped and they waited for the doors to unlock. The target looked at them. Kiyana smiled and said, 'Nice trainers.' He nodded, but without friendliness. The bag was on his back, both arms through the straps.

The school girls were getting off and they walked together in a gossiping bunch towards the metal stairs that would take them over the bridge to the road. Steve let the target go ahead. The train was pulling away, revealing the town over the rails. The wind blew coldly across. The boy stopped to zip his jacket. Steve stopped too and zipped his, ready to catch the boy's eye and comment on the cold. There was no sign of a waiting vehicle.

The boy was walking again.

Kiyana was at Steve's side, keeping pace. Steve reached in

his jacket pocket and shouted, 'Excuse me, son, I think you've dropped something.' The boy turned. Steve had a white EarPod in his hand and he held it out on the flat of his palm.

The boy tapped his ears, as if checking, and then said, 'I've got both of mine.' He moved on towards the bridge, walking more quickly.

A car was drawing up on the other side of the track: a black Audi. Two people got out: a man and a woman. The woman waved and Kiyana returned the wave.

The boy looked back. Kiyana smiled at him. The imaginary weekend in the country was only just beginning! But the boy turned and started to run. He took the stairs two at a time. Kiyana began to move forward but Steve grabbed her arm. 'He's armed.' She pulled away. 'So are we.' The boy tripped but quickly recovered. At the top of the steps, he turned left instead of right over the bridge and was out of sight.

Kiyana pulled her police cap out of her pocket and began to run. She was almost at the top, Steve two paces behind. The woman by the Audi had begun to run forward but the man got back into the car and she turned and followed him. The siren wailed and the car swung out in reverse. Steve pulled his cap on too. He saw a little gate on the left of the bridge, leading to an alleyway. It was an alternative exit to the station that must go into one of the neighbourhoods.

Kiyana began to move towards the gate. Steve pulled her back and she turned to him, furious.

'What the fuck?'

'He might be waiting for you.'

She unholstered her Glock, but Steve, reaching into his shoulder holster, pushed her out of the way. Just beyond the gate he saw the boy, face down on the pavement his hands cuffed in the small of his back. He put his own weapon back into its holster. A male officer stood over the boy with a gun and another officer was looking through the bag. A grey Audi was parked up with the doors open. They knew about the two exits and had been waiting for him. In another minute the black Audi was there too.

Steve held up his warrant card and stepped forward. The AFO with the bag said to him, 'No weapon. Can't find any ID.'

The boy on the floor wailed. 'I told you. What are you doing?'

Steve dropped to his knees. 'What's your name, son?'

'Go fuck yourself.'

Steve said, 'All right then, Mr Go Fuck Yourself, I'm arresting you under Section Two of the Modern Slavery Act.'

68

Lizzie pulled over in a loading bay beside a little café with a too-small green awning outside and red-and-white checked tablecloths showing through the window. Asha sat up straight, her back away from the passenger seat, and her hands clasped together tightly on her lap.

Lizzie said, 'I need you to wait here.'

'Why? What's happening?'

Lizzie drummed the steering wheel with her fingers.

'There's not much time. I'm asking you to trust me.'

'If you think Leif might be at the coach station then I want to come too.'

'I can't take that risk. If you insist on coming then the whole thing is off. It's a long shot, anyway.'

'I can get out of this car. You can't stop me. I'll call a taxi.'

'The coach is due in five minutes.' Lizzie looked at her watch. 'Actually four minutes.'

Asha slammed her hands on the dashboard. 'He's my son.'

'If you want to go to the coach station, get out. I'll drive on to Middleton without you. Because if you're there, I'm not there. I can't see any other way.'

'You could drive me to the coach station! What is the matter with you?'

'You have to make this decision quickly.'

Asha reached down angrily to get her bag from the

footwell. She stepped out of the car. Lizzie leaned towards the open passenger door.

'I'll text you. Soon as I know what's happening.'

Asha slammed the door. She moved around the back of the car towards the café. To the sound of blaring horns from oncoming traffic, Lizzie swung the vehicle back towards the town.

Two hundred yards down the road she pulled over and ran to the back of the car. She put her cuffs in her jacket pocket, and her asp in the back pocket of her jeans. In a minute she was back in front of the wheel and taking the feeder lane towards the bus station. Drizzle was falling. From the height of the road she looked down on the concourse. Small bunches of people queued at the various stands, bags at their feet. Others rested their bums on the narrow benches in the rain shelters. Several tired local buses waited: their doors closed, their lights extinguished. There were at least two possible pedestrian exits: one up some steps towards the ring road; the other, on the opposite side of the concourse, towards the town centre. A coach was large in her rear-view mirror feeding down a few cars behind her. She pulled to the right and parked on a double yellow. The coach overtook her and she looked up at the windows but they were too high and gone too fast for her to identify any faces. She walked quickly towards the station, slipping her car keys into her jacket pocket and zipping it shut. Definitely she should not be doing this.

69

The phone buzzed and Leif fished it out of his pocket.

Milton Drive.

He shifted in his seat. It had been five hours and his body ached. It took more than an hour just to cross London. Stopping and starting in heavy traffic, the coach huffing and puffing with the effort, constantly jerking to a stop and jolting forward. Leif's heart at first hammered at the thought of the revolver in the bag overhead, but then the ribbon of fields, hedges and trees streaming past endlessly lulled him into a different state.

A few hours in there was a forty-five-minute stop to change drivers.

In the coach station the disabled toilet was unlocked. Leif pulled the door shut and lowered the toilet seat. Like he'd been told, he put on the latex gloves that he had in his pocket. Then he took the spinner out of the bag. He practised cocking it and pulling the trigger. He sat. Resting the gun on the palm of his left hand, he slid the release backward. He reached down with his right hand into the bag for the other sock. It was awkward; he should have got the bullets out first. He stretched out the fingers of his right hand, placed the gun on the floor, closed his knees and put the five bullets carefully in the crease between his legs. He bent sideways and picked up the gun with his left hand, slid his thumb through the frame again, and fed the bullets in, one by one.

In the waiting area he sat alone with the bag on his lap, too self-conscious to get himself a drink or something to eat. The tannoy announced the resumption of the journey. The coach's windows lit up and the doors opened. Only a lone woman up front and a couple at the rear joined Leif to continue on towards Paxton.

His phone buzzed with another text.

There's a fed.

He looked out of the window: the coach was pulling off the big roundabout down a slip road to the station. He stood and reached his bag down from the overhead shelf.

Another text: he glanced at the screen.

On her own. White woman. Jeans. Turquoise jacket.

The coach was moving around the perimeter of the station. Leif moved across into the aisle seat. Behind him, the couple were lifting down their bags. He was shielded by the high seat. He slipped the spinner out of the bag and into his inside jacket pocket. He zipped his jacket up halfway, putting his hand in to be sure he could reach the little revolver. The couple were moving down the aisle towards him. He slipped out before them and walked towards the front of the coach. The doors opened with a hydraulic swoosh just as he engaged the woman at the front in conversation.

'Sorry to bother you, miss,' he said, mustering a smile. 'Do you know where Milton Close is?'

She was younger than he'd thought and had a nose piercing. 'I'm going that way,' she said. 'I'll show you.'

70

About a hundred yards away, the coach was disembarking. Lizzie saw no lone boys. A couple were walking towards her, hand in hand, and they obscured her view briefly. She moved past them. A girl and a boy were walking together towards the ring road. The bag on the boy's back was blue and had the Three Lions crest.

She reached into her pocket and retrieved her phone. Sarah did not pick up. After four rings Lizzie gave up. When she looked ahead her distance from the boy and the girl had increased. They were talking, heads turned to each other. Perhaps the bag was just a coincidence and she was making a fool of herself. She dialled Steve and quickened her step. Ahead was the dark mouth of a concrete underpass that would take the couple beneath the roundabout. She followed, and her phone lost its signal. Here was the familiar smell. The damp-stained walls. A man was sitting, back against the wall, with a dog and a cardboard sign. *Please help*. She walked briskly. Ahead the tunnel bifurcated. The couple turned right and disappeared.

She ran lightly, took the bend. Ahead, the girl was now alone. She turned towards Lizzie and Lizzie saw an ethereally pale complexion, thick red hair cut short and choppy. Lizzie slipped her warrant card out and held it up but the girl's face was blank and unfriendly. Lizzie knew instantly that there was no point stopping to ask her about the boy. The young woman would only enjoy slowing her down. She ran past, up the underpass towards the light.

He was 200 yards ahead. The area was residential: red-brick terraces with white cast stone arches over the doors and net curtains at the windows. A too-narrow pavement and cramped on-street parking.

The boy turned and looked at her for an instant. Then he began to run. She grabbed her phone and pressed redial. It went to voicemail and she closed the call and dialled 999. She ran too. Leif was young but she had run for her county and she was gaining on him.

'Police, please.'

The road descended, bent to the right.

'I'm a Met officer . . . Urgent assistance needed. Park Street. Paxton. Suspect may have a firearm.'

There was a T-junction, opening onto a dog-leg of a road. Ahead were black railings, surrounding a cemetery. She ran into the centre of the road, looked left and right along its length, and caught a glimpse of Leif disappearing into a tunnel that ran through the terrace.

'Right right onto Shakespeare Drive, and between numbers seven and eight. I am pursuing.'

She ran through the front garden, along the line of the low wooden picket fence. The damp brick of the tunnel between the houses closed around her like something ancient, the brightness of the back garden framed like a view through a keyhole. The first thing she saw as she stepped out were hens. Yellow-legged, dark-feathered, plump and glossy, they picked their way through the damp collapsed autumn grass. Beyond them a park. The next thing was Leif, who stepped out from the shelter of the ancient brick lean-to. In his hand was a small revolver.

The sensation was as if someone had thrown paint over a screen. Her mind filled with Connor, and nothing else.

She said, 'Just go. Go.'

Through the fog the boy nodded. 'So stop following me.'

But he did not move. Like a photograph developing, the boy's features resolved. He was small with plump lips, round brown eyes: a child, pointing a toy gun at her chest. He was terribly frightened.

'Leif, put the gun down.'

He waved it for a second and in that instant the wayward possibility of a bullet released just by accident seemed to separate her from her own body.

He said, 'Shut up.'

She could smell Connor's little head when she bent over to kiss it after his hot bath, see his feet in his dinosaur slippers. She focused on the boy's face.

'My son needs me. His dad's dead. It's just me, on my own.' Leif blinked. His bottom teeth gripped his upper lip. She spoke softly. 'If you pull the trigger you will kill me. Do you understand that?'

His hand tightened round the gun.

She met his eyes. 'It's very easy to fire by mistake.'

'I know that! I'm not an idiot!'

'I don't think you are. Some very bad people have tricked you.' She reached out her right hand, the palm up, the fingers open and soft. 'I know about your friend, Michelle. We can get justice for her.'

His eyes were very wide. He panted slightly, his mouth open in a little round O.

'Come on, Leif, give me the gun.'

Faintly they both caught the sound of a siren wailing.

He met her eyes again. Accusation blossomed across his face and the terror of it made her cold. He said, 'You called police.' He moved forward and pushed her in the chest with the revolver. 'Give me your phone.'

She saw behind him the rickety fence that bordered the park. He would hop it and be gone, and, in a slow instant, she pictured all that would swiftly follow. The helicopter whir-ring overhead with its infrared. The dogs. The armed police hunting him down. This boy would not know how to sur-render cleanly. He would probably be shot, not by a fifteen-year-old child with a converted starting pistol, but by trained adults with Glock 17 semi-automatic pistols and Heckler & Koch G36 assault rifles. However pathetic the little revolver in the boy's hands, they would know it could kill and they would all still need to go home to their families that night.

Leif jabbed her in the chest and said, 'Your phone,' but he was distracted. He followed her eyes, glancing nervously over his shoulder, thinking perhaps – as if this were a deadly game of grandmother's footsteps – that the police were already behind him. With his eyes turning towards the fence, the hand holding the gun travelled slightly too, following his eyes away from her and in the direction of the back fence. It was as if someone had injected something directly into her brain. She stepped to the side and knocked the gun away with her left hand. At the same time her right hand was reaching into her jeans' pocket. Her thumb instinctively found its place over the end of the asp to stop it racking and, gripping it tightly, she punched his forearm hard with the weapon. With a reflexive flick of the wrist he momentarily lost the strength in his hand.

'Motherfucker.'

She stepped forward and turning inside his fighting arc, her back to his, she dropped the asp and closed her right hand over the gun.

This boy had no real fight in him. But that was not the danger. The danger was that they would both be shot. Keeping her right hand closed tightly over the gun she stamped down on his left foot and then, swinging her left arm at the elbow, brought her clenched fist back into his face.

'Motherfucker.'

He sobbed the word, this time the consonants blurred by pain and snot. She had possession of the gun and she threw it as far as she could. The hens protested noisily, flapping up into the air with great offence and clucking.

Her strength was ebbing, the adrenalin giving way to shock. Two spots of crimson fell onto her hand. It was a messy business.

She turned and said, 'Do exactly as I tell you.'

Leif's nose was already swollen and blood was running down his lips and chin. She struck him with the heel of her palm twice in his sternum. His feet stumbled backwards, two steps further away from the gun which now lay in the long wet grass. To her left through the dark tunnel came warning shouts from the front garden.

'Armed police!'

She raised her own hands, fingers outstretched and clearly empty, high above her head.

'Put your hands up, Leif. Copy me. Show them empty. Do it now.'

71

The station at Middleton had never seen so many officers.

On Cheng's authority the tiny custody suite had been opened. A jailer and a custody sergeant had been recalled to duty and they drove in from Alnbridge. It was the revolver that had made the difference: a tiny little converted starter pistol, almost a silly gun, but perfectly lethal and evidence of serious criminality. Cheng didn't want World War Three breaking out on his watch.

Met officers on specialist units always had a way of making a place their own and Middleton police station was no different. Steve and Kiyana had pushed a bank of tables together. Their coats were on the backs of chairs. Fedden had dragged in an armchair from the station office. Steve's feet were on the desk. Steve and Sarah had nodded hello to each other and skirted around anything more that lay between them. Nevertheless, it was clear to them both that they would conduct the interviews together. It was something they had always enjoyed, almost reading each other's mind as to when to speak, when to introduce evidence, when to sit back and wait.

But if only Jaydn had been carrying the gun and not Leif. They had practically no evidence they could use against him and disclosing what they did have would put Asha and Leif in more danger.

After the formalities Jaydn's lawyer read out a prepared statement.

'As I have been given no information as to any evidence against me, my lawyer has advised me to answer no comment to all questions.'

Jaydn spoke only once in interview – to answer yes to the question whether this statement was indeed his. After that he sat in his fancy clothes with a face like stone.

The two detectives knew there was no point asking more. The interview was over in less than fifteen minutes.

His lawyer – a tiny woman with big brown eyes – stood in the little custody suite protesting the use of force and the grounds for arrest.

What kind of animal is she? Sarah thought. Looks cute but is ferocious, what's that? A weasel? A stoat? A pine marten? Harris will know.

'If you make absolutely no disclosure about the evidence against Jaydn,' the lawyer said, 'then you can hardly expect him to answer your questions. Any judge would rule that no inference can be drawn from his silence.'

Sarah said, 'We'll be keeping your client in custody while we investigate further. He'll be driven to Alnbridge in about five minutes. I'll walk you to your car.'

There was no way of disguising the activity in the station. At least, leaving via the back door, the lawyer wouldn't see anyone's face. With the Met and the local officers combined there were eight vehicles, both marked and unmarked, parked up in the yard. Three AFOs, who had started with an early shift and agreed to stay on, were asleep in one of the cars. The seats were tilted far back and they were dead to the world.

The lawyer said, 'Having a get-together?'

'Remind me, what it is you advise your clients to say?'

'It will be a no comment, then?'

Sarah tapped the code into the pedestrian gate and the latch slipped.

The lawyer said, 'Have to ask why you are taking Jaydn to Alnbridge? It will be inconvenient for him.'

'Twenty questions?'

'It's fair to ask. I'm his lawyer. He arrived here, not in Alnbridge. Is it even lawful?'

'Someone can drive him back in the morning, if he's not remanded.'

'Is it because you've got someone else in custody you don't want him to see?'

Sarah scratched behind her ear. 'I like you. You seem switched on. Maybe you could extend that into trying to imagine why we might need to protect the identity of anyone we might or might not have in custody.'

Sarah pushed the heavy gate open, but the lawyer did not move.

'I couldn't give a damn whether you like me. My job is to protect the rights of my client. So far, I've seen nothing to justify his violent arrest. Unless proved otherwise Jaydn is innocent. That's the law.'

Only when she turned back towards the building did Sarah notice that Steve was standing in the shadows of the yard smoking. He stretched out his hand with the packet in it, and she accepted a cigarette.

He said, 'Thought you'd given up.'

'Just for old times' sake.'

'I'm a bad influence now?'

'Ah, Steve.'

Sarah inhaled and those years of smoking together, while Sid the crow hopped about insisting on food, came back to her.

Steve said, 'Did I hear the brief right? Jaydn is innocent?'

She didn't want to get drawn in. She had hoped just to stand together for a moment, but Steve's words brought her back to the demands of the present. The best they could do with Jaydn was to hold him incommunicado so he couldn't tell NK everything and then run off back home to burn down Leif's flat. They might have to pay for that strategy by facing a suit for wrongful arrest, but so be it.

'We need to get him out of here pronto,' she said. 'Don't want him intimidating Leif, when he gets here from the hospital.' She stubbed the cigarette out, and put it in the wall-mounted cigarette bin. 'I'll go back into custody. Sort out a van for him.'

'They're all innocent, until they kill someone,' Steve said, leaning back against the wall. He took another drag. 'Sometimes they're even innocent then.'

'But what will the customers eat tomorrow?' Fedden asked, smacking his lips dramatically.

Harris's sister owned a local café and he had called in a favour. Everyone stumped up ten quid and the central table in the back office was now covered in foil boxes, all of which were worse for wear. There were the remains of flatbread and falafel, smears of hummus, pickles, three cauliflower pakoras, a lone grilled salmon steak, two meatballs, beetroot salad and green beans with butterbeans, a big empty tray with one last square of sticky toffee pudding.

Fedden reached out and put it on his plate. 'I hate to see it looking so lonely. Poor thing.'

'Seen this?' Kiyana said, holding up her phone. On the Middleton Facebook page, a photo of the police station and the caption, *Anyone Know What's Going On?*

Fedden stirred wearily in the chair that he'd dragged in from the front office.

'Doesn't matter. There were texts on the kid's burner from whoever was picking him up warning a police officer was at the bus station. NK has already figured out we've been busy.'

Lizzie was checking her statement. She didn't look up. She had barely spoken to anyone since she arrived.

With Harris tasked to assist the op, Eyebrows Patty was now the sole uniform cover for the district. Harris called her up and promised they were all listening out for her radio. 'You put up a shout,' he said, 'and you'll have a small army.'

'When have I ever needed one?'

'The Seventh can handle anything it meets,' Steve said.

'What's that?' Kiyana asked, grateful for some chat.

Harris glanced over. 'It's General Custer before the Battle of the Little Bighorn.'

Kiyana smiled widely. 'It'll be you I'm picking for the quiz team, then.'

Harris didn't return the smile. 'I don't think it's fair, actually. Patty's not declining reinforcements. We just don't have any to give her. It's not the Met here.'

Steve nodded without warmth. 'Sorry about that. No offence intended.'

Kiyana shot Steve a look and said, 'There are photos of otters on the Facebook page, too. Didn't know you had those here, Mark.' But Harris had already walked away.

Fedden opened his eyes.

'I don't want you out with the team tonight, Steve. If we get a rendezvous we've got enough without you.'

Steve got his phone out and started scrolling through.

Sarah came back in from the custody suite. 'Jaydn's on his way to Alnbridge. The phone work is showing two known Soldiers travelling from London. ETA two and a half hours.'

Two little round headlights flashed at the gate. Sarah keyed the code and a sweet little sixties sports car drove in. The man who stepped out of it had grey wispy hair and wore an old tweed jacket. 'Tony Saunders,' he said, offering his hand.

'Yes, I'd guessed. I asked PC Harris to find Leif a good lawyer.'

'Maybe you better call someone else then.'

Sarah laughed. 'I don't think so. Lovely motor. What is it?'

Saunders laughed too. 'It's a heap, is what it is. Please don't look too closely.'

'Don't worry about me. I don't know the first thing about cars. My girlfriend, on the other hand, is a traffic sergeant . . .'

'Thanks for the heads-up. I'll know to avoid her.'

Saunders sat in consultation with Leif and Asha for a good hour before Sarah took her seat beside Steve. Asha sat beside her son, with Saunders at the end of the table, notebook in hand. Leif's broken nose had spread to include two black eyes.

Sarah said, 'Leif, you've been arrested for possession of a prohibited weapon, that is a Section Five handgun, and for Section Seventeen of the Firearms Act. The allegation – the thing we are investigating here – is that you illegally

331

possessed a firearm and attempted to use it to prevent your own arrest. Do you understand that?'

He nodded.

'Can you answer out loud, please?'

Leif looked at Saunders, who nodded.

'Yes. I understand.'

'Thank you. I've explained to your lawyer that you could be charged with other offences. Attempted robbery; Section Sixteen of the Firearms Act, too – that you possessed a firearm with intent to cause someone to believe that unlawful violence would be used against them.'

Asha cleared her throat. 'I don't follow this, so I'm sure Leif doesn't.'

Saunders said, 'Detective Inspector Collins will explain.'

Sarah clasped her hands together on the table. 'I'm warning you that this interview is wide-ranging. It is investigative: we are trying to find out what happened. That means other offences may come to light in the course of questioning. We're interested in how the gun was obtained and what you were doing in Paxton. You must be clear that this is a recorded interview and anything you say can be used against you.'

Leif looked at his lawyer and then back at Sarah.

Sarah said, 'Let's keep it simple. Can you talk me through what happened today?'

Leif shook his head. Saunders cleared his throat gently and Leif mumbled, 'No comment.'

Sarah opened her book and took out a photograph of the revolver lying in the wet grass.

'This photograph was taken of a gun found ten feet from where you were arrested. The firearm has been the subject of an urgent forensic examination and has been confirmed by an expert as viable – that means the gun works. At the time it was seized it was loaded with five live rounds. Did you load the gun?'

Leif looked at the photograph.

Sarah said, 'Leif?'

'No comment.'

'Did you know it was loaded?'

'No comment.'

'Detective Constable Lizzie Griffiths says that you pointed the revolver at her. You told her to stop following you and you demanded her phone. That action could be charged as attempted robbery. Is that account correct?'

'No comment.'

Sarah put her hand on the exhibit. 'Don't know whether you know much about guns, Leif?'

He shook his head. 'I don't.'

'It's a Bruni Olympic thirty-eight revolver. It started life as a starting pistol – for running races, you know?'

'No comment.'

'There's a phrase, Leif, don't know whether you know it. Necessity is the mother of invention. What that means is—'

'I know what it means.'

'OK, so firearms are hard to obtain but, got to hand it to them, criminals are creative. Someone somewhere must have spotted that these little starting pistols would be easy to convert. Not only that, but the ammunition is a standard thirty-eight, so the bullets would be easy to source, too. Bingo. A while ago police started coming across these little revolvers in shootings. Any idea why I'm telling you this?'

'No comment.'

She leaned forward. 'Because, Leif, to me this converted firearm is evidence that you've got caught up in some very serious criminality. I've looked into your record and you've been arrested just the once, for shoplifting. You're only fifteen, but someone has supplied you with a gun.'

Leif interrupted. 'No comment.'

'I'm asking you about a very serious allegation – that you pointed a loaded firearm at a police officer.'

'No comment.'

'A firearm is defined under law. It's a "lethal barrelled weapon". Our expert says that this' – she tapped the photo again – 'is exactly that. Lethal means it can kill. You could have killed Lizzie Griffiths today. Then we'd be investigating you for murder.'

Saunders said, 'But that didn't happen, Detective Inspector.'

'You're right, thank you. I'm just trying to make clear to you, Leif, the seriousness of the allegation. I want you to think seriously about whether you want to talk to me.'

He nodded, looking, for all the bruising on his face, like a good boy accepting his telling-off.

'What I'm saying is . . .' She struggled to find the right words. 'That . . . that, Leif, you are only fifteen! Someone has put that lethal weapon into your hands. I don't believe the person who did that is fifteen with no more than an arrest for shoplifting. I would guess they're deep into the game, making good money, higher up the chain, but it's you, not them, who is sitting opposite me under investigation. If you protect them, you're taking all of their very serious criminality on yourself.'

'No comment.'

'Please talk to me, Leif. Tell me who gave you that gun. Tell me how you came to be in Middleton. There are protections for young people like you. Your lawyer has explained that to you?'

'I can't talk to you.'

Saunders said, 'I remind you of my advice.'

'I mean, no comment.'

Asha put her elbows on the table and rested her head in her hands.

'Jaydn Kelly. Tell me about him.'

Leif's eyes widened. He glanced at his lawyer again who shook his head. He looked back at Sarah.

'No comment.'

'NK?'

'No comment.'

'Yesterday I was called to a young woman in the river. I believe you may already know what happened. Her name was Michelle Barnes, but I think you may have called her Shell? We have evidence that before her death she was raped—'

Leif started crying. His chest heaved.

'Is that why you agreed to accept a gun, Leif?'

Saunders said, 'We should take a break.'

'Before we finish . . . Leif, look at me. I've watched the CCTV from the community hospital that night. If you were a witness to what happened with Michelle then there are legal ways to punish the perpetrators.'

But maybe Leif hadn't heard her. He was looking down, sobbing.

Steve said, 'We're pausing the interview.'

*

Saunders, Sarah and Steve stood inside the corridor of the custody suite. Leif was in the cell with his mother. The sound of his weeping carried.

Saunders said, 'I should have been put out to grass years ago.'

'Why are you still doing it, then?' Sarah asked.

'Habit, I guess.'

'I don't think it's that.'

Saunders looked at her. 'Leif's mother Asha is wanting to put in a complaint, about the officer who arrested Leif, Lizzie Griffiths.'

'OK.'

'I've suggested you have a chat?'

Sarah's phone began to ring. She glanced at the screen: a number she didn't recognise. She answered it. 'Sarah Collins, give me just a moment.' She turned to Saunders. 'I'm sorry. I'll have to take this in private.'

She pushed the back door open and moved into the yard. 'I'm listening.'

The person on the other end of the line was struggling to speak.

'Take your time.'

In a moment Steve was beside her, with a notebook and a pen.

Sarah said, 'Is that Wendy?'

'Shell . . . I feel so bad.'

'You knew her?'

Crying. Sarah moved the phone away so Steve could hear.

'She was working for the new line. Just delivering. They paid me a few baggies to trick her and the new boy. It was an ambush.'

'I need to come and see you. I can meet you in an unmarked car, anywhere you like—'

'I can't be seen with you. He'll kill me!'

'Who'll kill you?'

'NK.'

'The bruise on your face?'

'It would have been worse but he didn't want me marked. He's making me order from them tonight. Tit for tat, he says.'

'Where?'

'Same place. Some garages, near the Marsh community centre. Ten o'clock.'

'You got an address?'

'Mark will know it.'

'PC Harris? OK.'

A moment's silence.

Sarah said, 'How are we going to keep you safe, Wendy?'

Crying again.

'You mustn't go tonight.'

'I've got to.'

'If you were willing to give us a statement—'

'Fuck off!'

'We could offer you witness protection.'

'No, no, no. I live here. Me mum's here. I've never lived anywhere else.'

'Let us help you.'

The line went dead.

72

Steve wanted to be present when Asha made her complaint about Lizzie, but Fedden was adamant.

'Do I look like a man who's taken leave of his senses? No, drive Lizzie to the hotel. Then have a fag and calm down. Sarah and I will handle it.'

The Travelodge was fifteen miles away, along an A road that was too narrow and bendy for the traffic it carried. Steve drove too fast, and Lizzie told him to slow down.

'You'll be back in time for the showdown, if Fedden lets you anywhere near it.'

Beyond the road lay dark fields and woods. Then, ahead, the too-bright lights of the hotel. As they pulled into the forecourt Steve said, 'What you did, that's what Kieran tried to do.'

'I know that.'

'Take the gun, I mean. He tried to do exactly that.'

'I know what you meant.'

'And it makes me think of that children's recording. Did you have it? You know: But what if Peter hadn't caught the wolf? What then?'

'Shut up, Steve.'

'I'm thinking of Connor.'

'So am I. Shut up.'

Steve turned the engine off. 'It was very brave, too. I can't fault you there.'

'I don't need to hear it.'

'And you did it really well.' He laughed. 'Broke his nose! You've got a complaint from his mum for saving her son's life.'

'Honestly, I should care less.'

'I wanted to be there when she talked to Fedden.'

'I don't need your protection. But thanks.'

'Less of the kid gloves, more of the home truths.'

Lizzie released her seat belt and sighed. 'I'm very tired, Steve.'

'You going to be all right?'

'Yes. I'll call Connor and go to bed.'

'I'd offer to come in with you, have a drink.'

'I know: you've got to go. You want to arrest him.'

Steve didn't reply.

'You're sure it's him?'

Steve turned the engine back on. 'Of course it's him. NK killed a fed, didn't he? I'll call you if there's a result.'

'Don't.' Lizzie grabbed her bag. 'Don't call me. I need to sleep.'

73

They spoke to Asha in the interview room. Saunders took the seat beside Asha, and Sarah sat opposite. Fedden leaned, with his back against the wall, like a hibernating bear.

Sarah placed two CDs in the machine. 'Before we begin, I am recording this, so there's an objective record of what is said. Can you confirm that is acceptable?'

Saunders said, 'So long as it's clear that Asha is not under suspicion of any offence. She's not under caution, and none of this can be used in evidence.'

'Yes. And I expect you will intervene if you think lines are being crossed or evidence gathered unlawfully.'

'I will.'

'OK, so DCI Jim Fedden from the Metropolitan Police is also present. We'll start then? Asha?'

Asha looked around her as if casting about for an ally, someone who would understand what she had been through, but her face scrunched up as if she had found no one.

'Lizzie Griffiths has been awful from the start,' she said. 'Didn't take me seriously when Leif first went missing. She said he wasn't a priority and moaned about her childcare arrangements.'

Saunders made a note in his day book.

'And then today. I begged her to let me go with her to the coach station. If I had been there he would have seen me. I'm his mother! He wouldn't have run from me. He wouldn't have pulled a gun. None of this would be as bad for him.'

'You can make a formal complaint.'

'Why are we talking if this isn't that?'

'Because your son is still in custody. You are acting as his appropriate adult. There are things I want to disclose to you.'

'If you're trying to get me on side then it's way too late.'

'I'm asking for information from your son. There's the possibility of serious violence tonight and your son might be able to help us prevent that. Normally we would ask him after a charge, but tonight there isn't time. Talking to us could also be good for him. Not just legally, but in other ways. He can't handle this stuff on his own.'

Asha looked at Saunders.

He said, 'Just listen, like I said. Don't say anything until it's just the two of us.'

'I am afraid that your son is in very deep. But your lawyer is here, and he will advise you, not me. Do you understand?'

'I'm not talking to you. Forget it. I'd started to trust Lizzie. I actually believed you guys were finally looking out for him. Then she just dumped me at a café. I couldn't believe it. Now look.'

'When DC Griffiths called me,' Sarah said, 'I decided that officers wouldn't attend the coach station at all.'

'You did what?'

'We had intelligence that a firearm had been supplied and we didn't have resources, particularly at such short notice, to make a safe stop there. We can't go to places on a hunch. If there's a firearm, we need specially trained authorised firearm officers to make the stop. We had no information at all that Leif was on that coach. Our intelligence pointed to the railways, or a car. DC Griffiths, in her statement, says she went on her gut feeling. If Leif was there she wanted to arrest him before he joined the criminal gang that we believe has been running him.'

'So why didn't she take me? Why just dump me at some café in the middle of nowhere?'

'She couldn't put you in danger.'

'He's my son! Don't you get it? It was my decision—'

'Not really. She's a police officer, she can't put members of the public in danger. Someone else might have been on the coach. Someone more ruthless might have had possession of the gun. You being there might have even made things worse. Her going was, well, as her instinct turned out to be right, it was risky enough.'

'Did you even see Leif's face? She didn't have to do that. He's just a kid.'

The hibernating bear in the corner rocked slightly away from the wall. 'A kid,' Fedden said. 'But with a gun.'

'Leif would never have fired that gun. You don't know him. He's fifteen.'

Sarah looked at Fedden.

Asha said, 'What?'

Fedden said, 'OK.'

'What!'

Sarah said, 'Did Lizzie tell you she's a single parent?'

'Yes! Little boy called Connor. The dad died from cancer. He wasn't even with her, though. He was married.'

'Connor's dad didn't die from cancer. He was shot dead trying to disarm a fifteen-year-old kid with a gun.'

74

The standardised neatness of the anonymous hotel room – replicated, Lizzie imagined, in a thousand towns and cities – made her feel tiny, just a speck. She wanted to feel that she was somewhere real, somewhere she might matter. She got up and pulled the floor-length gauzy curtain aside but the window showed nothing but the brightly lit car park and beyond that the wide dark night. She sat on the bed and took a breath before making the call.

Kieran's mother picked up.

'Everything OK?'

'Yes, good. Can I speak to Connor?'

'Of course.'

Connor was distracted. He looked past the phone screen at something beyond.

'Mum, Granny says I can watch *Horton's Got a Hoo!*'

Ah, she was interrupting.

'That's all right. I'll be back tomorrow. Can't wait to see you! Will you give Granny a kiss from me?'

'OK.'

'Love you.'

'Love you too.'

The phone was framing the wall, rather than Connor's face. Lizzie could hear the film soundtrack in the background. Isobel took the phone back.

'Everything all right there? Have they put you in a good hotel?'

'Lovely. Thanks so much for this.'

'Always pleased to spend time with my little Con. They grow up so fast! Next thing you know he'll be off to college. Night night, dear.'

The line emptied.

People had been strangely silent about her actions. Fedden had muttered something about well done. She had caught Sarah watching her, but when she turned Sarah had looked away. Who knew what she was thinking?

At the scene, after the AFOs arrested Leif and made the gun safe, they put her in the back of a police car. There'd been a moment of verification: her warrant card in someone's hand. Conversations in which she had no part. They brought her a hot chocolate and a sandwich. She was one of them, but not one of them. What was she doing bringing this crazy shit to their town? That was how it seemed to her, even though that may not have been the truth of their response. The inspector leaned in to the car. Did she need a doctor?

'No, I'm fine. Really.' And then, remembering, 'But thank you.'

She had started shaking. Had it been just that split second, just luck really, the boy's inattention and the location perhaps – the chickens and the gusting wind rather than the confined and focused space of that little room; was it those chance things that had made the difference between Kieran dying and her living? She took a sip of the hot chocolate and regretted it. Her gorge rose against its thick sweetness. She opened the car door and spat onto the pavement. Uninvited came another thought: that Ryan, too, had been unlucky that day. A shard of difference and perhaps everyone might have walked away. She pushed this thought away. Was nobody guilty of anything any more?

The uniformed inspector was standing in the road talking on his phone. A van arrived. She saw the double doors at the back open and Leif, his face blank, his hands cuffed behind his back, stepping up into the little space with its metal shelf.

Round and round her head buzzed the risk that she had taken and, swimming through her, a horrible shame that she had taken that risk. What would they have said in the church? (The coffin draped in the Metropolitan Police flag maybe.) That she was a hero, no doubt. But little Connor would have lost his mother. She was flooded with the memory of him, wriggling in the pew at Kieran's funeral and dropping his wooden elephant on the stone flags, too young to understand what was happening. Connor was her VIP! Her one and only. Since Kieran's death her life had been set aside for him. What was that worth if today he had been nothing to her, not in her thoughts as she ran up that dark tunnel or when she moved to take the gun? Leif had been about to run away and she could have let him go. What frightened her most was that this behaviour had felt authentic, like a return to herself. It was how she was wired. She wasn't brave; she was impulsive. Faced again with that blank-faced frightened boy, sensing his imminent danger, she would do the same. That was why she could no longer be a police officer.

She got up from the tidy bed with its crisp white pillows and its sheet pulled tightly. She placed her forehead against the cold window.

75

'I don't know,' Sarah said. 'It's so hard to assess. Feels like NK is always ahead of us. He or one of his associates saw Lizzie at the coach station so he knows Leif's been nicked. Wendy doesn't even need to be lying to us. She can believe what he's telling her and be doing the right thing. Or he can have told her to ring us and to feed us this intel.'

The headlights of Steve's returning car swung through the room.

Harris said, 'I know that area, but it's not known to me for drug dealing. Does that make it more or less likely?'

Fedden said, 'Leif hasn't been able to give us much, but through his solicitor he has told us that's where they went to deal drugs.'

Sarah said, 'No time to make local inquiries or check CCTV.'

Fedden puffed out his cheeks. 'The absolute worst thing would be to make no decision. The phones are telling us they're getting closer. Something's about to kick off. I'm going to deploy the AFOs. We can always change our mind if we get different intel.'

Steve came in, threw the keys on the table. 'Hope you put paid to that woman's complaint.'

'Done and dusted,' Fedden said.

'Lizzie all right?' Sarah said.

Steve shrugged. 'She could have been killed today. I have no idea why you allowed her to come to Middleton.'

Sarah held his gaze for a second and then turned away.

Steve turned to Fedden. 'What's happening?'

'I'm deploying the AFOs. One team will aim to intercept the Soldiers on their way into town. The others will go to the garages to arrest NK. I want to prevent a meet.' He stood up and moved towards the door. 'I'll be on the ground. You, Sarah and Kiyana will stay here. We need back-office support. And, Mark, do you mind staying, too, so there's some local knowledge?'

Kiyana started clearing the silver trays into a bin bag and Harris joined her. Sarah sat at the edge of the room, in front of her laptop.

Steve took over Fedden's armchair and stretched out his legs. 'Do you know why Fedden really doesn't want us there, Mark?'

Harris shook his head. 'I think I'm getting warmer, but I don't really want to know.'

Sarah said, 'Steve, you are not free to share all our intelligence.'

Harris looked between them and then went back to clearing the table. Steve reached into his jacket pocket and said, 'Fancy another ciggy, Sarah.'

Sarah and Steve stepped out into the yard and moved together towards the far wall. Steve offered a cigarette but Sarah shook her head.

'Go ahead and say what you need to say.'

He took a cigarette out of its packet and lit it. His hands, to Sarah's surprise, were shaking.

'Fedden said you rang him about me. Said I was worked up about Ryan. Undermined his confidence in me.'

'I did speak to him, yes, in private. It was a conversation between old colleagues about my concerns.'

Steve held the smoke inside his chest. 'Might have been private, but did you make a note about it in your little book, in case things go wrong?'

'I didn't, no. But maybe I should have.'

There was a silence.

Steve said, 'I'm sorry, that was low of me.'

'You have no idea.'

She started to move away but Steve said, 'Sarah . . .'

She turned. He was offering the cigarettes again.

'Go on, have one. Like you said earlier, for old times' sake? You don't have to finish it.'

'Thanks, but no.'

Steve said, 'Do you remember that bloody crow?'

She paused. 'Do I remember him? What do you think?' Sarah folded her arms across her chest. 'That young DC, Jez? He gave me a framed picture of Sid when I left the DSI.'

'No way.' Steve smiled. 'I'm a bit jealous actually.'

Sarah laughed. And suddenly there was that longing: to be close again, to be forgiven and accepted. But on the heels of that desire came the need to be understood too, to be treated fairly.

She said, 'You can't have it both ways, Steve. You can't be cross with me for allowing Lizzie to be part of this and then angry with me for raising your suitability with your boss.'

'It's completely different.'

'Is it?'

'I'm not the only surviving parent of a small boy.'

'That's the difference, is it? Is it really?'

'Now, thanks to you, I'm stuck here instead of arresting Ryan Kennedy.'

'Jim's shout, not mine. Whether to deploy you or not was his call.'

Sarah closed her eyes momentarily. She wanted peace. She said, 'I feel responsible, Steve. For Kieran's death, I mean.'

'Well, you shouldn't. Things go wrong.'

'And you were right about Lizzie. I should have stopped her from having any part in this investigation. My guilt clouded my judgement. Instead of doing my job, I asked her what she wanted to do. For goodness' sake! She could have been killed today when she disarmed that boy. It doesn't bear thinking about.'

'Well, I'm not Lizzie. I'm a lonely old fart no one would miss. You and I go back. You should know you can trust me.'

'But I don't. That's the problem.'

Steve and Sarah moved together back into the office. Harris caught Sarah's eye and nodded some encouragement. She turned back to her laptop and pulled up the most recent phone updates. It took her a moment before she could concentrate. The Soldiers' phones were getting closer, moving steadily towards Middleton.

Harris said, 'We've got some dark spots for mobile coverage round here. We can expect to lose them for ten minutes on the way in.'

Sarah had another email from the phone guys and clicked on it. It was developing the work on the phone boxes outside Middleton. She scanned through. There were the calls she already knew about to the unregistered phone Jaydn had been using. They wouldn't be able to attribute that phone without Asha giving a statement. Then there were two more recent calls. Helpfully a call to the phone Jaydn was carrying at the time of his arrest. Then – a surprise – a recent call. She checked the time: fifty minutes ago. She double-checked the number. The call had been to the Soldiers. How did that work?

'Mark,' she said, 'how long to drive from the Wentworth estate into Middleton?'

'Not long. Thirty minutes. Blue lights and no traffic I could maybe do it in fifteen.'

She checked the Soldiers' phones. They'd gone dark.

'Take over with the clearing-up would you, Steve? I need Mark to talk me through this phone stuff.'

Steve got up. 'But I forgot my pinny.'

Mark pulled over a chair and sat beside Sarah. She showed him the map. 'The phones have gone dark, like you said.'

'I'd expect that. They should pop up again in about ten.'

'Something's not right. Hang on.'

Her jacket was over the back of her chair and she reached into the pocket. 'I was out at the Wentworth estate taking a statement and I got lost just by the phone box that's been making some of the calls. There was this little agricultural area, concreted over. Lots of spent shotgun pellets.'

'That's pretty normal round there.'

'But when a bird is shot, is it normal for it not to be retrieved?'

'Sounds a bit odd to me, but I'm not a shooter. It must have been recent, or a fox would have taken it.'

She opened her hand and showed the little red metal cylinder she had found. 'Any idea what this is?'

'No idea.'

She tapped the maker's mark that was visible on the side into Google. PEATY'S. She clicked.

Mark said, 'Looks like bike nerd stuff.'

Her eyes scanned quickly. *High performance products . . . we can all spend more time riding our bikes!*

She clicked again, scrolled down. Her eyes flicked between the metal cylinder and the photo. It was some sort of valve for a tyre inflator kit.

'Tubeless tyres,' Mark said. 'Latest fancy thing for our pedal junkies. We've got a lot of them round here.'

Sarah thought, He doesn't know we are onto the phone box. She said, 'I should have checked this out before.'

'What is it?'

She stood up. 'No time. I'll go with you, Mark, in the marked car.'

'What's going on?'

'NK called the soldiers. Fifty minutes ago. Why would he do that if it's an ambush? Mark, we need to make progress out towards the Wentworth estate. And I have to call Fedden.'

Steve had walked over to them. He already had his keys in his hands. 'What I said outside, Sarah.'

Harris looked between them. 'I'll wait for you in the yard.'

The door shut behind him. Sarah hesitated. No wonder Steve had made such a good UC. He had a way of getting under your skin.

Steve said, 'You need Kiyana and me. We're both armed.'

She shook her head. 'If they are there, we won't be stopping them. We'll wait for the AFOs.'

'You making that decision for your new friend, too? Deciding not to take armed back-up.'

She thought of Harris. She hadn't asked him about his family, his friends. She held out her radio. 'I'll use Harris's. Take the unmarked Met car.'

Steve smiled. 'Thank you.'

76

NK waited high in the barn with the loading doors ajar. The moon was huge and a cold light poured through onto the shotgun that rested across his knees. Out in the dark fields the White Walkers were moving.

He heard the car approaching and saw the headlights pause. The passenger got out to open the gate. Pointing the gun at his forked figure, NK thought, I could hit him now. He recalled the bird rising from the trees, the easing of the second trigger and the kick of the gun. Dreamlike, as if he and the bird had been tied together by some cord, it jolted in its flight and its direction changed as it drew a wide fluttering arc across the sky before it fell. He imagined the man, how he would jerk backwards suddenly as if kicked by a horse. The fall. His astonishment. The others would run. They wouldn't have the courage to stay.

The car pulled up into the yard and two men stepped out. One had a handgun. The man who had opened the gate joined them. They looked around. He could shoot the car windscreen out. They would run but the second cartridge would catch one of them. He would have time to reload.

It took them a seeming age before one of them thought to look up. He leaned back out of sight.

Their voices carried in the night air but only as annoyed sounds. Then he made out, 'Not here.' Two of them began walking back towards the car but the man with the handgun remained where he was.

NK moved down the ladder and stood in the lee of the door, the shotgun in his hands. He flicked the switch on his head torch.

The man who held the handgun stepped forward, his hand shielding his eyes. 'What the fuck?'

NK stepped out beyond the barn and levelled the shotgun. 'Let's both keep our distance.'

The car lights flared.

NK said, 'Tell them to back off. I'm here for business, nothing else.'

The man with the handgun hesitated.

NK said, 'You give a fuck about the boy with the sore arse?'

The man gave a cough that was almost a laugh. In the moonlight NK could see that he was thin with a narrow face and a little wiry goatee. He wore jeans and a parka with a furry hood.

NK said, 'I don't care about the bitch neither.'

The man turned slightly and stretched his arm out towards the car, the palm up: stay back.

'All right,' he said.

NK gestured with his head towards the loft. 'I was up there.'

'Well done.'

'I'm explaining so that you can trust me. If I was here to smoke you, I would have. We're in the same line of work. Like I said, it's business.'

The man glanced again towards the car.

'But don't be thinking you can leave without settling this. Can't have you going around acting the gangster and me with nothing to show for it. Don't watch the shotty. It's an insurance thing, same as yours. Only better, obviously.' He turned the shotgun slightly and the light gleamed off the barrel. 'Pretty, ain't it?'

'Thought you weren't showing off.'

'Just being clear.' NK pointed with the barrel towards the large piece of abandoned machinery that stood before the barn. 'Any idea what that is?'

'Fuck knows.'

'Yeah, me too. Anyhow, that's where the line is. Walk over there slowly and you can get a good look.'

Again the man glanced at the car.

'Like I said, if I was here to smoke you, I would have. I got real teeth in the barrels and turns out I'm a good shot. I never missed, in fact. But you don't have to take my word for it. You can try me. Way I see it, this goes wrong, we're all sorry.'

The man walked slowly to the machine that had been red in daylight but was now dark. The car slid forward, shadowing him. NK followed, keeping his distance, the gun still against his shoulder.

'It's just there,' he said. 'On that bar there on the bottom.'

The man picked up the phone.

'Take your time. Get a good look.'

The man scrolled through, the phone casting light onto his face. He looked back at NK, who took two steps closer and aimed the gun at his chest.

NK said, 'You know much about shotties?'

'What's your point?'

'I just don't want anyone to fuck up, is all.'

'How you wanna run this?'

'Put the burner back down. Both your men get out the car. One of your boys brings me the bread. He shows it to me, properly. There's a torch there, underneath where the burner was, in a bag. Everyone stays cool. When everyone's happy they're getting what they came for, your boy puts the bread on the ground in the bag. You take the burner. I wait here with my impressive friend. Everyone stays safe. You drive off. It's sorted.'

'There's three of us. We got a car and a spinner.'

'What is that? A threat?'

'A warning.'

'Any one of us screws up it's gonna be messy. I'm up for that.'

77

As Steve and Kiyana drew out of Middleton the street lights ended and the darkness expanded. Out here you could imagine how it had once been: little pockets of human life surrounded by wildness. Ahead Harris's marked car was doing ninety.

'I thought he wasn't supposed to draw attention,' Steve said.

Kiyana said nothing and looked out of the passenger window across the landscape.

Harris's car swung a left and they followed. Then, a few miles on, another turn. They were on a lane; potholed, bendy, and single track. Fields. High hedges.

Steve said, 'You want to tell me what's going on? Why you've got the hump?'

'I haven't got the hump.'

Kiyana's phone rang and she took the call. 'Go ahead . . . OK, I got that but I'm losing signal.' They bumped on. On the left a pond glimmered darkly.

She said, 'That was Sarah. Fedden says they've picked Wendy up on the way to the garages. No sign of anyone else. Soldiers' phones haven't reappeared. Not surprising really. We might as well have put an ad in the local paper to say we were in town.'

'What's the plan?'

'We're recon, in case Sarah's right. The AFOs are running to us, but they're the other side of town. Ten to fifteen minutes, they reckon.'

Harris's car pulled into a passing point and Steve drew in behind him. Sarah jumped out and ran to the window.

'The private road is up ahead, a couple of miles. There's no other turn-offs between here and there. You wait here. We'll cover the other side.'

She ran back and Harris pulled away. Steve turned the car and pulled in close to the hedgerow. He switched off the lights and darkness settled.

Kiyana said, 'I used to feel like we were working together. Now, well, it's anyone's guess.'

Steve scratched his head.

Kiyana said, 'You don't have anything to say to that?'

'At the train station, I didn't want you getting hurt,' he said.

'But it's OK for you to take the risk with George?'

'That was different.'

'How was it different?'

'In every way.'

The radio transmitted. 'Three up. Your direction.'

'Fuck,' said Kiyana. 'What now?'

Sarah transmitted again. 'The AFOs are running but they're at least fifteen minutes away.'

Steve took the radio out of Kiyana's hand. 'There's a warren of lanes. If they get out into them, they'll get away. How do you feel about trying for something that looks like a routine stop.'

The radios went silent.

Kiyana said, 'What now?'

Steve said, 'They're discussing it. They better hurry up.'

Sarah transmitted. 'OK. We're going to stop them. Lots of burglaries in the area, kind of thing.'

358

Steve threw the car into a turn. 'I'll drive towards you. They won't be able to pass.'

'Received.'

Kiyana said, 'Thought we were just recon.'

'Shit happens.'

'This is different again?'

'It is.'

Steve pulled out. A beam of headlights lit the hedgerow ahead, before a silver car rounded the bend. Steve made as if to give way, flashing his lights and reversing, but slowly, blocking the road. A minute behind, the marked car turned the bend, strangely dramatic here with its livery and blue lights creating a blinking pool of colour. A burst of siren broke the lane's quiet. The silver car stopped, trapped between the two vehicles. Steve killed the engine and the light from his headlights dimmed. The door of the police car opened and Harris walked up the lane.

Kiyana said, 'Mind telling me what we are doing?'

Steve leaned on the horn. Harris put his hand up, give-me-five style.

Steve honked again.

'I can't leave him on his own,' Steve said, freeing his seat belt. 'I'm going up. How long-you-gonna-be kind of thing.'

'Then I'm going too.'

'No, you're not.' He honked again and flashed his lights. Harris held his hand up again and shook his head at the impatience. Steve said, 'It will look more real if it's just one of us. The woman waits in the car. Like real life.'

He reached across into the dashboard and took out his cap, stuffed it into his back pocket.

'Oh fuck off, like real life,' Kiyana said. She released her seat belt.

Steve had opened the door and was walking briskly up the lane.

'Come on! Move over. I need to get to my mum's! She's not well.'

Harris said, 'Sir, if you wouldn't mind just waiting.'

Steve was almost at the car. He pulled his police cap out of his back pocket and onto his head. In an instant he had both hands gripping the Glock. Kiyana broke step, round to the passenger side. She had her firearm out, pointing into the car.

'Armed police. Show us your hands. Show us your hands!'

Kiyana had the door open and was pulling the passenger. 'Out out. On the ground. Do it.'

Steve shouted, 'Now!'

Sarah was in the car, gloved up, holding a torch in her mouth as she searched. Harris was filming on his BWV. The three men stood cuffed, facing the hedge.

Steve said, 'NK, was he on his own?'

'Don't know what da fuck you're talking about.'

'Sure you don't.'

Harris shouted out. 'She's found it. A shooter and a phone.' He moved back round the car towards the prisoners. The man with the goatee said, 'I don't know nothing about that.'

Kiyana said, 'Where was it?'

'Behind the pollen filter.'

Steve took Harris aside and said quietly, 'You got leg restraints?'

'Sure.'

'How far are the AFOs?'

'I dunno. Less than ten minutes now.'

'I'm thinking they could have shot him. He could be bleeding out. One of us should drive down and take a look.'

Sarah said, 'No, Steve.'

He said, 'I'm sorry, but you're not my commanding officer, and it's the right thing to do.'

The car plunged down the narrow lane and over the cattle grid, the lights bouncing off the concrete and on the hedge-rows. Lights came on inside a little stone house by the side of the lane. There was a dog-leg, then dark barns loomed on the left. Steve got out of the car and paused at the gate. He looked up towards the barn. There was a high window – a good lookout point – but he could see no movement. He pushed the gate open and walked forward. The sky was clear and the moon was low in the sky. He stopped again, listened. Nothing but wind and the movement of trees.

He unholstered the Glock and slipped the safety. He moved across the concrete concourse towards the barn, looking around him and up towards the window.

The door was ajar. He stepped in. He was gone. Why would he wait?

He ran back to the car. Turned down the lane deeper into the estate. This was surely the way Ryan would take on a bike. He accelerated. Over the hump of the bridge, then up the hill. A gate ahead, open. *Private. No Trespassers.* An avenue of trees. Another stone house, a woman's face at the window. He got out, holding his warrant card, shouted, 'You see anyone coming down here? On a bike?' She shook her head and drew the curtains.

Cedar trees. On the right a lawn and a winding drive, and

at the end of it, in darkness, a large house with stone porticoes. The land was flat here. Sheep stood in sleeping groups either side of the lane. He put his foot down. Another cattle grid. Possible footpaths to left and right. The drive was well tarmacked and swung down and right, back onto the public road. He took a left towards Middleton.

A little village nestled in a dell. Outside one house a sign: *Eggs for Sale*. A small church. A red phone box – this one full of books. He drove faster than the quality of the road, accelerating and braking: sixty, sometimes seventy miles per hour. He couldn't know which of the many cross-country tracks Ryan might have chosen but he could hope to get back before him or to catch him on the road. Forestry land now on either side. The road was climbing. A little car park on the right for walkers. Suddenly a plunging view over the town, its big Norman church, the remains of the town wall. He swooped down, taking the bends, crossing the stone bridge over the river, and climbing up past the empty market square. Dawn was beginning to crack a thin line of pale pink light across the sky. The courtyard in front of the hostel was empty. He sat on the bonnet of the car and waited.

After about thirty minutes the front door opened. Behind the building the dawn was fully red. Ryan stepped out, wheeling his bike. He looked across at the car. It seemed to take him a second to recognise the man sitting on the bonnet. Then he smiled. 'Long time.'

Steve got up and took two paces towards him. He said, 'What are you up to?'

'I'm out for an early ride. I'm working in a bike shop.'

FRIDAY

78

They were running on empty. The three Soldiers had been driven to Alnbridge to be interviewed by fresh officers. The AFOs had been sent home to their beds. Kiyana was asleep on the floor, her folded jacket under her head and Fedden's coat over her.

The CCTV in the hostel wasn't working, so they couldn't show whether Ryan had ever been out and returned.

Outside the police station window, a bunch of children were walking together towards school.

Fedden leaned back from his laptop and stretched out. 'CPS have come back with charges for Leif. Section Seventeen Firearms Act, Section Five Prohibited Weapon and a bonus ball of Possession of Prohibited Ammo. We need to get his brief and his mum in.'

Sarah sighed. 'There we are. Got the kid, but not the main guy.'

Fedden said, 'Lizzie can continue as liaison going forward. Steve, can you drive out and pick her up?'

Steve shifted in his seat. Since he'd arrived back at the station he'd hardly said a word.

'Sure thing.'

Sarah said, 'So it wasn't an ambush. NK was selling the line.'

Fedden said, 'Got out when things got hot. Sold at the top of the market, just before it crashed and burnt.'

Steve slid his chair back. He looked towards the ceiling.

'And now he's being allowed to disappear into the ether, just like he never existed.'

Sarah leaned forward, tired and irritated. 'You think I haven't tried to nail him?'

Steve said, 'He's not Keyser fucking Söze. He's a shitty little drug dealer. It's not too late to get a warrant.'

'You think we'll search his room and find a Purdey shotgun and ten grand in cash? The guy we can't link to anything?'

'It's worth trying. Anything's worth trying, considering who he is.'

'No one willing to identify him. No phone evidence.'

Steve got up, walked towards the window. He folded his arms and looked out at the waking morning. 'It can't be that difficult. If we give it some focus.'

Sarah started to speak, 'But he's gone quiet now. He's sold the line—'

'You could have done a lot more!'

Fedden said, 'Play nicely, please. Everyone's tired.'

Steve took a breath but he didn't turn back. Fedden continued.

'Steve, if we had limitless resources, I'd agree with you. You don't think I want him? But when we get back to London there'll be an endless stream of NKs needing our attention. No one will allow us to stay here and chase this. And the locals have already thrown everything they've got at it. No, we're firefighters and we're done here. Drugs line closed. Firearms seized. Mission more than accomplished. We should be pleased with the result. Those three in custody: their offences are as bad as anything we could have got NK for. We'll focus on them. And if it is you-know-who, this

366

shows he'll come again. This is intelligence: we'll develop it. We haven't given up on him.'

'You-know-who?' Kiyana said, stirring on the floor. She pulled herself to sitting. 'Who's that, then?' She grinned. 'Voldemort?'

Sarah and Steve exchanged looks.

'What am I missing?'

Fedden said, 'It's Ryan Kennedy, Kiyana. The toerag who murdered Kieran Shaw. He's on probation in Middleton.'

Her face blanked. 'You're kidding.'

Fedden shook his head.

She looked at Steve. 'And no one thought to tell me?'

Fedden said, 'Information like that, it's sensitive. You've got to understand that.'

'Everyone knew but me?'

'Not everyone. Only the people Sarah and I couldn't keep it from.'

'And that was?'

'Lizzie and Steve.'

Kiyana stood up. She put her hands behind her head and sighed. 'That explains a lot.' She looked at Steve.

A marked car drove past the window and indicated right into the yard.

Kiyana said, 'I'll go open the gate for Mark.'

Steve shrugged, looked back out of the window.

A couple of minutes later Harris entered, his arms full, pushing the door open with his foot. He started unboxing a coffee machine on the side. He said quietly, 'Kiyana's going to stretch her legs.'

Sarah caught Fedden's eye. Harris picked up the glance and looked between them. Sarah walked over to him with a smile, determinedly bright. She put her hand on the machine. 'Chief Constable's Commendation, I reckon, for getting hold of this.'

'No problem. We've an amazing little shop by the river. You could probably buy an orbital launch vehicle there if you needed one, just not from a brand you'd heard of.'

He filled the machine with water and inserted a pod.

'Fight you for the first coffee,' Sarah said.

Steve turned back. 'Usually their street names have meaning. Have we looked into that? Can't we use that to link him? Anyone know what NK is?'

Sarah said, 'Nothing gang related on the usual channels. I googled it, got No Kids. Not Kidding. Natural Killer. Any of those is possible. None of them help.'

Harris handed her a coffee. 'There's Night King, too.'

'What's that?'

'*Game of Thrones*?'

Fedden said, 'Goblins and orcs, is it?'

Harris said, 'Sounds like the Met.'

Steve tapped the table impatiently. 'Who is he then, the Night King?'

'Leads the army of the dead.'

'OK, what the fuck. What else? Where's he from? What does he want?'

Fedden got his phone out. 'Hang on, I'll ask DC Google.'

'No need,' Harris said. 'I'm a Thronie.' He pressed the button for the second cup of coffee, breathing in its smell theatrically. 'This cup's mine, I'm afraid.'

Steve waved his hand. 'Don't care. Tell me about NK.'

'I don't think any of it will help. Kind of the whole point is his . . . emptiness. He doesn't have friends, family. He's a, well, he's the first White Walker. Was a human, now he's something else. Sort of dead, but alive. He doesn't even seem to have a name any more. And what does he want? He doesn't seem to want anything, not in the way humans do, anyway.' Harris took the coffee and had a sip. He closed his eyes and seemed for a moment to have slipped into sleep standing up. 'Endless night, maybe. Maybe that's what he wants. Endless night.'

79

Lizzie took Asha, Leif and Saunders into the consultation room.

Lizzie said, 'Mr Saunders is present because this is all now pending and you need legal representation. Leif, you're going to face a number of charges relating to the possession of the gun.'

Leif nodded and looked down. He seemed strangely calm. Asha put her head in her hands.

Lizzie continued. 'You'll be referred to something called the NRM: the National Referral Mechanism. What that means is that evidence will be collected regarding how you came to be drawn into this. How you were approached, the promises made to you, that kind of thing. In all likelihood this NRM will be your defence.'

Leif looked up. 'But I can't talk about any of that.'

It was said plainly and Lizzie had to stop herself putting a hand on his shoulder.

She said, 'You won't necessarily have to give evidence against the people who groomed you.' She paused. 'Then there's Michelle – Shell. The rape. I don't think you understand how important you are in taking that to court. The DNA will only go so far, but you were a witness. You can say what happened.'

Leif shook his head. His face had set into immovable sadness. 'I can't.'

'Those boys don't know who you are. We can protect your

identity and you can tell the court what you saw. You cared about Michelle. That was what you wanted, wasn't it? For those boys not to get away with it?'

'You don't understand. I want to, but I can't.'

Asha said, 'My sister dropped Ari off at school today. When she was walking back to the car a boy came up. He told her everyone knows where we live. Where my sister lives, too.'

'But the boys who raped Michelle, they were from a different gang. They don't know you.'

Leif said, 'There's a debt, that's the thing. I owe NK money. I lost the gun. And other stuff, too. Drugs money when we was robbed.'

'What's that got to do with the boys that hurt Michelle? They were from the other crew.'

Leif looked at his mum, as if she should explain, but she turned to Lizzie and shook her head. 'I don't know. I don't understand it.'

Leif said, 'It's a principle for him. He told me. I'm not free. I need to pay him back. If I don't he can put my name out.'

'But it's not a real debt, you know that? It's coercion . . . a way of tricking you, enslaving you.'

Leif's expression didn't change. He said, 'Yeah, I know that. But still.'

Lizzie looked across at Saunders. He raised his eyebrows sympathetically. She said, 'We can move you anyway. Away from your ends. That's the first thing. Let's take it one step at a time.'

'Thank you, miss.'

Leif stood up. He was calm, and Lizzie thought of Michelle and whatever resignation it was that had taken her down to the river. Asha put her hand on her son's arm. She spoke gently to him.

'Will you wait outside with Mr Saunders for just one minute? I need to say something to Lizzie.'

'OK.'

Saunders and Leif stepped out of the room. Fedden was waiting by the custody desk to read the charge. Asha shut the door and stepped back towards Lizzie.

She said, 'Your boss – the fat man.'

'DCI Fedden,' Lizzie laughed. 'I'll tell him you said that. Yes?'

'He told me last night about how Connor's dad died.'

'OK.' Lizzie squinted. A familiar chill passed through her. 'I'd rather not talk about that, if you don't mind.'

Asha reached out and took Lizzie's hand. 'Just wanted to say that I read about it last night.' Asha's eyes filled up. 'And I wanted to say that I'm very sorry. That's all. Very sorry. And very grateful to you for going to get my Leif.'

A cold formality set into Lizzie's heart at the intrusion. 'That's OK. It was just my job. But thank you.'

Lizzie was about to move, but outside the door she heard the low murmur of voices. Asha was waiting here with her, she realised, rather than dashing out to be with Leif. Suddenly she was flushed with surprise, astonishment even. She put her hand to her face, and with her other hand she squeezed Asha's hand back tightly.

80

Steve sat in the Church Inn, a nearly finished pint on the table in front of him. He had walked out of the nick and escaped into another reality. A small fire was burning. At a table in the corner a couple were tucking into fish and chips. A loud group of men in jeans and jumpers over collared shirts stood at the bar making a big show of getting another round in. He'd been scrolling through his phone for a while. The Night King seemed an endlessly solemn fellow. It didn't look much fun being him; although, on the other hand, he did seem to be getting some sort of kick out of standing still in front of lots of scary dead people and doing mean stuff.

Steve downed his pint and went and got another.

He went back to the various fan sites.

Sadistic and bloodthirsty.

That sounded about right. He took a gulp of beer.

Despite his powers, he is not overconfident in his abilities and is capable of self-preservation, knowing his death ends his campaign.

That too. His death. Had that been what Steve had been hoping for, driving alone with his Glock through the countryside. If he'd come across him with a shotgun he'd have had the perfect excuse.

His phone started ringing: Kiyana. He picked it up. 'You talking to me again, then?'

'Enough to get you back to the nick. We're driving back to London and everyone's waiting for you.'

'What's happened with the boy?'

'Lizzie's charged him.'

'But is he giving evidence?'

'Not even in the rape.'

Steve glanced down at his phone.

Pressed a cursed dragonglass dagger into the captive's chest, turning him into the first of the White Walkers.

'Why not the rape?'

'Because he owes NK three thousand. Says NK will name him if he doesn't pay his debt.'

Steve knocked back his pint. 'I'll be there in about forty minutes. I'm a bit of a walk away.'

'But we can pick you up.'

'I'd rather walk.'

He closed the call.

In the bank he showed his warrant card and his card. It was surprisingly easy. Then he popped into the town's stationer's and bought an envelope.

The bike shop was a brisk fifteen-minute walk away, along a lane on the outskirts of town. A small lean woman in a blue beanie hat was at the counter.

'Can I help?'

He looked beyond her to the back of the shop where a young man had his back turned, working at a bike that was clamped into a work stand. Ryan looked round, wiped his hands on his jeans.

'Friend of mine,' Ryan said to the woman. 'OK for me to go outside for a minute?'

'Sure.'

They stood outside on the forecourt. Wind blew cold across from the open fields.

Ryan said, 'You wired?'

'No.'

'I believe you, sure I do.'

Steve smiled.

'Whassup?'

'NK. It's a good name.'

'What you talking about?'

'I've been studying him.'

'OK.'

'Did you know the Night King can turn male human babies into White Walkers just by pressing the tip of his finger to the baby's cheek? Seems like a useful power for someone running a line.'

'You gone crazy?'

'Maybe.' Steve reached into his jacket pocket. 'I brought you something.' He took the envelope out. 'That's what Leif owes you.'

'Don't know what you're talking about.'

'That's OK. I'll put it on the ground and walk away. No wire. No admission. Nothing.'

'Why you doing this? You're trying to prove you're a better man than me?'

'I'm just trying to give Leif a chance to get out. He's a kid, just like you were before . . . all this. And if he does give evidence about the rape – that won't hurt you, will it? My enemy's enemy, all that.'

Out on the field the White Walkers moved.

Ryan said, 'You're the Night King, man. You're the one who presses dragonglass into people's chests. I trusted you.'

'You're probably right. I definitely feel like that, have done for a while, but then I've been drinking.' Steve bent down and put the envelope on the ground. He put his foot on it against the wind. 'I'm leaving that there and I'm going. Up to you what you do with it, but I'm asking you to consider my offer. I'm sure our paths will cross again.'

PART FIVE

HOME

81

Everything about Meghan Clarke made Sarah smile. As if somehow all her magnificence – the long thick plait that fell down her back, the Scottish accent with its hints of hills and moorlands – was some sort of splendid joke. Meghan was a rat: a traffic skipper. She investigated fatal collisions for a living and they had met when Meghan was running the crime scene at the death of Lexi, killed by Ujal Jarral. Jarral was Shakiel Oliver's right-hand man – or his dog, as he was recorded calling him on a surveillance tape. Lexi had been hit by a car, but it was no accident. It was a punishment. Not even that, perhaps; her death was just business with no real passion attached. Shakiel needed to set an example. It was the rules of the game.

And standing at the crime scene Meghan had been: just right. Without apparently even noticing that she moved in a world of men, she was super-knowledgeable and competent. Disputatious and funny, too, but with just the right amount of deadly serious about convicting the bastard who had run skinny Lexi down in cold blood.

Meghan was like Sarah, but not like Sarah. She drove a motorbike. Well, more than one. She had a Ducati for fun but also a vintage 1959 Triumph T120 Bonneville, also for fun.

Sarah had learned to ride pillion. Excitement had overcome her fear. Sitting on the back of her girl's bike: that was how she arrived outside her parents' house.

Her father stepped out onto the street to look at the bike

and hear all about it. He had been a vicar for so long that there really was no separation between the dog collar and the rest. It was an embedded part of his character: this way he had of listening to other people's passions with great concentration but without ever sharing them. The smell of petrol, the heat of the engine: the Ducati contradicted every polite word, every answered question. So clearly the bike was about nothing but pleasure. As Meghan talked about how well the bike handled an unspoken understanding stood between Sarah and her father; that the machine was the wrong kind of joy. Her father's listening was always a gateway to somewhere else – to the presence of God's love in every beautiful detail of the world.

It was a mistake coming here. Sarah had fudged the issue; asked could she bring 'someone': avoided the word 'friend', but not used 'lover' either.

'I can take you for a spin,' Meghan said with a grin, while the exhaust clinked its way audibly down to cool. 'The roads are great round here. All twisty-turny and lots of hills.'

'Ah,' her dad said, 'I'm a bit old for that.'

'Never too old,' Meghan said with a steely look, and then, turning up that Scottish lilt that brimmed with irony and hidden laughter, 'I promise tae be gentle with you.'

'I think I'll pass.'

The subject of the motorbike had ended in some sort of unspoken disagreement. They moved together towards the house. Sarah's mother offered to take their bags up, but that was ridiculous.

The stairs were tall and narrow with short treads and steep risers. Meghan and Sarah had been put in different rooms at the top of the house. There was a white towel neatly folded at the bottom of each of their separate beds.

Meghan pulled her best disbelieving face. 'What's the idea of this, then?'

Sarah shrugged. What had she been thinking? She hadn't really warned Meghan.

'Don't they know?'

'Oh, I think they know.'

Meghan threw herself face down on top of her queen-size. She rolled onto her back and patted the mattress next to her and smiled. 'Still, there's plenty of room for two. What are they going to do? Arrest us?'

Sarah folded her arms. 'I've been on duty for days. Let's get some air.'

They walked to the Norman church and climbed its tall tower. There, with the wind blowing and the view over hills and fields, they kissed. But voices were ascending and the light tap of children's feet running ahead up the stone stairs.

When they returned, the smell of dinner wafted into the street. A fresh white cloth covered the table and soup spluttered on the stove.

Geoffrey and Grace had just finished sleeping rough for the week in the centre of the small town they had moved to when Geoffrey retired. It was part of a Christian action to raise awareness of the homeless.

'Retired!' Grace said, handing out the soup plates with Meghan, who was tough and strong but also gentle and courteous. 'He's always leading the service in some little church or other with only three people in the congregation.'

'And how was it, sleeping rough?' Meghan said.

'I can feel every single bone in my spine,' Geoffrey said.

'Maybe you needed to drink more,' Meghan said, lifting

her glass and catching Sarah's eye. 'That's how the homeless cope, I believe.'

'Spice isn't it, nowadays?' Geoffrey said, showing off.

Grace said, 'In the middle of the night some boys came up to us. I don't know whether they were drunk or . . .'

Sarah's thoughts drifted to the house of her childhood: a 1970s-built rectory. Metal-framed windows and the front elevation timber-clad. An A-line roof and dormer windows. Orange Formica tops in the kitchen patterned with sketched marigolds. Masses of foxgloves in the garden and not much else: no one had time to look after the beds. A set of three swings. The house had been full to overflowing. Parishioners, scripture, music; her mother played an upright piano, that, even when Schubert was being played, was always the joanna. And as the sisters grew older Suzy's many friends began to add a new element to the house. Teenage girls sitting on the swings with short skirts and bare knees. Once, caught smoking! It was a world Sarah had been able to slip through quietly. Her father and mother's gazes were on her but they had seemed content to let her be. Suzy was in charge of fun and mild controversy. Suzy had a boyfriend. Sarah did well at school.

But behind the tatty furniture and the old car with its panels faded to different shades, Sarah deciphered that there were reserves in hand. Geoffrey's father was a doctor in Yorkshire. Grace had been to Oxford, the clever daughter of a family with a tradition of both manufacturing success and religious dissent that had earned it a Wikipedia entry. When her parents retired it turned out there was enough put by to buy this tall narrow Georgian house, part of an all-sorts terrace of mismatched houses in the nice part of town. There was a tiny little garden in the back with a round table and a few pots with hostas and ferns. In the sitting room there was even space for a little spinet piano, squeezed to the right of the door and just fitting under an unevenness in the wall. Sheet music waited on the stand and Meghan asked Grace to play, but she protested. 'Oh no, it's out of tune, silly thing. It's always out of tune. I don't know why we keep it.' It would have been a blessed relief for her to play but instead they sat on the ancient furniture which, Sarah had eventually realised, was antique, and valuable, while Geoffrey interviewed Meghan about her work until at last the evening was over.

'Do you want hot-water bottles?' Grace said.

And Meghan grinned and said, 'I don't think so. We'll be warm enough.'

After Sarah had brushed her teeth, she found Meghan waiting for her in her bed. She had the covers over her head and she pulled them back and said, 'Surprise!' Meghan had that look about her: it had been a long evening. She'd been good for hours and now the separate beds told her that something she liked very much to do was forbidden.

'Come on in,' Meghan said. 'I've warmed the bed up.'

Sarah got in beside her but even though she had a go at kissing she couldn't concentrate.

'What's the problem?' Meghan said, with a grin. 'You don't find a candlewick counterpane sexy?'

'I'm sorry! I'm sorry I brought you here. I'm sorry I didn't stand up to my father . . .'

'Calm down,' Meghan said, leaning over and tracing a finger over Sarah's lips. What love there was in the gesture was coloured by definite impatience. 'Honestly, sweetheart, no one's going to come upstairs, you know.'

'I know, I know. I do know that. But I just can't. Not here. I thought you'd understand that.'

Moonlight fell through the half-open curtains. Meghan's sleeping breath from across the landing filled the two small rooms.

Sarah felt a flash of irritation about her mother's story of the local boys who had come towards them, threatening to piss on them. She could understand those boys. These pious people were just asking to be pissed on. And if they wanted to experience what it was like for homeless people – well, being pissed on wasn't the half of it.

No doubt Geoffrey was fast asleep too. She was the only one kept awake by the evening's shenanigans. She felt like she'd swallowed a frog and it was jumping around inside her.

She imagined her mother's thin old body hitting the stone of the buttercross like a canvas bag full of clamps and bolts. Her snatching little rags of sleep, only to be woken by some rough lads with their trousers undone, scaring and shocking her. Poor old thing.

Geoffrey and Grace had endured the death of her sister, and still somehow held on to their faith and their compassion for others. It can't have been easy. And now they were old. Where was her compassion?

Sarah shifted on the mattress. It was as if she was having an argument with herself. Because there was that impatience again. What had been the point of her father and her mother sleeping rough? What was the point of a bad night's sleep when you could simply give money and sleep in your own bed?

Round and round it went. Sarah shifted around and sleep did not come. Her father loved her, his one surviving child, she knew that. (And here she moved again, and pulled the covers up.) Still he sacrificed their time together! He was like Luther, nailing his ninety-five theses to the door. Here I stand, I can do no other.

She wanted something more capacious than this kind of love. In her own life, too.

She thought of her dog, dear Poppy, how she always ate the tasty morsels first. She was with the over-indulgent dog minder this weekend and would probably come back two pounds heavier. Good for Poppy. She thought of Lizzie and Leif and Kieran Shaw. And she remembered poor Michelle Barnes, just sixteen years old, her long brown hair thick with river mud. What to do with the terrible loneliness of that death? Sarah drew her hand across her face. Life was so precious, and so easily wasted.

Daylight was coming in through the tiny casement window. The room was stuffy. Meghan was already dressed – in her leather biking trousers. She leaned over the bed and kissed Sarah.

'I'm not cross, my love,' she said. 'It's just not for me, all this . . . whatever this is. There's a fantastic route just a short drive from here. Steep hills, panoramic views, and a lovely bed and breakfast by the sea. I'll be doing that today instead of going to the service, and you're so very welcome to join me. But I understand if you have to stay.'

*

Her dad liked to smoke a pipe at the little round table in the tiny garden in the back and Sarah joined him there with a cup of coffee. Her mother hovered at the window, and gave a little anxious wave.

'Meghan's my girlfriend, Dad,' Sarah said.

Geoffrey took a puff on his pipe. 'I know that. Your mother knows that.'

'But you put us in separate rooms.'

'I'm sorry, my darling. I can't make allowances for myself, much as I would love to. I have nothing against Meghan.'

'Dad—'

'I don't judge you, Sarah. Really, I don't. It's between you and God. You must do what you believe to be right. But I just can't allow it in my house. I'm ordained.'

She remembered how he had lifted her up and swung her round when she grazed her knee.

'I'm your only daughter, Dad. I'm what you have left. I'm living.'

'And I love you dearly. I admire you. I admire what you do. And what Meghan does, too; she seems a fine young woman. But I have no choice, don't you see? I can't preach one thing and do another. I can't make my own rules.'

Sarah slipped into the kitchen and took her mother's hand. 'So sorry, Mum. Meghan has decided not to stay for the service. And I've decided to go with her. I've been on duty non-stop and with our shifts it's so hard to get time together. We've only got two days' leave.'

Grace squeezed her daughter's hand. 'That's all right, dear. I understand completely. Please believe me. What makes you happy makes me happy.'

Meghan was revving the engine of the bike, impatient to be away. She was still smiling and polite but there was an edge to her courtesy. She was baffled by Sarah's parents and pushed, Sarah thought, dangerously close to rudeness.

Grace hovered outside the front door, sad-looking and kindly. She kissed Sarah and her skin was papery. She had shrunk and her spine was knobbly beneath her cardigan. 'Love you,' she whispered, as if it were a secret. Sarah climbed on the back of the bike and put her arms around Meghan. The Ducati's engine roared like an animal set free and Grace gave a bold wave that made her rise briefly on one leg, as if she might be carried away by the wind.

After a couple of hours, they pulled up at a roadside snack bar. It was a converted double-decker bus with a view over a valley that was green up close and blue in the distance. There were chairs in the lay-by, and they sat in those and drank bad coffee. A man with facial tattoos walked by and gave them a wink. He said, 'Nice bike, ladies.'

And Meghan said, 'Thanks,' and put her arm round Sarah's shoulders.

Sarah glanced at her watch. The service would be starting. She said, 'I feel so bad.'

'Ah, but there's more to you than that,' Meghan said. 'Much more. Let's not go and see them together again.'

Sarah said, 'I got a call from Lizzie. About that boy, Leif.'

'OK?'

'They've agreed to his referral. The judge has dismissed

387

the charge and they've moved out of London. He's going to give evidence in the rape trial.'

Meghan leaned over and kissed her. 'You see! You're my hero!'

Sarah laughed and kissed her back. 'I love you, Meg.'

'Stupid girl. I love you too.'

'I'm so pleased. So pleased. So pleased. I was thinking, what would be the point of it all if Leif was lost.'

Acknowledgements

Thanks to everyone at Corvus. Sarah Hodgson has supplied support and brilliant editorial guidance throughout and Alison Tulett is a wonderful copy editor. Thank you to my agent, Alice Lutyens, the Queen of Can-Do.

I am indebted to Professor John Pitts, Professor David Wilson, Robert McPhee, Mark Attridge, Sheldon Thomas, Gerel Falconer, Dr Charlotte Smith, Jules McRobbie, Isla Rowntree and Stuart Foreman. All errors are my own.

Many of the people who made this book possible cannot be named. I thank those people from my heart for trusting me with their experiences.

Thank you and love to my family. This book is dedicated to my mother, always a source of inspiration and love.